# Past Promises

by

## Jahmel West

# Indigo Sensuous Love Stories

**Genesis Press, Inc.**
315 Third Avenue North
Columbus, MS 39701

## Past Promises

First Edition

# Acknowledgments

*Everyone imagines thay the creative process is a solitary one. The images of the fevered writer hunched over a typewriter in a dark and lonely room is impressed in all of our minds. But for myself, I found that this book would not have been possible if it were not for the encouragement and support of my co-workers, friends and especially family. Far too many people to name them all, but I can't thank you all enough.*

*I would especially like to thank Lori Gillis, my attorney and E. Chris Edwards for his wonderful picture. A very special thank you to Kevin Carroll and all of the football players from Knoxville College and the Arena Football League who aided me in my research of this book.*

*This book is dedicated to My Mother, who taught me to read before I was enrolled in school. Gave me my first library card, and introduced me to one of my enduring loves...reading. Thank you Mama.*

*"You taste like butter, melting into honey..."*

At the first touch of his lips under her zipper, Nicole shot up. When Kevin looked in surprise at her suddden movement. Nicole shyly explained, I'm sorry. I just can't take anymore. It's been too long for me." Looking down in inexplicable embarrassment, she continued. "I just want us to be in this together." He continued to look confused and Nicole struggled to find words to explain what she barely understood herself. Giving up in frustration she reached for his shirt which he had yet to doff, and started lifting it off. "I don't want tonight to be just about me."

"But it it," he protested as she unzipped his jeans. "This night is for you."

"No," she stated firmly as she crawled hack unto his lap. Holding his head between her hands as she softly punctuated each word with a kiss.

*"Tonight is for us."*

# Chapter 1

Nicole Blakely desperately hoped that the blood racing through her veins did not translate to a look of nervousness on her face. By sheer strength of will she held her mask of a smile firmly on her face as she made her way through the equally nervous crowd. The auction had yet to begin and already the tension in the air was palpable. Surveying the crowd, she watched as the elegantly dressed attendees made their way around the ballroom discreetly eyeing the Tolleston College memorabilia that would soon be presented for sale. She laughed softly to herself as one smartly dressed woman coolly cut her eyes at another as they both admired the same item. Greed and wealth were in the air, the kind of wealth that was so old and distanced from daily needs that it was easily squandered on useless items. Smiling to herself again, she thought, *Everything is going according to plan.*

How many nights had she sweated over this plan? From the moment she had pitched the idea of a benefit dinner and auction to the college's board, it had been an uphill battle. True, the college was desperate for money, but to the considerably older and stuffy board members, an auction was one small step above begging. Nicole had only convinced them by promising that it would be an elegant and formal affair befitting Tolleston's prestige in the community, or at least what little prestige was left. Several items for bid were being presented by local celebrities and famous alumni. As the newly appointed dean of students, Nicole had worked day and night to ensure that the board was not let down. As she saw several members circulating with pleased looks on their faces, she knew she had not failed them.

"Hey, how come you didn't tell me?" Tyrone Reese, her student assistant, noisily interrupted her thoughts.

"Tell you what?" she responded with an absent-minded question. Having accustomed herself to his easy excitability in the months they had worked together, she had learned to pay him only so much attention.

"That Kevin Powell is one of the guest presenters tonight."

"Because he's not," she answered simply as she carefully adjusted the glass case covering a pair of antique lanterns.

"You mean you don't know?" he asked in disbelief.

"Tyrone," she spoke softly with her back to him as she continued with her adjustments, "once people heard that some of our more famous alumni would present items at the auction they naturally assumed he would be one of them, but I wasn't able to reach him." Possibly because you didn't try, she guiltily added to herself.

"No, Miss B., he's really here. When I first heard it, I couldn't find you so I went and asked the big H. myself, and he confirmed it."

"That's impossible...," Nicole started but even as she spoke her eyes searched the room hastily for Harold Wright, the chairman of the board. "He can't be here..." Even as the denial came to her lips her eyes locked onto Hal's, and the truth shone so merrily out of his eyes that she wondered how she had missed it earlier. Cursing softly, she quickly put the glass case back down before she dropped it. Betrayal so profound it rose like bile in her throat nearly choked her. After two years of doing everything she could to prove herself to the board, they still hadn't trusted her. Instead they had gone behind her back and contacted the one man who could have ended the school's financial problems single-handedly if he had chosen to do so. But when Kevin Powell left Tolleston College ten years earlier for a career in professional football he never looked back. It infuriated her to think that the board had gone begging to the arrogant jock. Why couldn't he have picked up the phone and called them if he had been interested in helping? The troubles at Tolleston College had been well publicized.

The media had fed like sharks as every meaty problem surfaced. First, it was discovered that the former dean of students had embezzled hundreds of thousands of dollars in student aid. While Tolleston was still reeling from the humiliation of that scandal, it was discovered that the athletic director had broken every rule in the book to attract star athletes to the school, resulting in a two-year suspension of all football and basketball. Lack of these sports programs, a major source of funding in a private institution, plus the embezzlement and falling enrollment had the historically black college on the brink of closing its doors for the first time since its opening shortly after the civil war.

Active as Kevin Powell was in the sports community, he surely had known about the suspension and what it meant to the school. Why would he suddenly appear now that it was nearly over, and they were at last able to recruit again for next year's fall semester, instead of two years ago when the troubles had first hit? If he was concerned he could have called and expressed it. But then, when had he ever picked up a phone when he should have? As quick as that thought came she squelched it. She would not let him make this personal. Tonight was about Tolleston College and not any failed relationship between the two of them. Steeling her spine, she prepared herself for the day she had dreaded for ten years, for in her heart she had always known that eventually they would meet again. Resolving to be firm and businesslike, she braced herself for the inevitable. No way would she let him see how unnerved she actually was.

If he had decided after all this time to help, she would take every penny. She would smile in his face and just as quickly turn her back and give him the cold shoulder. Damned if he would ruin this night.

"So isn't it great? I heard he's upstairs in a suite, waiting to make his entrance," Tyrone gushed.

"Well, since, as usual you seem more informed than I, have you heard what item he's presenting?"

"The book."

"*The first edition*?" Shaking her head in disbelief, Nicole's control nearly snapped. "The book *I* was going to present? The one it took me a month to convince the board to sell? The one that is upstairs right now under lock and key, along with all of my carefully researched notes? There is no way he is auctioning *that* book." Nicole fumed at the thought that all of her hard work, her pièce de résistance, could become his shining moment.

"Yeah, cool, huh?" Tyrone beamed his big Cheshire cat smile, totally oblivious to her angry sarcasm.

"Unbelievable," she muttered in disgust. Determined to keep focused she asked, "Weren't you supposed to be getting the description cards to the presenters and rounding them up so we can get started?"

"Right, guess I got a little sidetracked. Give me ten minutes and I'll have everyone lining up behind the stage. Then I'll be ready to go up with you. I'll be right back."

"Only ten, Tyrone, we've got to get this auction going." She spoke to his back as he dashed off in his usual energetic way.

At a signal from the chairman of the board, Nicole approached the microphone on stage. As the stage lights came up and the audience took their seats, she noted Tyrone was to her left offstage, giving her the thumbs up signal. Sweeping the crowd with her eyes, she saw David Spears, the interim athletic director, had finally made it. He looked devilishly handsome and charming in his tuxedo. Catching her eye, he sent her a mischievous wink while never seeming to take his eyes off the beautiful Carlista Cunningham, marketing director of Tennessee Peaks, a new, exclusive resort which was developing in the area. Smiling to herself she wondered what she would ever do without these two men who were always there for her, offering unconditional support. Unlike Kevin, her mind added bitterly. Taking a deep breath, and shaking off a sense of foreboding, she stepped to the microphone, welcomed guests, introduced the auctioneer, crossed her fingers and prayed.

"So far so good," Tyrone stated an hour later, unknowingly echoing her thoughts. "I still can't believe how people can spend good money on some dumb souvenir." He broke off suddenly and blushed as much as his rich ebony skin would allow. Smiling sheepishly, he continued, "I mean, I know it's for a good cause and all, but that man just paid four thousand dollars for a letter! I'd write him every day for half that price." Laughing at his own humor, he added, "I guess some people got more money than sense."

"Lucky for us," Nicole smiled, understanding his sentiment. When you came from a home where simple necessities were treasures, as he did, it was hard to imagine spending money on things that didn't clothe, feed or house you. But since the extravagances of the rich tonight would help secure good educations for the students at the school, she knew the money would not be wasted.

"I wonder how much the book'll go for," Tyrone said. "I was looking at it this morning and thinking, 'Wow, all this tonight is really for a stupid book.'" His slanted dark eyes rounded with awe.

"Tyrone Reese, tell me I did not hear you say you touched that book after I gave you specific instructions that that book was not, definitely not, to be removed from its case until tonight," she reprimanded in her sternest voice.

"Miss B. you know I couldn't help it." Smiling, he added, "I mean, how often does a man hold a hundred-thousand-dollar book in his hands? I just opened it to take a little peek. No harm, no foul, right? I mean, think of my children."

"You don't have any children, and if I kill you, you never will," she quipped back, not completely immune to his charm.

"Nicole Blakely," Chairman of the Board Harold Wright spoke from behind her. "I'm surprised at you threatening this young man. Where is that renown patience of yours?"

"Completely exhausted after one semester with Tyrone." Smiling, she relented and turned to Hal, "It's going well, isn't it?"

"I never had any doubt," he smiled in return while grasping her hand and squeezing affectionately. "Why even without the book we've hit the eighty-thousand-dollar mark. I'm sure you've heard by now that Kevin Powell is here." He broke the news casually, completely oblivious to Nicole's feelings. "When he steps on stage with the final item, he will carry us over the top." Rubbing his hands in anticipation, he reminded her so much of an eager student that it was hard to stay angry. Especially since she knew he was unaware of the past relationship between Kevin and her.

"You know, it was quite a surprise, hearing he was going to be here tonight. How did you manage to pull it off without my knowledge?"

"Actually he called me directly and insisted on helping, only he didn't want to interfere with too much publicity beforehand. I hope you're not upset by my little surprise. I would have told you but when someone of his caliber offered to work with us, I felt I had to respect his wishes. After all, he doesn't know you like I do, so even though I trust you completely, he has no way of knowing if you can keep a secret."

"Oh he knows all right," she muttered to herself. "A pity he didn't speak to me himself, then I could have told him exactly what he could do." She paused a beat before adding, "For tonight's auction."

"Luckily, I took care of everything."

"Lucky," she repeated, adding 'for him' under her breath.

"Are you ready?" Hal asked, looking at his watch.

Nodding in the affirmative, she put personal resentments aside for the business of the evening. "You go and get Kevin, and I'll meet you with the book in the foyer outside of the ballroom in ten minutes."

"All right," he quickly agreed as he rushed off.

When she left the hotel's ballroom and went upstairs, Nicole took with her Tyrone and two of the private security guards hired for the evening. She crossed the suite quickly, removed a key from her purse and opened the wall safe hidden in the closet. Withdrawing a heavy mahogany box from the safe, she set it on an end table. Slowly, she raised the lid and carefully pulled back the velvet to reveal its shocking contents: several cheap paperback novels! The rare antique book was gone.

"This can't be," Nicole cried in consternation. In

dazed confusion she looked again at the cheap mysteries piled in the wooden box. Frantically she pulled them out one by one, as if by some miracle she would find the priceless book at the bottom. But there was no miraculous discovery. Rushing to the closet, she pulled everything out, as if the book might have been carelessly dumped on the floor by mistake. It took her several minutes to accept through her shock that the book was truly gone.

"Oh, my God," she whispered softly while lowering herself onto the chair someone had thoughtfully placed behind her. Without that thoughtfulness she would have surely dropped to the floor. "What's going on?" She directed the question to Tyrone and the security men, hoping
desperately that she was the victim of some sick joke.

"I swear I don't know, Miss B.," Tyrone answered, his young face unusually solemn.

"Tyrone," she rose as she approached him, "you said you saw the book. If you saw it, you would have been the last person who did. Where is it?" In her frustration she crowded him menacingly.

"Miss B., I promise you I don't know. I did look at it, but I looked when it was in your office before it was moved to the hotel. I never looked after that, I swear it. You gotta believe me."

In his earnestness, he looked more like the seventeen-year-old boy he was than the man he was always pretending to be. As she carefully deliberated her answer, his eyes filled. She was his hero, the first person at the school to reach out to him, despite his rough background, and give him a second chance. Really a first chance, for no one, not even his mother, had really cared enough about him to give him a chance before.

"Tyrone," she said, taking his hand, "of course I believe you. I trust you with my life. I'm just in a lot of trouble right now, we both could be, and I need to find that book."

"Nobody could ever think you took it, Miss B. And even if they did, I wouldn't let them," he promised, her staunch defender as always.

The security guards returned to the sitting room from the bedroom of the suite. "Miss Blakely, I called hotel security and they are on their way up, along with Mr. Wright."

"Thank you," Nicole answered, still in shock.

"Nicole!" Harold could be heard shouting before actually barging through the door. "Nicole, what the heck is going on? They just told me the book is gone. What happened?"

"I wish I knew," she answered. "I came up here to get the book. When I opened the safe, the case was there. It was heavy and I didn't think anything was wrong until I actually opened it to find these." She vaguely waved to the novels. "I can't imagine what happened."

"Well, it's obvious to me. Someone either on this

hotel staff or this security force is responsible. And they are going to pay. I'll sue them both." He blustered on, more 'huff' than 'puff' in his shock.

"Now wait a minute," Eugene, the head security officer, spoke up. "Our agency has a spotless record, and we did everything we were contracted to do. Why none of our officers even came into this room before now."

"You, along with this hotel, were still responsible for getting that book safely to the auction," Hal maintained. "I'll have your job over this, along with your so-called spotless record!"

"Wait a minute, please," Nicole interrupted, actually afraid that the two men might come to blows. "Only one person was responsible for that book and that was me. It was my idea to remove it from the library where it had been safely kept for almost a century. It was also solely my idea to auction it off. So if anyone is going to lose their job over this, it should be me." Turning to look Hal squarely in the eyes, she added, "And I accept that. I'll tender my resignation in the morning."

"Now, let's not be too hasty," Hal spluttered. "That book was very well insured, and although we certainly don't want to lose it, we don't want to lose you either. We'll get the people who did this, don't you worry. Until we do, however, I think a little discretion is in order. We can hardly stand to have another negative bit of information released to the media. And I'm sure neither the hotel nor the security agency wants the negative publicity either. Am I correct in assuming that?" The security representatives nodded in confused assent.

"Good, then we're all in agreement. For the time being, while the investigation is ongoing, information regarding the theft will not leave this room." Hal looked at each person individually with a penetrating stare that demanded consent.

"But what about the auction?" Nicole asked. "Everyone is waiting for the auctioning of the book. What will we tell them?"

"Everyone is waiting for the final item up for bid. They all suspect that Kevin Powell is here and that he has something to do with that final item. What if, instead of the book, he were the final item?"

"What are you saying? We can't auction off a man." Nicole's mind moved slower than Hal's in her shock.

"Of course not. But what if we auctioned a day or evening with him. A day on the football field if a man wins or a romantic evening on the town if the highest bidder is a woman. That was my original idea when he contacted me but he preferred to do something else. Since we're in this jam, maybe he'll agree now. I know he wants to help any way he can."

Nicole didn't stop to wonder why the thought of Kevin having a romantic evening with some anonymous woman would cause a bitter taste in her mouth, but once again she pushed her personal resentments aside. After all, she knew it wasn't the first date he had been on in the ten years since she last saw him. "If he agrees, it would be a big help," she conceded.

"Good." Hal placed his hand on the small of her back as he ushered her out of the room.

"You go down and announce our little change. Say something along the lines of the board deciding at the last minute to withdraw the book. By that time I'll have returned with Kevin and that should settle everyone down. Trust me. And remember, tell no one the truth for tonight." As he hurried her onto the elevator, he added, "Don't worry, everything will be fine."

"Man, what a night," Tyrone exclaimed in disbelief as the doors shut. "First a book, of all the things here for auction, is stolen and now we are going to auction off Kevin Powell. I wish I had some money. I would definitely bid on the chance to learn some of his skills. Can you imagine me and Kevin Powell going one on one? Wouldn't that be great?"

Stabbing the ground floor button viciously, Nicole answered, "Just great." Shrugging off resentment for what seemed like the umpteenth time, she fixed her smile as she reentered the ballroom and prepared to give the greedy crowd what it seemed they had already anticipated: Kevin Powell.

Thirty minutes later it was all over with. The crowd which had been upset to learn that the book would not be auctioned was rapidly mollified when Kevin stepped on stage. Nicole had managed to avoid him by quickly exiting through the opposite stage door when he stepped up to the microphone. Harder to ignore had been her suddenly accelerating heartbeat when she had seen him again. Damn, he was still fine. But a fine face did not make a fine man, as she had learned the hard way. Luckily, the sudden burst of applause by the crowd had broken the brief tense eye contact before she hurried away, leaving Hal to wrap up the auction.

Later, while checking her makeup in the foyer mirror, she heard a group of ladies commenting on the fierce bidding that she had apparently missed. Carlista Cunningham had been declared the winner, with a bid so outrageously high she had forced everyone else out of the competition. Nicole, who privately thought that a shrew lay under Carlista's shrewd business exterior, felt they deserved each other. There was no reason to feel jealous, she reminded herself. Looking carefully at her reflection, she repeated, no reason at all. She was still an attractive woman and she knew it. She had dressed carefully in the 'ruthless red' color of her lip and nail polish. Her sequined dress fit so perfectly it could have been painted on her skin. She had 'dressed to kill' for the evening. Hopefully, she thought as she entered the ballroom again after one last look in the mirror, she wouldn't have to.

# Chapter 2

One million dollars, Nicole repeated to herself in disbelief. Kevin Powell had just announced a million-dollar donation to Tolleston College. Even though Nicole, like everyone else in the room, knew it was well within his means, she was still reeling with shock. Even more disturbing was the teaser that the crowd should expect an even bigger announcement from Kevin Powell and the Tolleston College board in the 'near future.'

Whispered speculation made its way around the room as everyone wondered what the mysterious announcement could be. Nicole watched Kevin from the opposite end of the room and marveled that his granite features gave nothing away. He coolly chatted with board members and even some alumni, but their disappointed faces showed that he had stoically revealed nothing.

She wondered if any of their classmates recalled the relationship that had once brewed between them and speculated on a possible romantic reason for his surprising return. She was under no such delusion. Whatever the reason for his sudden reappearance, she knew it was undoubtedly self-serving. Kevin Powell, she had learned, did nothing that was not in his own best interests. Even this donation was motivated by his desire for something; it was only a matter of time before he revealed what it was.

"Hello Butter, you're just as beautiful as I remember," Kevin said in a voice that was like honey pouring over gravel, his arrogant brown eyes sweeping her body from head to toe appraisingly as Nicole turned to answer.

The use of a once intimate nickname was an unexpected low blow to her practiced, polished mask. Recovering quickly, Nicole was still able to calmly reply, "Hello Mr. Powell."

As Nicole and Kevin traded stares, it was that arrogant self-possession of his that almost shattered the fragile hold she had on her control. In the ten years he had played professional football, before his early retirement just a few months ago, he had lost none of his animal magnetism. His rugged athletic face was softened by big brown eyes with eyelashes many women would have paid to own. His full sensuous lips had earned him numerous endorsement contracts, especially when he aimed that generous, down-to-earth smile at a camera. His cocoa complexion was as smooth as silk, and he had the kind of face that allowed him to sport his bald-headed look with confidence. Off the field his movements were characterized by the same graceful precision that made him a star on the field. Kevin Powell was simply a gorgeous man, who was certain of his own attractiveness. He was the type of man women chased and men admired.

She had watched him charm and regale the crowd which had surrounded him, wondering how she would respond when that charm was targeted at her. She tried to keep her mask of cool confidence as her eyes battled with his, but an unexpected surge of fire raced through her veins. Only long suppressed anger saved her from falling at his feet. Silently, she resolved that while Kevin Powell might have women all over the world making fools of themselves over him, she would never again be in that category.

"Oh, it's Mr. Powell now?" he asked teasingly, one seductive eyebrow lifting slightly while the brown eyes bored holes into her almond ones. "I mean, come on. It's been a long time but not that long."

"Well, you hardly seem like the Kevin I used to know," she answered sarcastically. Her eyes admired his hand-tailored tuxedo and diamond-studded cufflinks, which were a far cry from the well-worn jerseys he had favored as a student.

"You look as if time has stood still. Beautiful. Vibrant. Wonderful. Yet with just enough sophistication and class that you definitely aren't that same college girl." He smiled. "How have you been?"

"I've been well, and of course we all know from the media that you've done well, to put it mildly, for yourself." She paused to smile briefly before hardening her eyes to continue. "So why don't we cut through the small talk and you can answer just one question. And believe me, I don't mean to sound ungrateful, because your donation was needed and certainly appreciated. But what I want to know is, what are you really doing here?

"Butter, if you followed my career at all you'd know I never explain myself to anyone. But for you," he paused significantly, "for you I'm willing to make an exception."

"I stopped flattering myself a long time ago that I was ever an exception to you." She arched one delicate eyebrow appraisingly. "And your flattery only makes me more suspicious. So skip the pleasantries and tell me what's going on."

"Nicole," he answered with wounded brown eyes, "I'm here to help. This was my school, too, after all. If your stubborn pride hadn't kept you from asking me for help, I could have been here a long time ago."

"Funny, your feelings for my pride never stopped you before from doing exactly what you wanted to do. And if you had really wanted to help, all you had to do was put a check in the mail."

"True, so maybe we'll say it was my pride then." He looked at her pensively before continuing, "Maybe I waited to be asked."

"If that was the case, you'd still be waiting."

"What can I say? I was never one to wait too long," he answered, lifting his champagne glass in a mocking salute.

Before she could respond with an appropriately scathing reply, they were joined by a delightfully obtuse Hal. Always the life of any party, the merriment leaping from his eyes gave his fat cheeks a glow that made him look more like Santa Claus than the head of a university. Harold Wright, who stood six feet tall and almost as wide, was resplendent in a surprisingly elegant tuxedo and his frequently wild short "Afro" looked unusually neat, even austere.

"Ah...here the two of you are. I got shanghaied by some board members and couldn't get away. I've been looking for both of you to introduce you, but I guess I'm too late. Kevin, you have to forgive me if I've been remiss in my duties. But I should have known it would-n't take you long to find the prettiest girl here." Nicole's loud snort of disgust was Hal's first clue that something was awry. Quietly he assessed their faces before asking, "Is there some problem?" into the awkward silence that deafened their small circle.

"No, of course not, " Nicole answered. "I was just

thanking Kevin for his extremely generous donation."

"And of course discreetly pumping me for information about our forthcoming announcement," Kevin added.

"Well, naturally when Kevin contacted me about a little proposal he had for the school, I knew it would be perfect. Did he tell you all about it?"

"Not yet," Nicole prompted expectantly.

Hal looked to Kevin for direction. "I'm sorry. I saw the two of you engrossed in conversation and I just assumed you were discussing your little project. I hope I haven't said too much."

"No, Nicole is just a little impatient, but then she always was. So actually you showed up just in time. She had nearly wheedled the whole thing out of me. She always could wrap me around her finger."

"I didn't realize that you all had known each other before. Were you students here at the same time?" Hal asked as both Kevin and Nicole exchanged stares.

"Yes, and we were just catching up. It's a bit of a shock for both of us seeing each other again." Kevin smiled, "You know how it is."

Hal, who definitely did not know how it was, could only smile and nod dumbly. "Well, no matter," he said into the awkward silence that ensued. "I'm sure the shock will have worn off by Monday's meeting."

"Monday," she repeated, staring at him dumbly.

"Yes, at the board meeting," he replied, already distracted as he left them.

"You," she exclaimed. "You're going to be at the board meeting on Monday?"

"So it appears," he calmly answered in the face of her rising temper. "And before you start grilling me, I can answer all those questions I see floating around in your pretty little head with one simple answer." He paused to grin. "Wait and see." Satisfied with her frustrated silence, he walked away.

The questions ticking in her head suddenly went off like a time bomb. It was bad enough he had shown up on the most important night of her life. But his generous donation more than made up for it. With the way her luck was running tonight, it was too much to hope that he would give his money and just leave. Things with Kevin had never been that simple, which was part of the reason their relationship had not worked in the past. Now he was back, for God only knew what reason. But this time, she promised herself, she would not allow him to play his usual games. He would see, she vowed, the difference ten years had made. She was no longer a young woman awed by his prowess and charm. Lost in her thoughts, she had not noticed David stepping up from behind. So when he touched her shoulder she jumped noticeably.

"Sorry," he apologized. "You're not usually so jumpy. Is everything okay," he asked with concern.

"Yes, I'm sorry. I'm just tired. But God, what a night," she sighed with exhaustion.

"And that has got to be the understatement of the year. What with the book..., " he paused. "What happened with that, by the way? I was looking forward to seeing how much it went for, especially with all the hoopla and controversy over its sale. I remember how much trouble you went through to get the board to approve its sale. What happened? Did they get nervous and change their mind at the last minute?"

The adrenalin gushing through Nicole's veins seemed at that very moment to have found a convenient outlet in the throbbing pulses of her brain at just the mention of the book. In all the confusion of seeing Kevin again, she had nearly forgotten that the school had more serious problems. For a moment she allowed herself to wonder if it was an innocent coincidence that the first edition of a 19th century Nat Turner interview had disappeared with the reappearance of Kevin. In that same instant, however, she put the thought aside. Kevin Powell was undoubtedly a lot of things, but a thief was not one of them. Her heart froze at the thought that some long-dead loyalty on his behalf made her so certain of that fact. Then she realized it wasn't loyalty that crossed him off her list of suspects, but the fact that he could have outbid everyone in the room, especially since he was one of the first athletes in his sport to reach a multimillion dollar yearly income. Kevin Powell definitely didn't ever need to steal a thing.

"Nicole," David said, bringing her out of her fog.

"Uh, no. Nothing like that it's just... " As she struggled to come up with a smooth answer, her tired and stressed brain seemed to shift into slow motion. "It's just... David, in all honesty, I can't think right now. Can I tell you about it tomorrow? All the excitement has finally gotten to me. I cannot think beyond going home and getting into a nice relaxing tub with a cup of hot tea." She smiled sweetly to take some of the sting out of her unusually evasive answer.

"I understand. The excitement here is unbelievable. Carlista nearly fell out of her seat trying to meet Mr. Football." His green eyes feigned hurt. "I can't believe you managed to keep that secret to yourself. And don't tell me you didn't know Kevin Powell would be here tonight."

"David, believe me, there is no way on earth that you were more surprised than I was." She paused to reflect. "As far as I know, this was something between Kevin and Hal. I was as much in the dark as anyone."

"I heard murmuring in the rumor mill that we have more surprises to come from those two. I don't suppose they gave you any hint while you were talking to them, did they?"

"Not a thing. I know he'll be at the board meeting, hopefully just to get a formal thank you and then leave. But beyond that I'm not even going to let myself speculate. As I said, right now all I can think of is getting home."

"I'm sorry, you said you were beat and here I am interrogating you. Do you need a ride home? I have to take Carlista since apparently she didn't have any luck with Mr. Football tonight. She'll probably have better luck on her prized date. Did you see how she knocked out all the competition?" He shrugged cynically at the obvious play his date had made for Kevin Powell. "Anyway, I'll be happy to escort you if you need me."

"No thanks," she smiled, allowing herself a moment of gratitude for their genuine friendship. "But if you like, we can catch up on Monday after the board meeting."

"You're on." He grinned his response before continuing mischievously. "Now you run along home and I'll see if Carlista needs me to be her consolation prize." They both glanced to where Carlista was looking around impatiently.

"Have a good night, David."

"Oh believe me, I'm going to try." He winked before walking away.

She smiled to herself as she watched him make his way to his date, his confident swagger cutting a path through the crowd. Nicole couldn't help remembering when she first met David. He had started as the assistant football coach just weeks after she began as assistant dean. They had formed an instant friendship, which over the last six years had suffered some rocky moments, especially when their brief dating had ended disastrously. Serious-minded Nicole was not romantically compatible with life-of-the party David. But they had managed to salvage any hurt pride and secure a strong brother/sister relationship. He was one of the people on the campus that she trusted absolutely, and she knew she would tell him about the book, even if she had been instructed not to.

She truly was tired, she thought to herself. This had been one of the most stressful evenings of her life. She couldn't imagine what had happened to the book, and she didn't want to suspect anyone she knew, but any real rest would elude her until the culprit was caught. In the meantime, she would do her best to be prepared for Monday's meeting, a meeting where she knew she would have to answer plenty of questions. She hoped to have one of her own answered: What was Kevin Powell still doing here?

# Chapter 3

The most important meeting of Nicole's life started at eight o'clock; unfortunately she was already thirty minutes late. Silently damning Kevin Powell for the one millionth time in her life, Nicole prayed that for once the board meeting would not begin on time. Always scrupulously punctual, Nicole could only blame the disturbing events of the weekend for her tardiness. She had tossed and turned all night worrying about the stolen book and wondering what Kevin had up his sleeve. After finally managing to rest she didn't awaken until she was well behind on her schedule.

Flying into the foyer of the administration building's third floor, she smiled briefly at Rose James, the executive assistant shared by all the administrators on the floor. Rose returned the smile warmly. She was a big-hearted woman with an unashamedly voluptuous body to match. While she epitomized southern hospitality, she was just as likely to figuratively take a student or a staff member over her knee as she was to invite them to her home for a peach cobbler. Everyone loved her. She peered at Nicole over her wide-rimmed glasses.

"Honey, what happened? I've never known you to be late like this before. And today of all days..." She trailed off, looking around nervously.

"I know, I know, you can't say anything I didn't say to myself a thousand times as I practically ran over here. How do I look?"

After examining her from head to toe, Rose sighed, clearly not pleased. "Well, I suppose you'll do in a crunch and, face it, you don't have time to fix yourself up. Just get on in there while we still have a school. Right now it's nothing but a bunch of men in there making decisions, and that never leads to good. All you have to do is look at the world today to see that." She came from behind her desk to fuss with Nicole's jacket and hair while pushing her toward the big mahogany doors of the boardroom.

Taking a deep breath before Rose practically pushed her inside the room, Nicole steadied her racing pulse, reminding herself silently that she was doing an excellent job as dean, a position she had earned with years of dedication. Not only was everyone in the room a supporter but they were also friends. Everyone except Kevin, a lit-

tle demon inside reminded her. Firmly pushing that
thought away with the mantra she had repeated all weekend, *I can handle Kevin Powell*, she opened the door.

"Well, well, it's our little late bird," Hal said while
rising. His smile softened his words and the others
chuckled affectionately.

"Gentlemen, please forgive me," Nicole answered.
"A student emergency came up and I was delayed." She
silently crossed her fingers at the small fib. Everyone
answered with understanding words and gestures, though
Kevin looked as if he saw through her like glass.

"I hope I haven't missed anything important," she
added as she took her seat.

"Actually, you haven't," Hal answered. "We were
just discussing old business and bringing Kevin up to
date on a few things while we waited for you. I wanted
everyone present when Kevin made his announcement.
As it appears everyone is, I will turn the floor over to
Kevin Powell."

Twenty minutes later, Nicole sat in stunned shock.
Athletic director! Kevin Powell had somehow weaseled
his way into becoming athletic director of Tolleston
College. Not somehow, she corrected herself. There was
no somehow about it. He had bought and paid for it just
as he had probably paid for a thousand other expensive
toys over the years. That's all this was, she was sure, just
another expensive game for him. His generous donation
to the school on the night of the banquet had just been the

beginning. He had made a commitment to triple that original donation over the next five years. He also had arranged matching donations for an athletic fund which would allow for the complete renovation of the school's athletic facilities. By the time his five-year contributions and the matching funds from his corporate friends were totaled, he would have generated several million in much-needed help. Not added into the total at all was the as yet unspecified amount for ten, four-year athletic scholarships to be awarded annually. The amount of his generosity was staggering, and she could see why the rest of the board was clearly overwhelmed.

True, athletic director was usually no more than a figurative position; however their athletic suspension had changed that. Because they were fast approaching the end of the suspension, the new director would have the immediate task of completely rebuilding both programs, football and basketball, from the ground up. He would have free rein to start recruiting now for the fall semester when the suspension would officially end, recruitment that would entail staff as well as players. He would have the unique opportunity to put his personal stamp on every aspect of their athletic program. No wonder, Nicole fumed, he was so eager to step in. The program, *his program*, would be a lasting monument to his ego. She tuned out Hal's glowing praise as much as possible, until she couldn't take it anymore.

"The addition of Kevin Powell to our staff, along

with his donation means we can..."

"Forget about pesky things like GPAs, qualified teachers, books, buildings, or rather, academic buildings, computers, etc," she interrupted angrily.

The rest of the board looked at her in shock. Hal blustered, "What's that, Ms. Blakely?"

The use of her last name was clearly a subtle hint that she was overstepping her bounds but Nicole had to continue. "Don't get me wrong, a few scholarships and a new gym will certainly boost student morale. But, gentlemen, we have real and very substantial problems that these things will not fix. I think that it is very distracting and counterproductive for us to place too much credit on this superficial help and overlook, frankly, far more pressing issues."

"Well, now...," Hal stuttered.

Before he could respond, Kevin placed a silencing hand on his sleeve, making Nicole bristle even more. "I'd like the chance to respond to Ms. Blakely, if you don't mind." Looking at Nicole silently and seriously, he paused, as if carefully weighing his words. The firm look in his soft brown eyes almost had her feeling guilty for ever doubting him and she squirmed under their silent pressure. When he had commanded her complete attention with his eyes, he said, "Ms. Blakely, perhaps you question my commitment to this institution..."

"I'm not here to question you, or your *commitment*," oh how she despised him for using that word, "to anything. I'm just bringing up the facts..."

He continued as if he hadn't noticed her brief inter-
jection. "But let me reassure you and the entire board,"
he subtly emphasized the last word, "I sincerely want to
see Tolleston College take its place as one of the preem-
inent institutions of this country. As an alumnus of this
college I share your concern for its present as well as its
future. But change takes time..." He was cut off abruptly by Hal.

"And it's slow," Hal interjected nervously, not at all
comfortable with the level of tension he felt in the air.

Again, Kevin continued as if he hadn't been interrupted. "And I am after all only a man." He warred with
her eyes, daring her to interject whatever sarcastic
remark that her facial expression said she was clearly biting down on. "True, these changes may seem superficial
in the face of all that must be done, but, Ms. Blakely, I'm
sure you will agree that we must start somewhere.
Personally, I feel guilty, knowing that I have neglected
my moral obligations here for too long." He paused,
again daring her to say the sarcastic remark he knew she
was thinking. "But I decided not to let that guilt stop me
from doing what I can now. I'm old enough and, I hope,
wise enough, to realize that if each of us does just our little part we can hopefully make a big difference. I don't,
as you probably think, flatter myself that these few dollars will singlehandedly save the school. I believe that I
have a God-given talent in athletics that sustained me

through a successful career. Now that I have ended that career, I offer the board a chance to use me as they will." The humility of his last statement was belied by the arrogance in his eyes.

"Well said, Kevin." Hal was practically teary-eyed at the conclusion of his speech. "And in case I didn't mention it, Kevin is returning his salary in full to the school for use as the board sees fit." Because he had mentioned that earlier, no board member doubted whom that last comment was meant for. Thoroughly chastened, Nicole remained silent.

Softening somewhat as he looked at her, Hal continued, "Nicole, however, does raise a valid point, along with Kevin's. This is an excellent place for the school to begin its comeback but it is just a beginning. In speaking with Kevin, I know that he does have wonderful ideas to stimulate enrollment. We all know this is an issue Nicole has been working on as well. We've got to bring the numbers up by next fall, or there simply won't be a school." He looked carefully around the board. "Nicole, I think it would be wise to coordinate your efforts with Kevin's athletic recruitment efforts. I think together you two would make a wonderful team." He sent her a look that gave no quarter. "Bring him up to date immediately. Also, since you two will be working together on recruitment, please make time in your schedule to show him around and reacquaint him with our campus and staff. He'll also need to be brought up to date on all aspects of the athletic department."

"Perhaps Coach Spears will be helpful in that area. After all he has been acting director..." Nicole halted when Hal looked at her as if she were a student two months late with her term paper. Relenting, she said, "Of course some of those documents are in my office. I'll be happy to show him exactly where."

"Thank you," Hal replied. "I'm sure Coach Spears will be happy to do whatever he can. As for our push to increase enrollment, that really has been your project. And I'm sure your insight and help during this adjustment period will be more beneficial in general."

"Of course," Nicole agreed with a meek nod.

"Now," Hal continued, "I come to the regretful part of our meeting. Many of you called me to ask what happened to the sale of the Nat Turner book. I know speculation has run rampant and I'm sure my vagueness did not help. But I wanted to make the announcement today so that Ms. Blakely and I can respond to your questions together."

Nicole felt the anxious tension rise in the pit of her stomach as she waited with the others when he paused.

"As you know, for security reasons it was not displayed with the other items in the ballroom. Instead, it was held in the courtesy suite the hotel had given us for the night. Briefly put, the book was stolen from that same room before the auction."

Nicole squirmed uncomfortably as all eyes turned

toward her in stunned disbelief. All eyes except Kevin's, whose coolly assessing gaze never wavered, clearly having heard this information already.

"I'll ask Ms. Blakely to explain the events leading up to the theft and then I'll fill you in on what steps we will be taking for the book's recovery. Nicole, if you don't mind..." He waited patiently as she scrambled for a statement.

"Well, as you know, the book was kept in a locked case with only Hal and me having a key...," Nicole began. She summarized simply and concisely the pertinent events leading up to the theft, and ended with her reassurance that every possible effort would be made for the discreet recovery of the stolen book.

Hal added that the investigation was being led by the security firm, who also had a vested interest in the book's return.

"Let me get this straight," Kevin interjected. "The same company which could possibly be responsible for the theft of the book is leading the investigation?" he asked incredulously.

"Well," Hal stuttered, "as I tried to explain, they have a vested interest in finding the book. They don't want to be held responsible for its loss."

"It seems to me they could also have a 'vested interest' in making sure it's never recovered. I would suggest that an objective investigator be used." His smile softened his next words, "Someone with no ties to the theft and who could only benefit by the book's return."

"Well, of course we thought of that." Hal stumbled because of course he hadn't. "But the truth is, we simply cannot afford to let this leak out. Discretion in this case is just as important as recovery."

"In that case," Kevin replied, "I would like to volunteer the services of Michael Dix. Some of you may remember him as a teammate in my football days. While playing ball, Michael completed his master's degree in criminal justice and started a private security firm. I have used him on several occasions and can vouch for his discretion and his aptitude. And I would be willing to foot the bill myself." He looked around the table arrogantly. "That is, if there are no objections."

"Are there any objections?" Hal asked. The board members shook their heads. As there appear to be no objections, and I certainly have none, then we gratefully accept your generous offer."

"Good," Kevin responded. "I'll have Mike contact you by the end of the day."

The meeting adjourned ten minutes later. As everyone leapt at the chance to hover around Kevin, Nicole sat shell-shocked. Not only was Kevin going to be working with the school directly, he was going to be here on campus, in an office facing her own. To make matters worse, she was saddled with the responsibility of babysitting him! She hastily got her papers together. Before she could make a quiet retreat, Kevin's hand snaked out and grabbed hers with the lightning quickness he was known for on the field. The tingles radiating from his touch, more than his sudden action, had her looking up in shock.

"Are you leaving so soon?" he asked. "I was hoping we'd get a chance to go over a few things today." He added apologetically, "If that's possible."

"Actually, today is really not a good day for me," she hedged, hoping Hal didn't hear her trying to get out of her new assignment.

"Nicole," Kevin stated firmly, letting her know in no uncertain terms that this was not a request, "today."

"Fine," she replied, exasperated. "I'll be in my office." It was only then, after he released her hand, that Nicole could release the breath she hadn't known she'd been holding. She didn't have time to ponder how he could still affect her senses this way before she fled.

Three hours later she was fuming in her office. This was just like him! He had asked her to be available and now he looked like a no show. He probably was still entertaining his groupies on the executive board. Twenty more minutes, she promised her growling stomach, and then she would leave for her lunch date with David. When he'd called earlier to get the gossip on what happened at the board meeting, she didn't have the heart to tell him over the phone that he'd all but been replaced.

Since the beginning of the school year in August, when former Athletic Director Lyons had abruptly resigned, David Spears had been acting athletic director. Lyons, being unable to deal with internal and external pressure, had walked out on his contract. The staff had watched him go with mixed feelings. While he had not played by the rules of fairness he had worked so hard to instill in his athletes, everyone knew that he sincerely loved the school. David had reluctantly taken his place. Although he had known there was a possibility he would be replaced, everyone had felt sure he would be made permanent when the suspension was finally lifted. It seemed sad and very unfair for Kevin Powell to literally come in off the street and steal his job. And, of course, Nicole was left with the unpleasant task of informing David. It was just one more thing she could be thankful to Hal for.

She looked angrily at her watch wondering where her latest project was. Well, she told herself, she'd promised David she would meet him at noon and it was eleven-thirty. She would not, she silently resolved, be late just for Kevin Powell. Nicole was looking around for her purse when the knock on the door startled her. Without waiting for assent, Kevin entered.

Smiling boyishly, he nearly took her breath away. For that moment it was as if time had transported her back to the period when they had been friends and so much more. How many times, she thought, had he been running late and come to her apartment with just that look on his face. "Hey Butter," he would say, "sorry I'm late but the coach held us over working on plays." Of course, she would never instantly forgive him. They would go through their ritual where she would pretend to be mad, and he would tease and kiss her until she would laughingly give in. He would say, "I can always tell when you're mad at me because the freckles on your nose stand out." Then he would plant little soft kisses on her nose and cheeks until she would shoo him away. "I have to keep kissing them until they go back in," he would say as she continued swatting his kisses away until eventually they would compromise with a long, slow, passionate kiss.

"Sorry, I'm late. I got caught up with some people Hal wanted me to talk to for a minute and time kind of got away from us."

Shaking herself out of her reverie at his words, she stood up, even more angry for having remembered the past in such detail. "Well, I can't meet with you now. I'm on my way to lunch. So we'll have to meet some other time. Have Rose schedule you an appointment."

"As a matter of fact, I'm starving myself, so where are we going," he asked.

"I am going to meet David and you can go...well, let's just say, you're on your own."

"If by David you mean Coach Spears, I think now would be an excellent time for me to meet him. Just let me get my jacket."

"No, now is probably not a good time for you to meet

with him as I'll be telling him basically that you are replacing him. I think he deserves the respect of at least being told that in private. Don't you," she asked sweetly.

"All right, I can respect that. Can we meet after lunch then, say around two-thirty?"

"No." Placing the strap of her purse on her shoulder, she reached for her jacket in a way that was clearly dismissive. When he didn't seem to take the hint, she started advancing toward the door. She stopped in front of him when he didn't move. Having come this far, she could not retreat without seeming defensive. Instead, she looked up at him questioningly.

"Nicole, we need to talk," he said while locking her eyes in a firm grip.

"Do we? It seems as if you said everything you had to say back in the meeting. I got the message loud and clear. You are here, Mr. Superman, to save the school, and all of us mere

mortals who have been here struggling all along should just move gratefully out of the way. "

"You can be as sarcastic as you like, Nicole, but the cold hard facts are, that for all of your struggling, right now this school is in desperate need of a superhero to save it..."

"And that's supposed to be you?" she asked in disbelief.

"Hey, it was your analogy, not mine, but if the cape

fits I'll wear it. I'm willing to do whatever I have to do to save the school."

"Okay, say I accept that at face value. The question remains, Kevin, why? Why now after all this time? Let's get this one thing out in the open. What are you really doing here?"

"You really don't know the answer to that? You can't imagine why I'm here trying desperately to save the one thing that really means anything to you?" He paused, as if carefully weighing his words, before continuing softly, "Didn't I once promise you if you ever needed me I would be there for you?"

"That was a long time ago, Kevin." She sighed in exasperation as she moved nervously back to her desk, no longer caring if it seemed defensive. "A million things have changed since then. You can't possibly expect me to believe that..."

"That what? That I still care, that I've always cared? Just because you cut me out of your life doesn't mean..."

"Doesn't mean you can just walk back into it anytime you want!" she spit out angrily. "And let's not forget how willingly you went. You were more than happy to take the out I gave you. So let's have a little honesty for once. Tell me why you are really here." Nicole struggled to contain a quiet furor. "Long lost, undying love I'm not buying. Save it for the media and the people who don't know you."

"And do you know me, Nicole? Do you think you

still do after all this time?"

"As they say, a leopard doesn't change his spots."

"Hmm," he said almost sadly. "Well, maybe that's the problem. I'm not a leopard as you call me now. I wasn't a dog, as you called me then. I was a kid with a lot of growing up to do and I made a lot of mistakes. But since you don't seem any more interested in hearing me out now than you did ten years ago, I don't see any point in rehashing it all..."

"Neither do I since, as you say, I'm no more interested today than I ever was in hearing your sorry excuses."

"So if you feel we can just pack the past away, we should be able to work together with no problem. Especially if we are both true professionals."

"I'm nothing if not professional. So if there's nothing else, as I said before, I'm on my way to lunch." Nicole stood.

"You do realize that we will have to meet eventually and sooner rather than later?" he asked in a resigned tone.

"Yes," she agreed reluctantly. "But not today. I can meet with you tomorrow...," she paused as she leaned over to flip through her appointment book, playing the moment for all it was worth, "tomorrow at ten a.m."

He clearly saw through her ruse and smiled cynically. "Sure thing."

"And please be prompt," Nicole couldn't resist

adding.

"Yes ma'am," he replied sarcastically, letting her know that she would only be allowed to take the game so far.

"Just one thing, Kevin," she said as she came around her desk and he followed her to the door. "What's the real reason you think we need to hire Dix?"

"You're kidding, right?" he asked in disbelief. "You can't possibly be that naive," he continued as she looked at him in confusion. "Nicole, you must see that all the evidence right now is pointing to you as the thief."

"Don't be ridiculous...nobody would...," she stammered in complete shock.

"Anybody would," he stated firmly. "You talk the school into selling a priceless book, you alone arrange security, you have the book stored in your hotel room in your safe. Who do you think is the most logical thief?" Looking deeply into her eyes as she came to a halt within arm's distance of him, he added, "Instead of hiring you a detective, I should have hired you a dream team of lawyers, because I can't imagine anyone looking more guilty than you do. You practically have the smoking gun still in your hands."

"Well, if I truly look so guilty, why are you so sure I didn't do it?" Nicole asked curiously.

"You may not have really known me, but I do know you, Nicky," he smiled. "I know your loyalty will have you here on this sinking ship until you drown with it. I know that you would have put yourself on that auction block to save this school before you would have stolen one cent. I know you are so honest you are not going to put your lunch this afternoon on your expense account even though you will discuss business." He laughed softly as he traced an errant curl lying softly on her shoulder. He ran his finger over the few freckles sprinkled on her nose before she could duck away.

"I even know that with your big heart, it is killing you to hold a grudge against a grown man for mistakes he made as a kid." He pressed on when she would have protested. "But don't worry, I know you will hold on to that grudge as tightly as you can. And you should, for as long as you can, because you know that the minute you let that guard down, I'll do what I was too young and stupid to do in the first place."

"Which is what?" Nicole asked breathlessly.

He leaned down to whisper the answer so softly in her ear it took her a minute to fully grasp his outrageous comment. "Never let you go." With those final words he exited the office, leaving Nicole standing open-mouthed in shock as witty comebacks and erotic images danced in her head.

# Chapter 4

"Yo, Ms. B, can you believe it?" Tyrone asked, his face beaming at Nicole as she walked into administrative building.

Nicole realized from Tyrone's question and the awestruck look on his face that the day she had been dreading had finally arrived. Kevin was moving into his office today. Although it had been three days since he accepted the position of athletic director, Nicole had not held out hope that he would renege on his word. One thing she had always known about Kevin was that he was single-minded in the pursuit of any goal. Whatever goal he was going after here at the school, she was certain he was not leaving until he reached it. Feigning ignorance in response to Tyrone's question, she hedged, "Believe what?"

"Kevin Powell, here at our school. I mean, not like at the auction. He's going to be here, every day. I mean, didn't you hear?" His excitement was bubbling over so much even Nicole found it difficult to pretend indifference.

"Yes, of course I know," she smiled. "I'm just teasing you." She paused uncharacteristically as she continued uncertainly, "Um, is he inside?" She fiddled nervously with her suit jacket.

"Yeah, I met him already," he continued, not noticing Nicole's hesitance. "He is so down-to-earth. I mean, really a cool guy! I can't believe he used to go here." His quick mind was clicking away. "That was around the same time you were here. Did you know him? I guess you had to, what with the school being so small." He continued as he answered his own question, "What was he like then?"

Barely able to meet his eyes, Nicole answered, "He was..., I guess he was pretty much the way he is now. You know people don't change much." At least, that was honest, she thought to herself. Changing the subject, she asked what she had wondered all weekend. "What office did they put him in?"

"The one right across from you," he beamed. "Isn't that great?"

"Great," she responded to his back as he bounded up the stairs. After mentally preparing herself for the excitement, Nicole was still surprised when she arrived on the executive floor. The entire floor was crowded with spectators ranging from students and faculty to members of the press. Nicole's mouth gaped in shock. Kevin had promised to make his transition as smooth as possible and promised he would handle any excessive media problems. If this wasn't excessive, Nicole thought, she didn't know what was. The usually sedate executive floor had been transformed into a madhouse.

Tolleston's executive floor was situated in the top floor of the administrative building. All of the offices on the floor surrounded the secretary's station like spokes coming off of a wheel. Every office had a view of the Tennessee mountain landscape. Usually the soft elegance of the floor set a peaceful tone for Nicole's day. Today, she thought as she made her way to Rose's station in the center of the floor, was a glaring exception.

Bullying her way to Rose's desk, she smiled ruefully at the secretary. "Can you believe this?"

"I know it's a mess, but you can't help getting caught up in the excitement," Rose answered, standing on tiptoes to get a better view of all the commotion.

"Can't I?" Nicole queried.

Rose turned her sharp eyes, which hadn't missed anything in the more than twenty years she'd worked for the school, toward Nicole. One of the few people on the campus who knew the story of Kevin and Nicole's failed relationship, having played mother hen to both of them, Rose empathized with Nicole. "How ya hanging in there?" she asked with concern. Her dark eyes peered over her glasses. "I know this must be a little difficult for you."

"Just a little, you think?" Nicole responded. "No, really I'm all right," she smiled after seeing a frown forming on Rose's face. "I've had a few days to get used to the idea, and I can handle it. As long as all of this," she nodded her head in the direction of the crowd, "is going to benefit the school in some way."

"I'm sure it will," Rose assured her, reaching across her desk to touch Nicole's hand. "I don't know all of what happened between you, but I know that he did care," she affirmed as Nicole huffed in disbelief. "And I'm sure he still does, about you and this school. So, I'm going to give him a chance, and if he messes up, then he's not too big for me to knock him upside his head," she added, making Nicole smile.

"Can you do it anyway, just for me?" Nicole asked.

"Maybe later," Rose laughed. "Meanwhile," she adjusted her glasses and became professional again, "get to your desk. I left some messages on it for you and I'll bring you some coffee in a little bit."

"Thanks, Rose. And if you see Tyrone in this crowd somewhere, will you send him in? Kindly remind him that today is a work day."

"Will do, boss." She grinned as she turned back to watch the commotion.

Two hours later when Nicole was interrupted by a

knock on her office door, she barely had time to look up before the door opened. Entering the office arrogantly and without permission was Kevin, the object of Nicole's distraction all morning. Since she had been unable to concentrate on a single thing because of him, seeing him face to face did not improve her mood.

"Busy?" he asked, making himself comfortable in the chair facing her, obviously unconcerned with her answer.

"Actually, I am." She refused to acknowledge the betraying flutter in her heart.

"Doing what?" His devilish grin revealed that he was all too aware of her pretense.

"If you must know, I am going over my plans to increase school enrollment." Before her self-satisfied return smile could settle firmly into place for having thought of something so quickly, Kevin responded.

"Great, that's one of the first things I wanted to be updated about. And as you can see I'm right on time, just as you requested. So how's it going?"

"Requested...?" A puzzled look crossed her face.

"You told me to be here today at ten-thirty, sharp. And here I am. Ready to talk about
your plans. You did want me..., " he broke off to allow time for the double entendre to sink in. Grinning, he added, "For recruitment. That's what you said."

Nicole, who had not been thinking about recruitment at all, quickly rallied. "Yes, of course." She pretended to miss his innuendo. "Basically, the first phase of our plan involves traveling to various high schools and presenting group orientations, including a very nice slide show the communication department has put together. From these orientations, hopefully we'll get groups whom we will sponsor to come and visit the school on weekends. We hope that if we get more students to actually visit our campus they will fall in love with this school and want to attend." She broke off when she noticed that Kevin seemed to be looking at her with disapproval.

"Is that it?" His usually expressive dark eyes were shuttered, making Nicole fidget unbecomingly with the neckline of her suit.

"Well actually, I was thinking that since you will be a member of the staff now that perhaps we could have you make a few personal appearances at some of..."

"No," he interrupted before she could finish. Personal appearances from Kevin Powell are absolutely out of the question."

"Do you mind if I ask why? After all you were the one who spoke with such passion of your commitment to the school."

"Believe me, I'm refusing because of my commitment to the school. The media, the security issues, the confusion will all take the focus off the school and place it on me. And trust me, the last thing we need right now is a bunch of hero-struck kids enrolling because Kevin

Powell said to do so. We need good kids who are here because of a concern for their education and future. I'm not saying I won't meet with the kids ever," he continued as she started to interrupt his passionate refusal. "But if I have to do it, I would rather do so here in a more controlled environment." He looked at her squarely, as if daring her to come up with an argument against his logic. She couldn't and he knew it.

"Well, what do you think of the plan in general, besides leaving you out of it?"

He uncharacteristically dodged a direct answer. "We can talk about that some other time."

"No way. You insisted we meet now," she reminded him, "and you obviously disapprove, so let's have it. What holes in the plan does the Great Kevin Powell see?" she goaded.

"Fine," he responded angrily. "First of all, I think your plan totally underestimates the intelligence of the students. Today's kids aren't likely to be swayed into picking their college by viewing some slide show."

"But just a minute ago, they were unintelligent enough to be swayed by some has-been football player," she spat out, tapping her ink pen in agitation

"Secondly," he continued as if he hadn't heard her, "It sounds like the same boring presentations they will hear from every other school. C'mon Nicole, you have more creativity than this. Where's the pizzazz?"

"...the pizzazz?" Nicole fumed. "How dare you

come in here and judge me?"

"Face it. You haven't built in any way upon the uniqueness of the school. This is a historically black college with a rich cultural history. Kids today respond to products related to their own unique culture. Just look at the popularity of the hip-hop nation."

"So what are suggesting I do, go on stage and rap about the school?" she asked sarcastically.

They both paused for a moment, looked at each other stoically and then burst into laughter as the mental image struck them both at the same time.

Kevin stopped laughing first, and sat for a moment in complete silence, his dark eyes capturing the unguarded warmth on her face. He seemed mesmerized. For a moment the silence continued as Nicole struggled to control herself and put up the shutters against his penetrating stare. "Do you know," he finally said, "that is the first time I have seen you laugh or even genuinely smile since I've been here. For a while you almost had me convinced that maybe I had waited too late, that the real Nicole was gone, leaving some hard-hearted ice queen in her place."

Disturbed by his words and the conflicting feelings they evoked, Nicole clung desperately to her defenses. When she finally exhaled softly and spoke, her words were firm and sure. "The Nicole you used to know *is* gone, if you are referring to the Nicole you could easily lie to and manipulate. Or the Nicole who used to hang onto every word as if you were the last man on earth. Or the Nicole who thought you could walk on water. Well, she's grown up. So if you came here looking for that pure, fawning adoration you used to get, then you might as well move on, you have fans all over the world. Now I see you for the man you really are."

The deep brown of his eyes bored holes through hers and he spoke through a facial mask as enigmatic as her own. "I hope that's true because that's what I want. All I want is for you to see me as I really am and give me a chance to show you how much I've grown."

Nicole wondered how words she had meant to be biting and sarcastic had been twisted so skillfully to his own defense. Minutes ticked by as Kevin waited for a response. Nicole merely hardened her eyes and refused to give him another opening. Their eyes battled silently, and to Nicole's surprise, hers eventually won. When his eyes lowered, he took a deep breath and returned to business. His words drowned out Nicole's sigh of relief.

"Look, Nicole, contrary to what you think, I don't presume to have all of the answers. I just know that if we don't get that enrollment up by the fall, there will not be a Tolleston College for anybody. I don't want to see that happen." He paused before saying softly, "You know, I always kind of hoped our children would come here, like we did." At Nicole's look of startled surprise, he added, "Just because I didn't say it then, didn't mean I didn't always picture you as the mother of my kids."

"Well, isn't it just too bad and too sad that you find that so easy to say now, when it's too late?"

"It's only sad if it is too late," he responded. "But now is neither the time nor place to discuss what could have been in our relationship. We were speaking about your plan. I do feel it could work, even if it does lack the creativity and pizzazz I personally think it should have." "And," he continued, ignoring her outraged expression, "all of the media attention from today should help. It's the main reason I didn't insist on a complete press black-out."

"Oh that's right, how could I forget? 'The Great Kevin' is here to save the day. They didn't forget to put that nameplate on your office door, did they?" she asked for the sheer joy of seeing his hackles rise.

"Well, I'll let you get back to what you were doing. You were sitting in here...," he paused for effect, "work-ing, weren't you?" Arrogantly certain that her thoughts had been solely on him he rose and exited .

Exhausted, Nicole went by Rose's desk as she left for the day. She stopped short as she noticed that Kevin was already there ahead of her, apparently with last minute instructions as well. When he finished, Nicole asked, "Rose could you make sure we order those pizzas for the lock-in on Friday night."

"What lock-in?" Kevin asked, clearly not embar-rassed by his blatant eavesdropping.

"Nicole didn't tell you?" Rose looked at him in disbelief. "She had a great idea. She and some volunteers are going to lock themselves into the gym on Friday night and make recruitment packages. It's going to be like a little party with pizza, music, even some games Nicole made up to put a little fun in the evening. The lock-in's purpose is to get at least two thousand packages made up so that she can take at least one hundred to each of the twenty schools she'll be visiting in the coming weeks. It's an initiative she's calling 'twenty schools in twenty days.' It's going to be big fun. You should come."

"I would have mentioned it to you," Nicole said in answer to his unspoken question when Kevin's eyes swung accusingly to hers. "But it just didn't seem to have enough *creativity* or *pizzazz*."

"No, actually getting the kids involved sounds like the best part of your plan so far. So of course I'll be there. In fact, the pizza is on me."

" 'Great Kevin' to the rescue again," Nicole muttered ungratefully.

"Something you wanted to say...?" When he received no response to his rhetorical question, he continued, "I thought not. Anyway, ladies, it's certainly been an exciting day for me and I am calling it quits for the evening."

"Goodnight, Kevin, sweetheart. And welcome back." Rose's voice dripped with such sugary genuineness that Nicole almost gagged.

"Goodnight, Rose," he returned. "And goodnight, Nicole, sweetheart," Kevin said with mocking lightness, just as Carlista Cunningham came up the stairs and shook her artificially long hair out over her full-length fur coat.

Her high-glossed lips managed a pretty pout as she asked, "Kevin Powell, you haven't changed your mind, have you?" Just then, as if taken by complete surprise, her contact lens- colored blue eyes widened in shock as she looked at the other two women. "Oh, I'm sorry. I hope I haven't interrupted some sort of *business* meeting." Her subtle emphasis was purely to let the other two women know that her reason for being there was pure pleasure.

"No, not at all," Kevin responded. "I was just finishing up for the day. Have a good night, ladies."

Nicole watched in shock as he walked off with the stunning business woman without a backward glance. Rose interrupted her reverie by saying, "I wouldn't let that worry you any. She's been calling him here all day. I could hardly refuse to put her through, since she won the date with him. She said she wanted to talk to him about business, and, honey child, she would not take no for an answer. I think he eventually took the call just so he could get the date over with as quickly as possible. Then when he finally agreed to dinner tonight, she had the nerve to ask me if I would make the reservation! So like I said, I wouldn't worry any about her. I'm sure

Kevin has met enough of her kind to see straight through her."

"Believe me, Rose, I'm not worried," she mumbled as watched the couple drive away from the rotunda's window.

# Chapter 5

Flicking through channel after channel with her remote control, Nicole finally tossed it into the corner of her bedroom in frustration. Nothing was on television anyway, she thought in disgust. Not that she could have absorbed a single thing anyway, with her mind still ticking away in anger. As she walked restlessly from her bedroom to the bathroom her big floral house shoes made scratching noises on the floor. As she carefully scrutinized herself in the mirror she wondered if she'd really become an ice queen? Her reflected image in the bathroom mirror gave her no comfort.

Sure, her long flannel nightgown looked more like something a haggard old maid might wear, but it was comfortable. It wasn't like she would wear it in public. And tonight she had twisted her shoulder-length hair up into a simple ponytail, but even with its sloppy casualness, she thought she still looked appealing. True, she often went to work in one of the many starched and staid suits she had hanging in her closet, her hair in a neat and respectable bun or french roll. Makeup disguised her sprinkles of freckles and her lipstick was usually modest and toned down, but for goodness sake, she couldn't very well go to work dressed like a cheerleader.

Disgusted with herself for even considering Kevin's stupid comment, she turned off the bathroom light and headed to the kitchen for cheesecake. "Oh my God," she said aloud, "I'm like a bad episode of *The Golden Girls.*'" But just as quickly she banished the thought. Some days only cheesecake would do. Curling up in the middle of the couch with the whole pie, she couldn't escape the depressing thought, Have I really changed so much?

§§§

Nicole had been a nineteen-year-old sophomore when she first met Kevin. She could recall the day as if it had happened yesterday. She had been sitting on the bench in the middle of the  school's historic quad area when he had come running by trying to catch a football. He and a group of his friends had been tossing it around on that beautiful spring day. Each had been oblivious to the other—Nicole engrossed in her book and Kevin in his game—when their two worlds literally collided. Nicole had not been impressed at all by the six-foot-six, boisterous, popular player. But after months of dogged persistence, his good-natured smile, handsome looks and soft brown eyes eventually won her over. Nicole laughed to herself as she recalled how he'd worn his hair then in a high-top fade which had looked oddly appealing on his rugged face.

They'd been an odd couple from the very beginning. He was the most popular guy on campus and she was the girl whose name evoked, "Nicole who?" With popularity came problems. His groupies, as Nicole had called them, were not happy with the blossoming relationship, nor were his friends, for whom he suddenly had much less time. Whenever they walked around campus holding hands, catcalls were sure to be heard echoing out of doorways and bellowing down from windows. At the end of an evening when he walked her to her dormitory and kissed her innocently on the lips, guys could be heard chuckling as they walked by and girls clapping and sighing from the windows above. Eventually everybody realized that this was no 'flash in the pan,' and that the relationship was rock solid. After those first few months, they were like an old married couple nobody noticed anymore.

Looking like an old married couple or not, the physical side of their relationship had progressed much more slowly. Although Kevin was an experienced lover,

Nicole was not, and her strict upbringing kept her from taking that final step for a long time. One of the things that had endeared him to her had been his patience. He'd often repeated, "I love you and I never want you to do something you're not ready to do. Besides, we have the rest of our lives, 'cause I'm not going anywhere." In retrospect, it had probably been just a line. But line or not, he did wait lovingly and patiently as month after month went by chastely. In fact, it was not until the following year when Nicole had moved into her own apartment that things changed.

One day after an intense session of love play, Nicole worked up the courage to tell Kevin she was finally ready for a more intimate relationship. Ironically, it was Kevin who balked, saying, "Butter, think it over, I don't want this decision to be made in the heat of passion. Like I've told you, I can wait." No amount of arguing could convince him on that night of her sincereness. So she finally changed the subject by asking him again why he called her *Butter,* a question he had always refused to answer.

This particular time he chose to answer. "Easy," he said, reclining once more onto her couch, pulling her down on top of him. "Your skin is like butter." He placed kisses on her cheeks and neck before continuing. "Your touch is like butter." He grabbed her hand and kissed each finger for emphasis. "And when I kiss you, your kisses taste like butter." He placed a soft deep kiss on her lips already plumped by his previous kisses.

When he came up for air, she teased him by saying, "Always ready with a good line. Can't you come up with something more original than that?"

To her surprise, he didn't immediately respond with a joke as he usually did when she teased him about some of the sweet things he said. Instead of rising to the bait, he just looked at her silently for a long time. Finally he said, "Do you know I lifted three hundred pounds today in practice?"

Puzzled, Nicole struggled to follow his line of thought. "No, I didn't..."

"When I was finished, I was amazed at myself. It really hit me how strong I am. You know, people always tell me, 'Kevin, be careful, you don't know your own strength.' But today I really did. I felt so strong, so powerful..." He looked down as if embarrassed and confused. "You are the only thing that makes me feel weak. And you don't even know the power you have over me...I love you so much. So much it actually scares me sometimes and I haven't been scared of anything since I can't remember when."

Too choked up with tears to respond, Nicole could only hug and kiss him. Finally she tearfully managed, "I love you too, just as much. It's just as scary to me and it makes me feel just as weak." Quiet wrapped around them like a warm blanket as the two of them found comfort and refuge in each other's tight embrace on Nicole's sagging and lumpy, second-hand couch.

Nicole remembered his anxiety as they waited for the weekend of the draft pick. A big party was planned on campus and all of his teammates would wait with Nicole and his immediate family members for the announcement of his draft pick. The countdown to that weekend had been fraught with tension as everyone knew Kevin was being drafted; the only doubt was how high he would go. As they sat at her apartment eating fast food and laughing, Nicole had looked at him and suddenly asked seriously, "Will it always be like this, no matter what?" The question which had been wreaking havoc with her insecurities all week just seemed to burst from her mouth and could not be taken back.

Kevin, seeing her unsaid anxieties, had answered carefully. "Butter," he took her hand before continuing, "I don't know what the future holds. But I know I don't have one without you." He had leaned forward to give her a quick smacking kiss with their lips still greasy from food. "I can only promise you this. I'll always love you. No matter what, that'll never change."

Nicole, fool that she'd been, had believed him and his stupid lines. She had loved him too much to imagine anything else. Well, Nicole thought in disgust as she rose from her couch, angry that she had allowed herself to slip into the past so easily, I will never be that big a fool again. With that thought firmly in mind, Nicole got into her bed and mentally prepared for another night of tossing and turning.

🙐🙐🙐

Boxes lined two walls of the gymnasium with papers to be sorted on one side and completed packages on the other. Nicole looked around the room in pleasure. Most of the school had turned out to help. That was no big surprise. She knew that the reason for the sudden commitment to the school had been sparked by the quickly-leaked rumor that Kevin would be here tonight helping out. What had surprised her was how well he handled the crowd. At first he had made a slight speech as all of them seemed to expect it. His light and jovial manner put all of the students at ease. Afterwards, he had 'worked the crowd,' meeting and greeting every student personally. He was not too busy for any question, autograph or picture opportunity.

Nicole had been initially angry by what she perceived as his showboating. But it soon became obvious that there was a method to his madness. As the evening went on, the crowd had thinned, leaving only those who had truly come to work. Kevin left and returned with another round of pizza, chicken wings and soda. By now, he was on a first name basis with almost all of the remaining volunteers. And they were too flattered by his recalling their names to mind his harmless ribbing. Even Nicole was the victim of some of his jokes. Watching her as she got up to retrieve cups for everyone, he let out a low whistle and said, "Nicole, how did you remember to wear my favorite outfit?"

Nicole, who had never intended to dress for his pleasure, whirled around in disgust. "I certainly did not! I don't have on anything except jeans and a sweatshirt."

"And you never looked better," he answered. Turning to their captive audience, he added, "You all don't know how Nicole used to look." Winking to some of the guys, he continued, "Butter would walk around campus every day in those jeans and I swear traffic would stop. None of those shapeless blue suits she wears now. And not those baggy, sagging jeans girls wear now. Those were jeans that fit. She would have to beat the men off with a stick."

"Kevin Powell, I can't believe you can sit here and tell that story to these students." She protested with heavy emphasis on the word *students*. She turned to the volunteers as she sat down in the only seat available, one so close to Kevin that their knees were bumping under the table. "Do not listen to him. I was an honor roll student who spent more time in the library than anywhere else."

"A likely story," Kevin continued with his humoring. "If you all want to know your dean's never-told secrets, just stop by my office one day." He winked as he finished.

"Oh yeah, well, two can play that game," she vowed, giving as good as she got. "Don't let me get started on how Kevin was always trying to borrow some girl's pantyhose. The day before any game, Kevin was sure to be somewhere on campus asking for hosiery."

"You know I needed those to wear under my football leggings to keep warm," he laughed.

"I know that's what you used to say you needed them for..." She rolled her eyes. "But I heard stories of what really went on in that football dormitory and you guys were always just a little too close. Have you talked to Allen lately? Your old roommate?"

"Well, yeah but..."

"Case closed," she interrupted, much to the student's amusement.

"Hey," Tyrone asked, "why do you call Miss B., *Butter*?"

His innocent question caught them both by surprise, and they looked at each other as the same mental picture popped in their minds simultaneously. It seemed nearly a full minute before they broke eye contact and Kevin was able to respond. "That's because Nicole would look all innocent and sweet when something happened. Say she didn't do her homework. She would stand up in class and tell the most outrageous whopper of a lie, with the straightest face. My mother used to describe a person like that by saying, 'Butter wouldn't melt in their mouth.' Now to this day, I swear I don't know what that means, but it just seemed to fit. We would all just watch her in amazement.

"Kevin L. Powell! How could you tell that story and give these kids the impression I was a liar?" Nicole protested in outrage. "I am not a liar, nor was I ever. Do not listen to this man," she begged while laughing with the rest of the table.

"Did you miss me last night," he asked under the cover of laughter.

"Absolutely not," she whispered.

"See, what did I say. I know a good liar when I see one."

"Then how did you get the name, Miss B.?" Tyrone repeated.

"It was because of my complexion, that's all. And believe me," she said looking at Kevin, "I didn't like it then and I don't like it now."

"Liar," Kevin repeated for her ears only. After that, the tone was set for the rest of the night. The ribbing went on and Nicole had no chance to resume her usual stern, professional facade.

Finally around midnight, they looked around in wonder at their completed project. A box for each of the twenty schools Nicole would be visiting was neatly filled and securely taped. All Nicole would have to do for each trip was retrieve the box from the storage area behind the gymnasium stage. Well satisfied with the evening, the participants headed out in their various directions.

"Miss B., you need me to walk you home?" Tyrone yawned his question while stretching his long arms.

"Don't worry about it, Tyrone," Kevin responded before Nicole could. "I'll take her."

The easy camaraderie Nicole had felt in his presence all evening began to rapidly fade as the gym emptied. Shutting off the last of the lights as she prepared to lock the door, Nicole looked tiredly toward the exit. "Kevin, I'm okay. You go on. The faculty housing is only a block behind this building."

"Nicole," he growled in a low voice filled with impatience, "turn off those lights and let's go. You must be crazy if you think I'm going to let you walk anywhere after midnight."

"Let me?" she repeated in exasperation at his chauvinism. "I think I'm old enough to decide for myself where I will walk and who with, thank you very much. I have lived on this campus for the last eight years and I've never had any trouble getting home. No matter what time it was."

"And I suppose you spend a lot of nights coming home this late?" His brows rose in disbelief.

"A few, after late games and during homecoming."

"Yeah, well, I wasn't here then. So get your stuff and let's go." His lids lowered seductively when Nicole seemed to be slowing down in protest rather than speeding up. "You know, actually I'm not really in that big a hurry. I believe this is the first time we've been completely alone since I've been back." His smile widened with sensual promise. "Maybe we could sit down on those bleachers back there and..."

"You know what, I'm ready." Grinning, Nicole interrupted before he could finish his suggestive statement.

"That's what I thought," he answered before they both started laughing.

"Where's your car parked?" Nicole looked around curiously as he began walking toward her home.

"It's in the north lot. I'll walk back and get it after I see you home, since you don't live too far," he reminded her in a mocking voice. Stopping suddenly, he stood still and looked up in wonder at the endless sea of stars on the black velvet canvas of the Tennessee night sky. "It really is a beautiful night." Grabbing her hand quickly, he pulled her close to his side and before she could protest, he pointed. "Look, a falling star."

"Where?" Looking in the direction he pointed, she couldn't see anything. She glanced at his face and saw him silently laughing at her. Feeling foolish for her naivete, she said, "Oh, you..." Trying unsuccessfully to snatch her hand back and pull away from the inviting warmth of his body, she protested, "I can't believe I fell for such a childish trick. You ought to be embarrassed at your age to have to resort to such foolishness just to get a girl's hand." Seeing that her words meant to be humiliating were having no effect, she added, "Oh, grow up!"

"You're right. I should be embarrassed." Continuing his hold of her hand, he brought his other arm around to enfold her securely in his embrace. "But I'm not. Sometimes you have to use whatever opening you can get. Desperate times require desperate measures. And I was pretty desperate to do this." *This* turned out to be the lowering of his head towards her lips as he pulled her closer.

Nicole, who had seen the kiss coming, had time, she admitted to herself, to evade it if she had really tried. But for once her heart overruled her head and she found she couldn't resist. Seconds before his lips actually touched hers, she changed her mind suddenly, remembering how powerful his kisses could be. But by then it was much too late. Shock waves coursed through her body at the first electric touch of his lips. Merely butterfly caresses nibbling at the outside creases of her mouth at first, his soft kisses soon had her yearning for the full mastery of his tongue as her senses discovered that time had not robbed him of his powerful physical effect on her. When she softly moaned in protest to his gentle teasing, he deepened the kiss. For Nicole, the first meeting of their tongues, the feel of his strong embrace, his hand softly caressing the nape of her neck was like coming home after a long, long trip away. It was he, not she, who remembered where they were and finally pulled back. "Like I said," he repeated, releasing her from the bonds of his arms yet clasping her hands, "this is a beautiful night."

Nicole silently agreed. Remembering times they had

walked the campus in years past, holding hands and just reveling in being together, Nicole sighed wistfully.

"Yeah," Kevin sighed in response, almost as if he could read the silent path her heart was moving along. Within minutes the short walk was over. Both felt its loss because for a few moments they had been transported back in time.

"Well, I guess we're here." Kevin looked at Nicole for a long minute before saying, "You know, the night doesn't have to end here. You could always invite me in."

For just a second, Nicole contemplated it. As he stared at her with the sensuous look she had seen so many times just before their most romantic interludes, Nicole was sorely tempted. Sighing with regret for all that could have been, she found the strength to refuse. "No, I don't think I could do that."

"That's all right, one day you will." Before she could protest, he continued. "But meanwhile, I'll have to content myself with the fact that I really enjoyed tonight." He shook his head softly as if to clear it.

Because it was the exact thing she had seen him do countless times in the past, Nicole was transfixed. Awakening from a deep, comforting sleep, his guard down, he had always looked so sweet, so vulnerable.

He sighed as if he didn't know how to frame his words. "I know you don't believe this right now, but I've really missed you. I missed just talking and laughing with you. I missed the way you kept me in line." When

Nicole's eyes widened at that remark, he explained, "Oh Butter, you don't know. I've met all kinds of women in all kinds of places doing everything you could imagine. But nobody has ever made me feel the way you do. I wish I could say I could be satisfied with just your friendship because we had a great friendship and I've missed it." Reflecting quietly he added in a voice tinted with warm memories, "Today was so nice because I felt like I was with my friend again."

"Are you asking if we can be friends?" Nicole wrinkled her nose in puzzlement. She had turned in her doorway to look at his face while he spoke, and now she waited for his answer, unsure what her response would be.

"No, I'm not." All trace of wistfulness was gone as his voice grew firm with purpose. "Like I said, I wish I could be satisfied with just friendship. And I guess if I had come back here and found you happily in a relationship, I would have tried to respect that. But instead, I find you are just as beautiful and as sweet as you ever were. And I know that friendship will not be enough. Not now, not ever.

"I don't know what to tell you, Kevin." Looking within herself honestly, Nicole took a chance and told the truth. "I've missed your friendship too. That was part of what really hurt me. I thought we were sincere friends." Shaking her head in remembered pain, Nicole stuffed her hands into her jeans pocket out of fear they would betray her confusion. "But I don't miss the feeling of insecurity, the mistrust, the jealousy. I don't miss being the little woman in the background. I'm very happy here now. I feel like I've made a place for myself where I'm really doing some good things. Where I'm needed..."

"I need you..."

Nicole shook her head again to refute his words. "And I just don't want to go back. Not now, too much time has passed. And if you truly care about me...as a friend, you would just go away. Today was nice, but it can't be repeated. And the bottom line is, I don't want you here."

"I just can't believe that." Kevin stepped closer to her and took her hands in his. "I still feel that magic between us, Nicky, and as long as it's there, I know there's got to be a chance for us. And if you won't fight for it, believe me, I will."

Looking down at their entwined hands, Nicole cursed hers for betraying her by shaking. "I'm sorry, but there's just nothing left to fight for and nothing more to say," she said gently as she turned away.

"And what about our marriage?" Kevin asked gruffly to her back.

Nicole whirled around in surprise, angry at him for stooping to such a low blow. Their short-lived fiasco of a marriage was the one secret they had both kept to themselves. They'd never discussed it again after its abrupt ending ten years earlier. Nicole had been satisfied to maintain her legally separated status forever. Then as

Kevin's fame grew, Nicole had realized it would be impossible to file for an anonymous divorce without bringing tabloid sensationalism into her life and had never taken the final step. At least that was how she had rationalized her inaction to herself. She'd never known what Kevin's reasons were for maintaining his legal unavailability. From the moment he returned she'd known she was going to eventually have to discuss their marriage. However, when he didn't immediately mention it, she'd thought the subject would remain taboo and didn't mention it either.

"We will have to talk about it sooner or later. You do realize that?" He watched pointedly as she retreated two unconscious steps into her doorway.

"I wondered when you would finally get to that subject. Is that why you're really here? To settle it once and for all?"

"It depends on what you mean by settle. If it means that I'm here to get our marriage back on track, then yes, I'm here to settle it."

"Just like that? Do you think it could be that easy?"

"No, I don't imagine it will be easy. But I'm willing to do whatever I can..."

"...Whatever you can." Nicole shook her head in disbelief. "Can you go back in time and keep all the promises you broke? Like the promise to love me..."

"I do."

"Cherish me every day..."

"I did"

"So much so that you never sent a single letter. What about a card for my birthday?" Nicole continued angrily. "Can you go back in time and make up for missed holidays, vacations, for times when I was sick and needed comfort? Or times when I was down and needed support? Can you do all that?"

"Okay," Kevin stopped her in exasperation. "I admit it. I made mistakes. Your hero had feet of clay. But maybe I needed you to see me as a man and not a hero. It's the man who is here now trying to..."

"Don't even try it. Kevin, you always wanted me to see you as my hero. That's the role you wanted to play, so don't blame me if you couldn't live up to the high standard you set."

"I admit that too. I did like your hero-worshiping. And then when I needed you to see me as the man, I couldn't do it without toppling myself from my own pedestal." He shook his head in self-disgust. "But can you do it now? Can you see me as a man with faults?"

"I do. I see all your faults..."

"*And* as a hero? Can you see someone you admire, love and most importantly, trust?"

"I did. If anything I trusted you too much. And right now I don't know if I could do it again and frankly I don't know why I should try."

"Because I love you; then, now and forever, just like I promised. I believe you feel the same. Building a relationship is like building a house. We laid a solid foundation of love. But what we built up around it had to fall, because it wasn't real. It was a storybook house of fantasies that crumbled. Now we have a chance to build something real. We have that same foundation. All we need to do is get to work, both of us, building it up. Can you do that?"

"I don't know. I do know that even if we try it will take time."

"I can give you some time." Kevin hedged, "But it took me ten years to come to this point. I can't give you ten years to catch up."

"Can't or won't?"

"Either way. I need you too much. I know how selfish that makes me look, but that's part of the real man. The hero would have waited patiently, but the real me wants to just snatch you up. Whether you can live with a man who loves you that strongly is another question you'll have to ask yourself."

"I realize that," she responded, angry with his impatience. "But you are not going to take ten years to decide our marriage is important and then rush me into a decision in one week. So goodnight." And with those words, she entered the house and closed the door in his face, not caring when or how he left.

# Chapter Six

"Nicole," Rose's voice came through on the office speaker phone on the corner of Nicole's desk, "Tyrone is on line five. He says it's urgent."

"I should hope so. I sent him to get the recruitment packages for Wallace High School almost thirty minutes ago. He knows I have to be at that school in an hour," Nicole grumbled in complaint.

"Yeah, well, you know how easily he gets side-tracked. He's probably just calling to say he's running late," Rose soothed, trying to calm Nicole's ruffled feathers.

Nicole, who had not been in the best of moods, was not easily mollified. She quickly picked up the line Tyrone was waiting on. "Tyrone Reese, what is going on?"

"Miss B., you're not going to believe this. I think you need to get over here right away."

Expecting to hear his usual light, teasing voice, Nicole was struck immediately by the seriousness of his tone. Alarmed, she asked, "What's wrong?"

"You wouldn't believe this mess if I told you." She heard him say something to someone else before he spoke into the phone again. "Look, I've got to go, just get down here right away." And with that cryptic instruction, he hung up.

In an instant Nicole went flying out of her office, barely taking time to grab her jacket and purse before racing to the gymnasium. Unable to answer any questions, she could only say to a worried-looking Rose, "Please tell anybody who calls that I'll be right back."

Pushing aside the crowd that had already begun to form on the gym steps, she bulldozed her way into the gym. Immediately all of her haste came to a complete halt as she stood still in absolute shock. The scene that greeted her was like something from a bad movie. All of the carefully prepared packages were scattered throughout the gym. "What is that smell?" Nicole asked, covering her nose.

Tyrone answered from behind her, "Ammonia. It looks like someone dragged the boxes out, threw the packets around and then dumped cleaning fluid or something all over them."

The viciousness of the attack stunned Nicole. "How

is that possible and why would anybody do such a thing? What did they think they were proving?" Tyrone had no more answers than she did as they both looked on in puzzlement.

"This is just how I found it," Tyrone finally spoke. " I got here expecting to get the one box just like you asked. But when I got the door open, I walked in and found this."

"Was anybody here when you arrived?" Nicole asked.

"Nope, and after we all left on Friday night, everything should have been locked until classes this morning. You know everybody uses the old gym in the rec center for shootin' hoops." He frowned in confusion, "Nobody was even supposed to be in here until I opened it up this morning, and Coach Spears walked in right behind me. You could ask him. This is just how we found it. We haven't touched anything."

Looking around, Nicole could see David walking up from the back of the gym where the athletic offices were. "David, what's going on?"

"I don't know," he answered, looking concerned. "I just finished checking the offices to see if anything was touched back there and it wasn't. From what I can tell, no equipment is missing or damaged either. And you know we have some really expensive things back there, so whoever did this, it definitely wasn't about money."

"How did they even get inside," Nicole wondered

aloud. "Tyrone said the door was locked when he got here. And only you, the maintenance man, and I have keys to this gym. I gave my key to Tyrone before he came down here. Other than that, it hasn't been out of my possession."

"Neither has mine." David continued her train of thought, "And once maintenance cleans the gym on Friday night, they don't come back until classes have let out on Monday evening." Scratching his head in disbelief he surveyed the shambles. "But you're wrong. You know there is someone else with a key."

"Who?" Nicole wondered aloud, then answered her own question. "Kevin." How could she have forgotten that with his new appointment to athletic director, he had been given a copy of keys to all of the athletic facilities? For a man who had shown up to help, she thought in disgust, he seemed to have brought as much bad luck as good. There were increased donations, she admitted, but there had also been the book theft and now this vandalism. One thing was sure, everybody in the world knew Kevin Powell did not need money. But then the echo of David's words hit her. Whoever vandalized the gym hadn't done it for the money.

The very nature of the attack seemed more personal. Besides the boxes, the second most damaged thing in the gym was Nicole's own reputation, as she would obviously be unable to keep any recruitment meeting she had planned for the early part of this week. But who, Nicole thought, would want to make her look bad and why? Thinking of Kevin again, she wondered if maybe she knew why.

"Guys, I don't think we should touch anything for right now." Moving quickly, she added, "There may be some evidence in all of this garbage." She walked toward the exit. "Meanwhile, Tyrone, I need you to go outside, keep your mouth shut and move that crowd along. David, lock these doors back and cancel all the gym classes for today. I don't want anything touched until we discover what's going on. I'll be right back," she called as she walked out. To herself she added, "After I get a few answers."

"Is Kevin here?" Nicole asked Rose as she raced up the stairs toward Kevin's office.

"Yes." When Nicole didn't slow down for her answer, Rose yelled out, "But he's in a meeting right now. What's going on? What happened?"

She ignored Rose completely, leaving her hastily thrown questions hanging in midair as she burst into Kevin's office. Nor did she pay any attention to the man seated in front of his desk. "What's going on, Kevin?"

"Hello, Nicole," Kevin greeted, cool as a cucumber in the face of her accusatory tone. "We were actually just discussing you."

"Kevin, I just came from the gym. Do you want to explain what's going on?" she asked furiously.

"I don't know. Why don't you tell me."

"All of the recruitment packages have been destroyed." Her chest was rising and falling rapidly with righteous indignation.

Pointedly, he sat back in his chair, folded his arms and tilted his head challengingly before responding, his quiet manner far more menacing than her riotous explosion had been. "And from your tone and your manner, I'm assuming you think I had something to do with that."

"Who else would have a reason? You were against my idea from the very beginning.
And I think it's a little strange that since you have been here we seem to gotten a sudden crime wave, or is it just sudden bad luck?"

"First of all, this school had bad luck before I came, so don't blame that on me. Second of all," he continued with a quiet resolve, "I don't know any more about what could have happened to your precious packages than you do. Even less, in fact, as this is the first time I've heard about it. So before you run around flying off the handle and accusing me of anything, why don't you take a moment and remember that I came here to try and help save this school."

"Oh yes, lest we forget, 'the Great and Wonderful Kevin' is here, our knight in shining armor. A little late, yes, but still right on time."

"I can't believe this," he angrily forced out from between stiff lips. "What possible reason would I have for doing anything to destroy this school. I don't need the money, so I wouldn't have stolen the stupid book. And tell me just how destroying this school will get me one step closer to what I really want."

"That's just it, Kevin. Nobody knows what you really want. Not even me. So why don't you enlighten me."

"I thought I told you Friday night. But if you want me to say it again, in public for everybody to hear, I will. I'm here, once and for all, because I want you. And I'm not stupid or petty enough to think that destroying the one thing you really care about will get me that."

"You're not going to get me anyway," Nicole retorted.

"Look, Nicole, calm down and think." He took a deep breath to calm himself down, running a hand over his smooth pate in exasperation, before continuing. "I know you are upset and I understand. I spent just as much time as you did working on those packages. But Nicole, tell me, what possible reason I have to hurt you, especially after Friday night when the door that has been closed for so long finally showed a little crack. What sense would it make for me to slam the door shut on my own foot?" Quieting his voice a little more than Nicole would have thought possible, to barely a whisper, he continued, "You know what, I don't believe you really think I could have done it. I think you are just looking for an excuse to pull back. And it's not going to fly. You are just going to have to look a little further."

He stopped talking for a long moment and watched

the play of emotions across her face. "Now as you can see, you interrupted me in the middle of a meeting. And if you don't have anything more constructive than that to say, you can leave, because I won't ever answer such ridiculous accusations again." Taking a deep breath, he continued in a soft tone, "I know you don't trust me yet. But you better learn how, because I'm not going anywhere." And with those words he dismissed Nicole and turned back to his guest, who had been watching their fiery display of tempers with rapt interest.

Nicole, who had ignored the guest entirely because of her anger now swung her eyes toward him in embarrassment. "I'm sorry to have interrupted you..."

"Mike Dix," he said, jumping to his feet and offering his hand. "And please, don't apologize." He grinned amiably. "This is the most fun I've had in a long time. I love seeing Kevin on the hot seat. I think it does him good to know that not everybody sees him as Mr. Wonderful. It keeps his head from getting too big. Although," he looked at Kevin again and laughed before continuing in a teasing tone, "it may already be a little too late."

"Well, it was rude of me just the same," Nicole apologized. "I presume you are the same Mike Dix that Kevin said he would bring in to investigate the theft."

"The very same," he answered. "And please call me Mike." Pulling a chair up for Nicole, next to his own, he motioned for her to sit down. "Actually, Kevin was just

telling me a little of what happened before you, ah..."
He broke off as if searching for the right words. "Before
you came in," he finally finished tactfully. "I planned to
meet with you as soon as you were available because I
need to find out from you some of the details of what
happened. Kevin could only give me a sketchy outline.
And if there is some other problem, I'll need that information as well. The two incidents could be related. So,
what exactly happened?" Mike grinned nodded his head
in amusement in Kevin's direction. "He may know what
happened if he was involved, but believe me, I don't."

"Oh, don't you get started too," Kevin shot at his
mocking friend, not finding any humor in Nicole's accusations.

"Basically, we have a big recruitment push under-
way," Nicole answered Mike, ignoring Kevin's comment. "Our plan was to hit twenty schools in twenty
days. That campaign was to kick off today.
Unfortunately, now all the packets are destroyed. And
since the only new person on this campus with a key is
Kevin, I felt I had to ask..."

"Asking would have been okay, not accusing,"
Kevin interrupted.

"So, since Kevin has a key, I'm assuming the door
was locked and thus the natural conclusion," Mike clarified.

"Exactly..."

"That was not a natural conclusion," Kevin rebutted,

refusing to be kept out of the conversation.

"Have you reported this matter to the police?" Mike asked.

"Not yet, I came straight here..."

"Couldn't wait to accuse me, could you? I'm surprised you didn't feel you had enough circumstantial evidence to do a citizen's arrest."

"Anyway," Nicole continued, ignoring Kevin, "it all happened so quickly... I'll go and call right now."

"Well, if it's all related and you still intend to do as Kevin said and keep the whole thing quiet, it might be best to let me look into it first," Mike inserted. "Because if it was just kids being mischievous, it shouldn't be too hard to track them down. But if it is actually part of some sort of sabotage plot, then the last thing we need is to complicate matters by having any bumbling police or media types muddying the water."

"It's up to you, of course. You are the expert," Nicole answered. "And if Kevin says we should trust your judgement, then I guess we have to."

"Oh, now I'm to be trusted," Kevin said mockingly. "I guess I can find some comfort in that at least."

"Kevin," Nicole at last acknowledged his presence again, "if I owe you an apology..."

"If," he practically shouted.

"Then... "

"Please save it," he stopped her. "*If*," he said, stressing the word nastily, "... if there's some question about whether you should apologize, then I don't even want it."

"Well," Nicole rose gracefully from the seat she had taken across from Mike and smoothed down her crisp navy blue skirt, "I have meetings to cancel and reschedule." Her pride refused to allow her to back down completely. Dismissing him expertly, she turned to Mike. "After that, Mike, I can meet with you and give you a complete update. Meanwhile, I'm sure Kevin will be happy to show you over to the gym."

"Of course, boss," Kevin said sarcastically.

"See you later. It was a pleasure." Mike again stood and shook her hand as she exited.

Laying her head on her desk, Nicole barely registered her phone ringing beside her. What a long day, she thought as she finally picked up. She was pleasantly surprised to hear David's voice.

"Hi, how's it going?" he asked cautiously.

"You can ask me that?"

"Yeah, I guess I can imagine how your day went," he said before adding, "you'll be happy to know that we finally did get the mess cleaned up. And classes for tomorrow will go on as scheduled."

"Well, that's one piece of good news, I suppose."

"I met Mike and unfortunately he said he didn't think it was the work of vandals. We looked for any sign of evidence before we started cleaning up. There was nothing."

"Great," Nicole sighed despondently. "I just can't

imagine who would do such a thing. Rose and I spent all day working on getting more packets together for next week. And we'll still have to work on it again tomorrow. It was a good thing I saved all of the originals on disk. Otherwise, we would have really been in trouble. I had even our sample 'dummy' packages in that storage room as well. I can't believe I was so stupid."

"I wouldn't beat myself up over it. There was no way you could have expected what happened. And anyway, it wasn't a complete waste. Just thank God you had the originals still on a disk." Changing the subject before she could continue her self-flagellation, he asked in concern, "How are you holding up? You sound tired."

"Tired doesn't begin to cover it," she replied while rubbing the back of her neck.

"Then go on home and get in the bed. There's nothing more you can do tonight." He paused before adding in a teasing voice, "You know if you need me to come over and tuck you in, give you a hot bath, rub you down..." The smile in his voice clearly transmitted itself over the phone. "I'm there. You only have to ask, or not ask, just point your pretty finger. Your wish is my command."

"I wish to have all of these problems wiped miraculously away." She felt her mood lightening in the face of his teasing.

"Oops, sorry only minor miracles are available on Mondays and Wednesdays. For major miracles you have to call me tomorrow."

"You promise?" She played along with his teasing game.

"Of course, would I ever lie to you, the woman I love truly, madly and deeply?"

"In that case, I will have to see you tomorrow," she answered, smiling.

"See you tomorrow."

Groaning, Nicole stood up and stretched. Mentally preparing herself for what she had avoided all day, she gathered her belongings, turned off her light and closed the door to her office. Peeking over, she confirmed that the light was still on under Kevin's door. Silently she acknowledged what she had to do. She straightened her spine before knocking softly on his door. This time before entering, she waited for his invitation.

At his grunted assent, she quietly entered. "How's it going?" she asked fidgeting nervously with the lapels of her suit.

Not responding, he continued to stare at her expectantly, waiting for the real reason she had come to his office.

"I came to apologize," Nicole finally said under the weight of his silent gaze. Instantly that provoked a response as Kevin put his ink pen down and gave Nicole his full attention. "I *am* sorry. I just saw that mess and I went a little ballistic. It's been a rough week for me." She shifted her feet at his continued silence. "That's no excuse, I know. And if the situation were reversed, I wouldn't blame you for cussing me out and never speaking to me again."

He finally spoke up. "Didn't I tell you that you weren't getting off the hook that easy?" Standing, he came closer to Nicole and took her hand, leading her to the two chairs in front of his desk. Like a recalcitrant student, she followed meekly and allowed herself to be seated. He took the seat directly facing hers.

"Nicole, don't you think we can call a truce? This bickering back and forth is not good for the school or anybody else, for that matter." He looked at her intensely with a sincerity and warmth oozing from his eyes that Nicole was afraid to trust. "You told me on Friday you missed my friendship."

"And you told me that wouldn't be enough for you," she responded quickly.

"No, but it's a beginning. All I'm asking is for a chance. Let's sit down and talk it out. We never once discussed what happened between us. It was just suddenly over. Even if we never move past it and restore our relationship, at least let's be able to say we did discuss it as adults. Ten years ago, we wouldn't have been able to do that."

"After this morning, I don't know if we can discuss it even today."

"Oh, but I have more faith in us." He leaned forward in his chair and squeezed her hands softly. "Can't we at least try for the sake of what was once between us?"

"I won't be hurt like I was before."

"Nicole, I wouldn't hurt you again for anything in the world," Kevin promised earnestly. "All I'm asking is for a chance." At her stubborn silence, he continued, "What if we start with dinner. Right now I'm not asking for anything beyond that. Let's just have dinner. For the sake of the school," he added in desperation as she remained impassive.

"For the sake of the school...," Nicole repeated. As she thought back on her shameful behavior, she admitted to herself that she would have to make an effort or ultimately it would be the school which would suffer. "Okay, I'll go, but not tonight. I'm beat."

"Okay, tomorrow then," he pressed, not willing to lose his hard-won advantage.

"Tomorrow," Nicole agreed. As she left his office, she comforted herself with the thought, What harm could one innocent dinner do?

# Chapter 7

No matter how hard she tried, the 'roll' in her french roll refused to cooperate, and after three frustratingly futile tries, Nicole finally gave up. Slicking her hair back with gel she managed to tame her cinnamon-spiced curls into an elegant bun at the nape of her neck. After all, she reasoned, it was only a harmless dinner with Kevin. What did it matter how she looked? Purposefully ignoring the traitorous whisper in her heart that screamed it did, Nicole checked her reflection in the full-length mirror again, to see if the last minute decision of the long black dress was a still a good one.

The slip dress was deceptively modest. It was nearly ankle length on her five-foot-nine-inch frame and was one of the most beautiful dresses Nicole owned. The bodice was detailed with nearly invisible silver beading, giving the top half of the dress an aura of silvery fairy dust. While the straight drop of the dress's bottom half would be considered decent by any standard, it was the way that the material clung to Nicole's well-shaped lower half that made the dress positively 'x-rated.' It gave Nicole the confidence she needed to face Kevin in so intimate a setting.

Grabbing her black-beaded purse, she quickly double-checked it, then reached for her keys, glad that she had insisted on driving herself tonight. The last thing that she needed was for Kevin to see how unexplainably nervous she felt on leaving the house. As Nicole left for Kevin's hotel, she coached herself to relax and just enjoy the evening.

Kevin had moved into the penthouse suite of the same hotel where the auction and theft had taken place. He had insisted that the only way they could possibly have any privacy was to dine upstairs in his suite. Since her only other choice was to invite him over to her home, Nicole had reluctantly agreed. Stepping into the posh mirrored elevator that was specifically for the penthouse floor, Nicole wondered briefly if her decision to come had been a mistake. After all, what could they really have to discuss other than their marriage?

The marriage had been more a last minute fluke than an actual commitment made by two rational adults. The day after the draft, they had flown in to Las Vegas together, to meet with Kevin's agent and team owners. Nicole remembered vividly Kevin's return to their hotel room. She smiled ironically to herself as she recalled that it had been a penthouse suite that night as well. His excitement had bubbled over more than the champagne he had brought to surprise her with. Toasting each other, they had celebrated in the most elemental way possible, the way lovers have celebrated good news since the beginning of time. Later, Kevin had opened the curtains of the hotel room.

Lying back down, they had lounged in the huge bed that looked out over the world and shared dreams all night. After Kevin's adrenalin had worn off and he had fallen into an exhausted sleep, Nicole had lain in his arms and worried. What, she wondered, would the future hold for them? She had already seen the speculative glances from other women as they walked into the hotel after exiting the limousine the hotel had placed at their disposal. Even before he was officially signed, he had already been approached by several companies looking for his exclusive endorsement of their product. Friends they had gone to school with the last four years had started treating them both differently. Nicole had found herself frequently being pushed awkwardly into the unimportant background. Equally disturbing was the fact that Kevin didn't seem to notice. How long, she wondered, before she was pushed completely out of the picture?

She had heard all the stories of how athletes change. How could she express to Kevin her fears without sounding like an insecure clinging vine? That was the worst part of it all. Always before they had been able to be honest with each other about anything. Their friendship was such that no matter what the problem was they had been able to discuss it. But how did she tell him of her worries without pushing him away with her insecurities, sounding unsupportive or worse, jealous. Confused and scared, she had silently said nothing. She had hugged Kevin tightly to herself when she felt a chill come over her, trying vainly to ignore a terrible premonition. Bravely, she had promised herself that no matter what happened in the future to tear them apart, she would never regret loving Kevin. He was her world and she would just do the best she could, for as long as she could, to hold on, no matter how rocky the ride got.

As she held him, soft tears had slipped down her cheek as love and fear mixed in a potent brew that nearly overwhelmed her. Ironically, it was the tears landing softly on his oak ribbed chest which had alerted him. "What's wrong?" he had asked sleepily as he groggily came awake.

"Nothing," Nicole answered, quickly wiping her face.

"Were you crying?" he asked as he squinted his eyes. "What's wrong?"

"Nothing," she replied. "Just happy, I guess."

Looking at her face, which was illuminated by the garish lights from the Las Vegas Strip, his scrutiny penetrated her facade in pursuit of the truth. "You don't look or sound very happy," he commented as Nicole had begun squirming under his intense stare.

That maple syrup gaze was her undoing and some small part of Nicole could only observe with horror as suddenly every horrible thought she had worried about came flooding out of her mouth as if a dam had just broken loose inside her. Kevin had listened patiently for a long time and quietly anchored her through the flood. Responding at last, he asked, "Don't you think I have the same worries?" When she looked up in stunned disbelief, he tried to reassure her with his eyes. "I know that all of these wonderful things mean big change. On the one hand, that's great. It's what I've worked for, prayed for, just about my whole life.

"But on the other hand it is still change." Raising up on his elbows to look at her face, he had shuddered in one of the few times that he seemed humanly vulnerable. "Sometimes I feel like I'm at the roulette wheel downstairs. And I can either win it all or lose it all, and none of it is in my control. It's scary, even for me. I'm not so naive as to think that everything will stay exactly the same. I also know I'm going to have to sacrifice something." Leaning down he had kissed her softly on her lips to emphasize his words before enfolding her in a tight embrace. "I just don't want it to be you."

The next day, Kevin had suggested what seemed like the answer to all of their problems. "Let's get married, right now. Let's just do it." Grinning at her surprise, his enthusiasm was infectious as he tried to convince her. "I know we both wanted a really special wedding we could share with our families and friends. But we can always have a second ceremony later. Let's marry right now, before I sign anything." Taking her hand, he'd dropped to his knees in the middle of the busy casino floor. "I want to marry you right now, before the money, without a dime in my pocket. When I'm just a nobody. I want you to marry me."

"You would never be a nobody to me," Nicole laughed as she tried unsuccessfully to pull him up as onlookers began to stop and stare. She laughed until she began to realize that this offer was not just a reckless joke. Then she glimpsed again the uncharacteristic vulnerability as he solemnly waited on his knees for an answer and realized the offer wasn't just his reckless joke. She gave the only answer she could. "Just plain Kevin Powell without a dime in his pocket is good enough for me."

"So you'll do it then," he pressed. When Nicole had impulsively nodded, he finally stood up. "Someday we will look back on this day and laugh and tell the world about it. But for right now, this moment belongs only to us."

The only problem, Nicole thought as she came back to the present, was that someday had never come. Just as she'd worried, the whirlwind of fame had swept Kevin

Powell up and taken him away from her. Stepping off the luxurious elevator directly into the foyer outside of his hotel suite, Nicole rang the bell and waited anxiously. The door opened immediately and she was let inside by the man who was, at least legally, her husband.

Smiling nervously, Nicole looked around discreetly as he took her black wrap. He led her directly into the dining area of the suite. Whoever had decorated the table had done so with an eye for intimacy by skillfully creating the illusion that the dining table was the center of their own very private world. It took Nicole a full minute to realize that Kevin had been waiting patiently for her to absorb everything as he held her chair out for her to sit down.

"Everything is so lovely," Nicole said as she unfolded her cloth napkin into her lap, paying more attention to the task than was needed to cover her nervousness.

"I wanted everything to be absolutely perfect. I'm glad you're pleased." Taking the silver lids off their plates they began.

Looking down at her plate, Nicole gasped. "Crab legs?"

"Yes." He looked up in confusion. "Aren't they your favorite food?"

"You know they are." How, she thought in dismay, was she to maintain her image of aloof haughtiness with messy finger food? Although the creamy pasta dish and accompanying salad looked wonderful, there was just no way she was going to ignore those crab legs. Resigning herself to a little loss of dignity, Nicole cracked a crab leg as expertly as any aged bayou fisherman. Ignoring her dainty miniature fork, she pulled out the succulent meat with complete disregard for her expensive manicure. Dignity be damned, she thought again, as she swirled it in butter and tucked it into her mouth. Peering up at Kevin to see if he had witnessed her undignified enjoyment, she could see from his grinning eyes that he had.

"I'm sorry for staring. I just always loved to watch you eat crab meat." He looked at her with a teasing, sensuous light in eyes that focused on her sweetly sticky mouth. "Imagining you slurping that butter off in your mouth always turned me on. Remember when I used to feed it to you?"

"I remember going to the gym to work off all the fat," Nicole answered, trying to keep the mood light by refusing to be drawn into his licentious memories.

"If I remember correctly, we had a pretty good workout routine of our own going."

Unsure of how to respond to that without getting drawn into more sexual innuendo, Nicole said nothing. The awkward silence between them grew until finally Kevin broke it.

"So, how do you like this weather?" Kevin asked.

Nicole had to laugh. It was such a lame attempt at neutral conversation that it was funny. Her laughter was so infectious that he quickly joined in. When he stopped,

Nicole looked up from her mirth to catch Kevin just staring at her face.

"Oh, Butter," he said wistfully. "You are so beautiful when you laugh. I mean your whole face just lights up. I could never get enough of seeing you laugh."

"Apparently at some point you did get enough of it, or we would not be in this position, would we?"

"We're not in this position because I got tired of you. Believe me, nothing could be further from the truth."

"All right. Then here is the million dollar question. What happened?" she asked, suddenly serious, all trace of laughter gone.

He looked at her with probing eyes before answering. "Do you really want to know, after all these years?" Before she could jump in with a hasty answer, he quickly continued. "Let me rephrase that. I want to tell you, but I guess what I need to know is, are you ready to really hear me? I tried to tell you what was happening many times, but you never really heard me."

"Well, I'm listening now," Nicole said, laying down her fork.

"Do you remember when you pledged?" he asked. When Nicole, nodded in the affirmative, he continued. "Remember that feeling of walking around campus? You just got your 'greeks,' and suddenly everybody on campus was coming up to you and congratulating you. For those first few weeks, especially, it was like you went from being nobody to somebody." Locking his gaze onto hers he went on. "Do you remember the feeling of accomplishment that went with it? Can you imagine that feeling, only one million times more powerful? Gifts a thousand times larger? The whole country like your campus. Can you imagine feeling that sense of power?"

"Kevin, anybody other than you, I could see it going to their head. But you were so level- headed and 'down to earth.' You'd been preparing for that moment for nearly all of your life. Do you really expect me to believe, now, that you weren't prepared for it when it finally came?" she asked, her eyes searching for the truth in his.

"How do you prepare for something like that?" Since he didn't expect an answer, he wasn't disappointed by her silence. "At the time, I thought I handled it well. I was doing all the right things. I kept my girl, I wasn't sleeping around." He ignored her disbelieving snort. "I wasn't. I thought I had the only woman I would ever want." He gave that a moment to sink in. "I continued going to church, I gave to my community, I remembered my family."

Nicole cut him off. "Skip the local boy does good story. What changed the little choirboy into anything but? No, don't tell me. It was the evil seductress," she sneered.

Ignoring her skeptical expression, Kevin spoke as if he hadn't heard her question. "And everything was good for as long as I was in training camp. That first camp is so hard. It's like you are pledging again. All the rookies go through a hazing period, whether you were drafted number one or number ninety-nine. You can't imagine how much I looked forward to every letter you sent me. Sometimes, it was the only thing I could hold on to when things got really tough. Once training camp is over, though, it's like you're released on the world. And brand new rules apply."

"Like the one that says no wives or girlfriends on road trips?" she asked sarcastically.

"Exactly..."

"Because that's where you pick up the most women?" she queried, pleased that he had walked right into her fully-loaded question.

"Exactly." Before she could gloat in triumph, he explained. "But it was not like that with me, at least not at first. I followed the rules and I didn't let you come. And it was hard because, believe me, road trips get lonely when you're on the road four days out of the week."

"Poor baby," Nicole cooed insincerely. "Imagine how hard it was for me, not knowing what the heck was going on. All I knew was that the man I loved, the man who I thought was my husband, was suddenly unavailable. I'd call your hotel, and you would never there."

"Usually I was in team meetings, going over films. You should have known the routine from college," he snapped back in a brief display of temper.

"You weren't always in meetings," Nicole volleyed back, not willing to let him get away with the pat answer he had given her years before. "I would call your hotel room and there was always a party going on. You couldn't talk, but could I call back? I'd call back and you'd be gone or worse, the phone would just ring. Where were you at two in the morning the night before game day?"

Taking a deep sip of his wine, Kevin waited before responding. Aware that tempers were rising, he took a long minute to cool his own off. Carefully considering his words, he finally spoke. His agitation showed only in the carefully-measured stroking of his wine glass by his broad fingers. His normally deep voice sounded gruff as he spoke with precision. "Nicole, I want to tell you the truth. And I'm not going to lie and say it's pretty. There, truthfully, is no innocent explanation I can give you. I was in the wrong. I lied to you many times and I realize now how much I hurt you. You will never know how sorry I am." He paused again for a long time after she rolled her eyes in disbelief before he continued. "But I was never unfaithful to you. At least not until you left me for good. When you said you were finished with me..."

"Wait a minute." Nicole sat up straight-spined in her chair suddenly angrier. "I know you are not going to give me that tired line about how this was all my fault!"

"No, I wasn't going there. It was me. My immaturity, insecurity, pride, egotism, whatever you want to call it. I was out of control. The night you dumped me, I went out and got good and drunk. That was another thing that was out of control, my drinking. When I sobered up three days later, I was disgusted with myself. I realized then that I didn't deserve you. I could see I was only hurting you and I felt powerless to stop. You wanted to go and so I let you. I thought I was being noble and generous. Really, it was weak. I realize that now, you don't have to say it," he added as he saw her about to jump in. "Of course the right thing to do would have been to save my marriage. 'To straighten up and fly right,' as the old saying goes. But I just wasn't mature enough to do it. No matter how much I loved you, I couldn't make myself grow up."

"Did you even try?" Nicole asked with a mouth suddenly gone dry.

"I thought I tried. Looking back now, I can see I didn't try hard enough. I was a stupid kid. But I give myself credit for one thing."

"Hmph," she grunted in disbelief. "What was that?"

"Dumb as I was, I never took the step to completely let you go." Holding her eyes captive until he was sure she would absorb the full weight of his next words he added, "Yes, I got your 'dear john' letter in the mail, asking me for a divorce. But I refused to give up the hope that maybe someday I could work it all out with you."

"And I'm to believe that's why you're here now?"

"It is why I'm here now, and for the school of course." His reference to the school as if it were an afterthought had her rolling her eyes in disgust. "I just decided we'd played this game long enough. And for all these years, the loser has been me. And I'm tired of losing. I was a kid, just barely out of my teens. How was I to know what I really wanted. But the man, the man you see before you today, he's very sure of what and whom he wants."

"That sounds pretty good, but how am I to know the difference? You always claimed you knew what you wanted. But to hear you tell it now, when you got what you wanted you didn't know how to handle it. How can I know that anything has changed?"

"By giving me a chance. That's all I'm asking. Open that door just a little bit and give me a chance to show you how much I've grown up." He reached across the table to hold her suddenly damp hand.

Taking a deep breath, she tried to calm her pounding heart. "Kevin, I won't lie and pretend your actions didn't devastate me. And that kind of hurt is not easy to put aside. But I can't lie to myself either and act like I don't know that the reason it hurt so deeply was because I cared so much. I want to give you a chance. I'd love for you to show me that after all of these years, there is something still there worth saving. But where is my assurance that I won't be hurt again?"

"Do you want my word? I'd give it. But I gave it before, along with vows and promises and tokens and all of those things I can give again. But in the end, it will still boil down to you giving me a chance to show you that I can be trusted."

Acknowledging the truth of his words, Nicole reached for the courage lying in the depths of her soul and answered after releasing a long shaky breath. "Okay, Kevin, you have your chance."

He gave her hand a reassuring, grateful squeeze before he released it. Smiling into each other's eyes, they sealed their truce with a communication deeper than words.

# Chapter 8

Sinking deeply into the plush couch in Kevin's penthouse suite living room, Nicole relaxed. Grateful for the open waist empire bodice of her dress, Nicole exhaled a big sigh of relief that she could breathe without the necessity of unbuttoning anything. Full and replete, she closed her eyes and wondered how she would muster up the energy to return home.

"You're welcome to stay the night," Kevin said as if reading her thoughts. "You look so comfortable I hate to see you disturbed."

Deigning not to answer, Nicole instead chose to stare at him in silence.

He smiled sardonically in response, correctly interpreting the path her thoughts had wandered down. "I can't say I'll happily take the couch, but I can say I'll be willing to take the couch...if you insist."

"No, you won't have to go to the trouble. I'll peel myself off this couch and scoot along home in a minute. Don't worry." Closing her eyes, she returned to the warm cocoon she had snuggled herself into in her mind before he interrupted.

"Believe me, I'm not rushing you. You could stay the night or forever, as far as I'm concerned. I just want you to be comfortable."

"Believe me, I am. That's my problem." Nicole sighed again, sleepily.

Sitting down next to her on the couch, Kevin gently pulled her feet onto his lap. "Do you remember when I used to give you foot massages?" he quietly asked, slipping her black pumps off her feet.

"Mmmmm." Nicole wiggled her toes in contentment in answer as he began massaging the soles of her stockinged feet.

"I always thought you had the prettiest toes." He looked at them playfully before resuming his ministrations. "Yup, you still do."

"What did you think, I would have run them through the shredder?" she asked without opening her eyes.

"A man has to be sure of these things because we never know what foolishness a woman might commit in the name of making herself look better. You know you all take it into your heads to do all sorts of crazy things, like cut your hair."

Nicole, whose hair had hung past her shoulder blades when he'd last seen her, ran her hands over her much shorter locks self-consciously. "You don't like it."

Looking at her closely, as if he'd only noticed the difference today, he finally gave a nod of approval. "Actually, I do like it, but I loved it before. When she again closed her eyes, he added, "But I'm glad you kept some things the same." His breath brushed softly over her toes, sending a shiver up her spine, as he brought them closer for further inspection. "Yup," he repeated. "Absolutely perfect." Leaning down he kissed the bronzed knuckle of each toe through her sheer stockings.

Each soft caress of his lips shot a corresponding arch of pleasure up her spine but Nicole felt duty bound to offer at least a token protest. "Stop it," she commanded, half-heartedly trying to twist her feet out of his grasp.

"You always had the prettiest legs too. I wonder how they've fared over the years?" He sent his questioning hands over her ankles and up her calves. When his hands reached the back of her knees and began to idly caress, Nicole shot into an upright position on the couch. The back of her knees had always been a ridiculously sensuous spot for her and he knew it. "Just as I thought, exactly the same."

Now that she was seated straight up, Nicole found herself in even greater jeopardy. Her thigh brushed his intimately and she found herself trapped in the corner of the couch. Sensing her dilemma, Kevin pressed his advantage home. "I made a big mistake on Friday."

"What was that?" Nicole asked breathlessly. With his face only inches from hers, she sat spellbound, like a deer caught in headlights.

"I mistakenly thought if I just had one innocent kiss, it would be enough to drive those haunting memories away. Now I can't sleep for wondering when can I get another." Leaning forward with his question, his face was so close that his breath fanned the bangs on her face sensuously, emphasizing each word. "Can I get another one, Butter?"

In direct defiance of what her sensible mind had decided was the smarter course of action, her head nodded its own assent, and then completed the rebellion by lifting up softly for the coming kiss. The quick moment of anticipation sweetened the kiss for both. The breath-taking kiss scorched with so much flaming fireworks that Nicole wondered to herself if her lips were actually singed. Coming up for breath, Kevin continued his passionate attack by raining kisses all over her face. Gliding his lips down the side of her face, he followed its natural curve under her high cheekbone. Needing the taste of his lips once more, Nicole turned her face quickly so that again their lips collided in an intimate embrace. Tongue sought tongue, as each tried to dominate and titillate the other. The intimate battle raged until Nicole thought she would incinerate.

Hungry for more, Nicole leaned forward slightly as

Kevin found the hidden zipper in the back of her dress. Easing it down softly, he pulled back to look into her eyes, non-verbally asking her permission. Well past the point at which she could make a rational decision, Nicole silently assented. Easing the front of her dress down, Kevin exposed her to the waist except for her thin black lace bra. Normally reserved and shy, Nicole felt no shame because of the unadulterated admiration and pleasure in his eyes. Arching her back sensuously, Nicole reached up to pull his lips back down to hers. He seemed mesmerized for a moment and unable to move.

Kevin returned to his ravenous assault, scorching brands of fire from her lips to the base of her throat. Turning her head to the side, Kevin nuzzled his lips in the hollow spot between her neck's base and collar bone, running his tongue back and forth, up and down the ridge of her collarbone.

Nicole let out a soft, sensuous giggle. "Tickles," she said by way of explanation before his lips found hers again and silenced any laughter.

Lifting his head to look at her breasts for a moment, Kevin raised his fingers to trace over the sprinkles on her skin. "I love your freckles," he said softly, deftly removing her bra and tossing it aside.

"I only have a few," Nicole replied self-consciously.

"That's enough for what I have in mind." Kevin began tracing a pattern on her breast with his tongue.

"What exactly do you have in mind?" Nicole asked,

finding it increasingly hard to concentrate.

"Connecting the dots," he whispered mischievously as he wiggled his eyebrows in a wicked parody of a Saturday morning cartoon villain.

Laughing softly, Nicole was completely caught up in the sensual moment. Laying her flat out on the couch, Kevin tried to arrange room for his six-foot-six inch frame alongside hers. Giving up in frustration, he sat up, pulling Nicole along with him.

"There's just not enough room on this tiny couch for what I have in mind. I don't know how they expect a grown man to be able to stretch out on these miniature things." He stood up and reached down for Nicole's hand.

Accepting his hand, Nicole stood up as well. Because the top of her dress was already unzipped and free of her arms, when she stood her dress sank gracefully to the floor in an elegant pile. The unplanned disrobing caught them both by surprise as Nicole stood in her matching black lace panties before a fully dressed Kevin.

Muttering a sexy expletive under his breath before he swallowed hard, Kevin was momentarily at a loss for words. When the moment passed, he burst out of his trance in an explosion of activity. Scooping Nicole up, he kicked her dress carelessly out of his path as he carried her to his bedroom. Sweeping the cover off the bed in one smooth stroke he placed Nicole gently in the center of the gray satin sheet. Swiftly taking off his own shirt and shoes, Kevin joined her.

Taking out the few pins remaining in her hair, he plunged his hands into her curls and gave her another blazing kiss. Whatever doubt that had started to raise its ugly head during the moment while he was undressing quickly faded quietly away beneath the onslaught of kisses that Nicole returned measure for measure. Running her hands up his back, she finally settled them caressingly on his broad shoulders.

They both jumped when the ringing phone startled them. Answering the unspoken question in her eyes, he said, "There is nothing on earth which will make me answer that phone at this moment." Returning to kiss her lips again, he broke off groaning when she turned her head in distraction at the phone's insistent ringing.

"Get it," she coaxed. "It could be important."

"This is important."

"I'm not going anywhere," she promised.

"You better not," he sighed before sitting up to answer the phone. Rolling to the bed's edge he answered it. After listening a few minutes, he excused himself and went into the living room, saying over his shoulder, "Just give me a few minutes."

Self-conscious now that she was alone, Nicole got up and retrieved the covers from the floor. As she tucked the comforter into the space provided between the massive bed and the bedside table, she noticed a business card sitting next to the lamp. The name jumped off the card and grabbed her attention: Carlista Cunningham.

Picking up the offensive card, Nicole turned it over and read it in disbelief.    Written in bold red ink was Carlista's home phone number with a note. *Call me anytime.* Tramp, Nicole thought spitefully.

Had Carlista ended up in the very same hotel room and bed? After their date and a night of passion had she left this card for Kevin so that they could continue their tryst on another day? He claimed he had grown up, but he never actually claimed he was celibate now. Just a little more mature, whatever that meant. Maybe it meant he had just learned how to juggle his many women a little better. That was easy enough to believe, she thought, reflecting on just how easily she had fallen into his bed after a good meal and just a little sweet talk.

For all of his fine words about giving him another chance, he hadn't wasted any time getting her into his bed, had he? She wondered if that had been his game all along. Now that he had presumably conquered every woman in the world, was he back for round two with 'the one who got away'? It probably was another of his women on the phone with him right now, while she waited like a naked fool in his bed. Why else would he have to go into another room? Oh, he was good! she angrily thought.

Unwillingly, Nicole recalled another time when she had been on the other end of the phone; the night that had been the proverbial straw that had broken the camel's back. After trying unsuccessfully for days to get in touch with Kevin, she had finally tracked him down at his hotel room. After several rings he had finally picked up the phone, claiming he hadn't heard it ringing because he'd been in the shower. Blaming the distance in his voice to tiredness, Nicole had wondered why he hadn't sounded pleased to hear from her.

She'd noticed that their phone conversations had grown shorter and they saw much less of each. He'd claimed it was only because of problems coordinating her student schedule with his as a player. Despising herself for sounding like a whining child, Nicole had nevertheless struggled to pull from Kevin much needed reassurances. Why haven't I heard from you? Haven't you missed me? Can't you come see me? Can't I come there? It sickened her now to think of all the pathetic questions she had thrown at him because of her desperation. At one point, she had even considered dropping out of graduate school to spend more time with him.

During their last phone conversation, though, he hadn't been in the mood to hear her whining. Abrupt and short, he tried several times to rush Nicole off the phone. Finally, he'd gone to the door to pay for his room service, while leaving Nicole on hold. While he was gone, a woman's dark sultry voice had immediately come on the line. She'd laughed at Nicole and advised her to quit being a fool. No, she'd answered, she wasn't Kevin's woman now. But that was only because she was smart enough to not get caught up in the game. Men come and go, she'd advised, and any woman who thought she could nail down a man like Kevin Powell was either crazy or naive. And with those words the woman had disconnected the line. Nicole had cried herself to sleep that night, futilely hoping against hope that Kevin would call her back.

It had taken him three weeks to acknowledge that Nicole had ceased her daily calls. By the time he finally decided to find out what had happened it was too late. Nicole had faced some hard facts during that time as she wondered daily who he'd been consoling himself with. Even if it wasn't Ms. Sultry Voice, Nicole faced the reality that it was probably someone else. Refusing to even give him the satisfaction of arguing with him, she'd told him it was over and cut her losses. If she'd expected him to come to his senses and come crawling back, she'd been mistaken. Over the next few years he'd been seen in various publications, always with a new and prettier starlet on his arm. That first year, he had taken the time to send her a birthday card. In the card, he'd enclosed a note saying he hoped she was doing well and he wished her all the best. The second year she got a card with just a hastily scrawled signature at the bottom. After that she'd never heard from him again.

Well, she thought, growing angrier by the moment, she wasn't going to make it that easy for him to just walk back in the door. Thank God for whoever was on that phone, even if it was another woman. She'd just done Nicole a huge favor and stopped her from making a big mistake. Disgusted with herself for falling for him so easily, Nicole walked boldly back into the living room. There was nothing to do but to brazen it out. What else could a woman do when she found herself practically naked with her clothes stuck in the other room.

Entering softly, her hope that he was in the dining area was quickly dashed. He stood with one leg propped up on the couch while he spoke into the phone. His eyes which had lit up when she first opened the door now squinted in suspicion as she didn't return his smile.

Ignoring him completely, Nicole quickly crossed the room and reached for her dress, which was still lying on the floor. Ending his phone conversation, Kevin watched her with a piercing scrutiny which was all the more intense because it was completely silent. All the while she struggled back into the long dress, which suddenly didn't want to cooperate, he said nothing. Finally as she began looking around for her shoes, he spoke.

"Leaving so soon?" he asked cryptically.

"Yes, I think that would be best," she answered, avoiding his gaze by looking for her shoes.

They both spotted them at the same time. With his lightning quick reflexes he was able to retrieve them before she could. "Funny, I had begun to imagine a different end to this evening. Do you want to tell me what happened?"

"Nothing," Nicole lied blatantly, not willing to even discuss the matter with him, knowing from previous experience that she would come off looking jealous and petty. "I'm just ready to go home. You could have continued your conversation with whomever you were speaking to."

"Ah, now I see," he nodded in sudden understanding, "you're feeling a little neglected, maybe a little jealous. You don't have to be, that was business. I only took that call because it was from someone overseas I've been trying to catch up with for days."

"It doesn't matter to me." Nicole reached her hand out for her shoes.

"Then what's wrong?"

"Nothing," she answered, dropping the card she'd been hiding down on the table, like a gauntlet between them.

"Oh, I see. Been doing a little snooping, huh?"

"I was not snooping," she responded, incensed at the implication. "I was trying to make up the bed, anything to keep busy, since it was obvious you weren't exactly rushing back."

"Look, regardless of whatever thoughts might be running through your mind, why don't we sit down and talk about it like adults?" His quiet tone shouted a reasonableness that should have been hard to argue with.

However, it was his very reasonableness that made Nicole even angrier. Feeling frustrated and disgusted, she just wanted to go home. "I want my shoes; may I have them, please?" She stressed the final word. When he didn't immediately move, she added, "It is the *adult* thing to do."

"Let me at least walk you down," he sighed in defeat, while handing Nicole her shoes at last.

"No, thank you."

"Nicole, I thought you were going to give me a chance."

"Maybe it's still too soon."

"After ten years?" he blew out in disgust. "After ten years, you say it's still too soon?!"

"I'm sorry, Kevin," she apologized. "But I'm just not ready."

"But you didn't realize that until you saw that card." He pointed to it in frustration. "What are you 'just not ready for'? To trust me?"

"Exactly."

The look he held her with had so much contempt that Nicole squirmed in shame before he finally stated, "You know, I worked really hard to grow up. But maybe you should have put a little effort in that direction yourself."

"Wait a minute," she exclaimed. "I know you are not trying to turn this around on me. I'm not the one who..."

"Who what?" he asked. "You don't even know, because you haven't given me a chance. You would rather cling to your foolish fears than take a chance and trust me. You didn't really give me a chance ten years ago because you let your fears and insecurities get the best of you. And I could understand that. We were both young and I had a little trouble controlling those things myself. But what's your excuse now? And don't try to blame it on a stupid card. The truth is, you started feeling the ice melt on your precious facade and you got scared."

"I am not afraid of you," Nicole refuted, angry at him for turning on her.

"I don't think you are. I think you're scared of yourself. But when you go home and you console yourself in your lonely bed by thinking, 'I couldn't trust him anyway,' remember the person you really didn't trust was you. And ask yourself if maybe, just maybe, that wasn't always the problem."

By the time he finished his angry tirade, Kevin had walked Nicole to the elevator and closed the door on their evening.

# Chapter 9

"Rose, could you have copies of this memo sent out to all of the resident assistants when you get a chance?" Nicole asked as she approached Rose's desk. Head bowed over her notes and not looking where she was going, she practically walked into Kevin, who was standing near Rose's computer station talking to her. Awkwardly coming to an abrupt halt, she paused uncertainly. "Sorry, I didn't realize you were busy. I can come back some other time." As neither Rose nor Kevin said a word, Nicole felt even more uncomfortable.

Kevin breached the taut silence first. "Good morning, Nicole."

"Good morning Kevin," Nicole responded, wondering why she should feel so suddenly defensive.

Rose reached out her hand by way of rescue.

"Nicole, if your memo is ready, I'll be happy to get right to it. Did you want to proof it before I send it out?

"No, just go ahead and send it. I trust you."

"Well, Rose, I guess that makes you one of the lucky few," Kevin stated sarcastically as Nicole turned to walk back to her office.

Turning around and fully prepared for a battle, Nicole said, "Some people have earned their trust."

"If they had to earn it, then it was never trust in the first place, was it?" With that cryptic comment he turned as if dismissing a stubborn child and arrogantly turned back to Rose, who was watching them both with undisguised interest.

Tired of his dismissals and his always getting the last word in, Nicole refused to be so easily dismissed. "You know what, Kevin, I didn't ask you to come here. You invited yourself. You didn't consider what was going on in my life nor did you care. You came to this school, set yourself up as its great hero and expected that I would, I guess, come falling at your feet. Now when I don't, you have the gall to try and act like the reason I'm not tripping over my feet in gratitude is because of some failing on my part. I gave you all the trust I had to give and you misused it. So don't look at me as if I am the person with the problem. This is the bed you made with your own admitted immaturity. So while my insecurities may have played some small part, never forget that it was your own personal failing which put us in the position we are in today. So I don't feel guilty about not cleaning up your mess. Nor do I owe you any more trust." She added meanly, "Because in your case, you would definitely have to earn it, and you have yet to even try." And with that last parting shot, Nicole turned her back on him and returned to her office where she shut the door with finality.

An hour later Nicole was still riding the high she felt from getting in the last word. Ever since Kevin had arrived, she'd felt as if she were always on the losing end of the stick. She was so tired of feeling as if she were the person who was responsible for everything that had gone wrong in their old relationship. Somehow Kevin had skillfully managed to make her feel almost as if she needed to apologize and explain herself. But after the fiasco of the previous night, she had resolved not to feel apologetic anymore. Kevin had been directly responsible for the irrevocable breakdown in their relationship. There had been times during those first few years that Nicole had wondered if maybe her insecurities had been the cause. But ultimately, by his own admission, it had been his immaturity which had caused the real problems. If he had truly matured, as he wanted her to believe, then he would understand why her trust would never be given to him unconditionally again. And why, she asked herself, was she wasting time even giving him one more thought?

Entering Nicole's office Rose said, "Nicole, I got

everything all typed up, but I noticed the date you set for the meeting with the residence assistants conflicted with your rescheduled date for Wallace High School. So I went ahead and changed it. Is that okay?"

"Sure," Nicole replied absently. "No problem."

Standing quietly, Rose finally caught Nicole's attention when she did not immediately exit. "You wanna talk about it?" Rose asked quietly.

"About what," Nicole answered as if she didn't know.

"C'mon, honey. The whole school has noticed the tension between the two of you. Being in the room with both of you together is like being in a room with a powder keg and matches."

"It's that bad, huh?" Sighing with shame at her own uncharacteristic behavior, Nicole asked, "Do you really think it's noticed around the campus?" When Rose nodded in reproachful affirmation, Nicole added embarrassment to her sense of shame. Never before had she let any hint of her personal problems involve the school at all. And she had tried never to willingly be a contributor to the school's active rumor mill.

"Well, maybe not everybody," Rose soothed gently. "But they soon will, the way the two of you keep going at it. Now, I didn't want to be the one to bring this up, but I was here when the two of you were an item. I remember how close you guys seemed as you walked around campus together. Even for an old lady like me it was so romantic."

"So you're admitting you are an old lady?" Nicole could not help interrupting. Rose's determination to keep her true age a well-guarded secret was an on-going joke between the two of them.

"Never you mind about that," Rose skillfully evaded. "My point is, I would have bet my last dime that the two of you were truly in love."

"And that's why we're both broke today. We'd have had a better chance at winning the lottery."

"Naw, I just can't believe that." Rose shook her head firmly. "Kevin Powell was a good man. And I think he still is." Refusing to let Nicole interrupt her, she continued, "Now, I'm not saying he is perfect. But what man is? Why you can tell he's a sweetheart just by how he's helping out the school. Any man who could donate that much..."

"Huh! A tax write-off," Nicole could not help throwing out.

"Nicole, honey, he can't write off his time. Now tell Aunty Rose the truth. What can you possibly find wrong with this man? He's gorgeous, rich, successful, sweet. What part of this picture am I not seeing? If I was twenty years younger, I'd take him myself."

"Rose, he just can't be trusted. Believe me, I know."

"Like I said, I don't know what happened back in the past. But I do know enough time has gone by that maybe you should consider leaving it in the past." She held her hand up to forestall any protestations Nicole might have. "Ten years is a long time. I remember when you first came to work here after getting your master's degree. You were so starchy and formal. You would summon me into the office like you were the president of the country." Mocking a young Nicole, Rose continued in Nicole's prim northern accent, "Ms. James, would you please take a letter." Resuming her own more sedate southern drawl, she said, "I hate to say so, honey, but to use my mama's words 'you were full of yourself.' And many was the day I nearly told you so. But you grew up and matured. I've watched you. And I don't hold against it against you now for how you were then."

"It's not the same thing. Sure, I might have been a little cocky, but I never actually mistreated you."

"I know it's different. But the result is the same. I had to give you a chance. Can't you do the same? Love is nothing without trust. I know you used to love him very much. And I think you still do." Raising her voice and her eyebrows in one well-practiced movement when Nicole was about to interject a strong objection, she added, "And you still must or you wouldn't let him rile you so." Taking a deep breath, she deftly changed the subject. "Now I didn't come in here to get you started again. I just wanted your approval before I sent these memos out."

Knowing perfectly well that Rose felt perfectly free to organize Nicole's life however she wanted to, Nicole still accepted the gracious way out, approving the memo to preserve the pretense that Nicole was actually in charge.

David's call moments after Rose left her office was a much appreciated distraction. Agreeing to lunch, Nicole comforted herself with the thought that at least somebody was still on her side.

"Hey babe, how's it going?" David teased, deliberately using the title he knew always raised Nicole's ire.

Seating herself at what had come to be thought of as their table in the faculty cafeteria, Nicole refused to rise to the bait twinkling in his green eyes. "Fine, what's the special for today?"

Finding it odd that Nicole was not engaging in their usual teasing banter, David answered her question, then asked seriously. "Hey, is something wrong?"

"You mean other than the fact that we apparently have someone deliberately undermining the school, destroying recruitment packages and stealing our antiques?" She'd added the last part in a quiet tone, well aware that although she had not told David of the theft he had probably found out via the efficient grapevine. "Other than those things, I would have to say no, nothing's wrong."

Taking her hand, he squeezed it reassuringly. "Everything is going to be all right. Trust me." His green eyes gave Nicole the much needed support she relied on him for. "And hey, if it's not, my offer to run away with you is still good."

"Thanks," she murmured sincerely as she squeezed his hand back. "Wait a minute! Didn't you tell me today was going to be 'miracle Wednesday'?"

"Yes I did, and I have one for you right now." The student server approached with their plates as if appearing by some magical command of David's. In sotto voce he answered the question in her eyes. "The meatloaf is actually edible."

"That's my miracle!" Nicole exclaimed in protest. "Edible meatloaf!"

"Babe, if you knew how hard it was to conjure up this, then you would understand why there'll be no more miracles for the rest of the year."

Laughing at his silliness, Nicole enjoyed the easy comfort of their friendship, grateful that she always had David to depend on. What would I ever do without him? she wondered to herself as his teasing banter kept her entertained for the rest of their lunch. Thinking of how easily the school had cheated him out of his rightful position as athletic director with the return of Kevin was just one more wrong she could lay on Kevin's doorstep.

Walking her back to her office from the faculty cafeteria, David continued his light repartee. Practically in stitches when the elevator reached the top floor, Nicole reached unself-consciously for his hand as they stepped onto the office floor. All merriment abruptly ceased as they both faced Kevin, who stood watching them as if they were wayward children. Refusing to have her mood broken by his uncompromising stance, Nicole turned to David and said, "Thanks for lunch. Let me know the next time you can conjure up some more of that edible meatloaf."

"Anything for you, babe." He winked and gave her a friendly hug and kiss on the cheek before she turned for her office beneath the weight of Kevin's glare.

"Coach Spears." Kevin's commanding voice came booming out before either had gone very far. The thundery gravel in his voice halted both of them in their tracks. "Since you seem to have nothing important to do, do you think you could spare a few moments to meet with me concerning work?" His uncompromising posture and stress on the word *work*, made it clear what he thought of their jovial manner.

"Wait a minute...," Nicole broke in to defend David, shocked and outraged by the unwarranted attack.

Nicole was silenced by a shake of his head as David indicated he didn't need her help.
Instead he responded, "Sure, no problem." His smile was still in place as he followed Kevin into his office.

Locking her office door for the evening, Nicole stopped by Rose's desk and waited as Rose finished up to ask the question that had been on her mind. "What time did David leave his meeting with Kevin?" Nicole had wondered why he hadn't popped in on her before returning to his gymnasium office.

"They finished about a half hour ago," Rose answered.

"You're kidding me. Kevin kept him in there all that time? What could they possibly have to go over that would take that long?"

"I don't know," Rose answered, then continued in a conspiratorial whisper, "but whatever it was, it wasn't pleasant. When David left, he definitely was not smiling. He didn't even stop to tell me good-bye. And you know how odd that is for him. I think Kevin might have been a little hard on him."

"I see," Nicole said thoughtfully, all too afraid that maybe she did see what had happened, all too well. "Well, you have a good night."

"Aren't you leaving too?" Rose questioned.

"I was, but now I think I may need to have a little talk with Mr. Powell."

"Okay. But remember that we don't know what actually happened in there," Rose warned to Nicole's back as she knocked on Kevin's door.

"Yes, ma'am?" he questioned formally when Nicole entered his office.

"What happened with David?" Nicole asked, getting straight to the point.

"What business is it of yours?" Kevin mocked. "Or does he need to hide behind your skirts whenever he gets in trouble?"

"I want to know why he would be in any trouble,"

Nicole said, refusing to be sidetracked.

"Again, what business is it of yours?"

"I'm the dean of students..."

"Exactly, you're the dean of students, not teachers. Now, I don't tell you how to do your job, so don't tell me how to do mine."

"You have got to be kidding. You got your job because of one generous donation. You can't possibly think that qualifies you to know anything about how this department should actually be run."

"Whether you think I'm qualified or not, it's still my job. And I don't owe you any explanation about how I execute it. The board *trusted* me with this position and I intend to do what I feel is best."

"And what did those feelings have to do with David?" Nicole persisted.

"If you must know, I had several questions about what's been going on in his department. Like, why do we have football players failing English 100? When we know that most of them will miss at least 40 percent of their classes due to their athletic responsibilities, why are there no study sessions or tutors arranged for any of our athletes? Why are there athletes who haven't had physicals since they first enrolled? And I could go on and on. So no, I might not be qualified by your standards, but even I, a lowly professional athlete, can look and see more holes in this program than in a pair of fishnet stockings. And I want to know why he didn't see the same thing. Or was he too busy looking at your lovely face to notice?"

"Kevin, you have to understand that Coach Lyons ran the program in a different way," Nicole tried to explain while ignoring Kevin's last question.

"And he's been gone for months," Kevin responded, clearly not caring to hear any excuses.

"David just needs a chance. He's been working really hard."

"Apparently he hasn't been working too hard if he has time to lollygag over lunch playing footsie..."

"Admit it, that's what this is really about, David and me going out to lunch together."

"This is about the fact that I want a complete program for our athletes. One that will insure that when they leave this school they are prepared for their future. I've seen firsthand what happens to athletes who don't get that preparation."

"So all of this concern has to do with the kids?" she asked disbelievingly. "Nothing to do with David and me going out to lunch together."

"Don't be conceited. I don't care who you go out with or have gone out with. Although I do find it odd that the person who holds a grudge against me because of things I did while married isn't exactly walking around acting like a married woman herself."

"Well, that's easily solved. If I don't meet the high standards of how you think your wife should act, then all you have to do is divorce me." As soon as those words left her lips, Nicole recalled the lesson she had learned early in life: That words spoken in anger could never be taken back, and her angry ones seemed to literally stand on the tense air between them.

"I don't want a divorce," Kevin eventually stated. Sighing deeply, he looked into her eyes for affirmation that she felt the same. Uncomfortable under his perusal, Nicole looked away. "If I did, I would have gotten one long ago."

"Why didn't you?" The question which had been searing a hole in the back of Nicole's mind for days came out shakily.

"Because I never considered that I would marry anyone else," he said softly, as if compelled to tell no more than the simple truth. "And I guess I just always hoped that someday, there would be another chance for us."

"If you really meant that, you would give me time to learn to trust you again."

"Trust shouldn't take time, Nicole. I could give you a million years or one second and the bottom line would still be either you trust me or you don't."

"This, I believe, is where we ended yesterday." Buttoning up her jacket she shrugged and added, "And since I have no desire to go over this same issue with you again, goodnight."

"Goodnight, Nicole," Kevin finally answered after holding her gaze captive for a long moment before releasing it. Nicole left for what promised to be another long night.

# Chapter 10

The ritual packing of her briefcase on Friday was especially satisfying to Nicole, who breathed a sigh of relief as she snapped the gold-plated locks shut with finality. This Friday officially ended what had been the longest week of her life, and she looked forward to a tranquil and relaxing weekend. Although she had nothing more exciting planned for the two-day vacation other than 'vegging out' in front of the television, even that was a welcome change from the stress of the past week. Tension between her and Kevin had not lessened, and as Rose had warned, it was noted by the entire staff. How long, she wondered, before the rumors of dissent reached Hal's ears? Luckily, the icy politeness with which they treated each other could pass for a nominal working relationship. But she missed the friendly, peaceful environment she'd always previously enjoyed with a variety of different colleagues over the last eight years. Wishing Rose a good night, Nicole left the Tolleston campus with a relief she hadn't ever felt before.

Nicole had fallen in love with Tolleston's beautiful Tennessee landscape as a freshman. Later returning as assistant dean, when she was first hired by the school, she knew immediately where she wanted to live. Located on the outskirts of the campus, the two-story Victorian house she called home sat generally in the faculty housing area but on top of a hill with the best view of the mountains that the campus allowed. Its relative isolation yet nearness to the campus afforded the perfect synthesis of privacy and convenience.

Walking up the stairs to the porch, Nicole sat for a moment in the old-fashioned porch swing and watched the sun set in the mountains. Slowly rocking herself, Nicole was glad she had this home to come back to after a hard day of work. As the sun set with its silent fireworks show, Nicole relaxed as she had not done all week. Kicking off her navy pumps to curl her stockinged feet up on the hunter green and cream-striped cushion, she wondered about her relationship with Kevin.

All week thoughts of him had left her feeling angry and frustrated. Why, she wondered, couldn't he have decided his marriage was important years earlier? If he had, would her answer have been any different? He claimed he had grown up, but if a person matured, did that mean you just forgot all the things they did before? Did marriage vows mean that you were then committed to try extra hard to forgive a person? And if so, was there a time limit on how long you were obligated to try? Questions that had plagued and angered her all week posed less of a threat in the early evening hours with her legs propped up in the swing. Taking a deep breath before she finally rose and let herself in the house, she wondered, Did I ever really give him a chance?

By Saturday night, Nicole was restlessly pacing her hardwood floors. Not accustomed to dealing with such nervous energy, she was considering returning to work when her doorbell rang. Grateful for any interruption to her seemingly endless day of doing nothing, Nicole raced to the door. Leaning against her front porch rail was Kevin, the object of her mind's preoccupation.

"What are you doing here?" Nicole asked in an unfriendly tone, the first question that came to her mind.

"Good evening to you, too," Kevin responded, mocking her rudeness.

"Good evening, Kevin. Nice to see you," Nicole answered sweetly. "Now, what are you doing here?"

"One might think, Nicole, that you were not happy to see me."

"Since we didn't exactly part on the best of terms, I think one could be forgiven if that was true."

"Can't a man visit his wife?"

"Okay," Nicole said, thoroughly disgusted with him.

"I'm closing the door now. I don't have time for your games." She followed her words with the appropriate actions.

Quickly, he jammed his foot in the door before she could complete the swing that would slam it shut in his face. "Okay, okay. Give a brother a chance. I'm actually here to apologize," he shouted through the crack in the door caused by his foot.

"Apologize?" Nicole slowly opened the door a little further.

"You were right. I was being a little presumptuous and maybe a tiny bit arrogant."

"Just a tiny bit?"

"Just a little," he replied in the affirmative. "I did think that maybe it would be as easy as me showing up and apologizing, and I never considered how arrogant that was. And although I haven't changed my feelings about trust," he interjected firmly, "I do feel that maybe I could try and understand how you might need time."

"Oh...I see, maybe you understand...," she mimicked.

"Give me a break, Nicole. It was hard enough for me to admit I was wrong. It never occurred to me that just admitting that wouldn't be enough."

"And it's not!"

"That's why I'm willing to give you time. After all, I took the last ten years. I figure that I owe you at least a couple of days."

"A couple of days!" she shouted, rising to his bait before she saw the teasing gleam in his eyes. "Well, I thank you for coming and apologizing..." She broke off as she began slowly closing the door. "But if that's all..."

"Nicole," he teased before she could completely close the door, "I brought food."

Opening the door fully for the first time, Nicole responded, "Now why didn't you say that to begin with?" Before he could enter, she barred his way with her hand on his chest. "Wait a minute, wait a minute...cheesecake?"

"Of course, do you think I could ever forget?" He turned and motioned to the hotel's van out by his car. The van which had gone unnoticed by Nicole while she and Kevin talked, suddenly burst into action.

"What's going on?" she asked as two men in the white uniforms of the hotel's dining staff suddenly appeared. Nicole moved to the side as they briskly brushed past her with a dining cart loaded with sparkling silver utensils, flowers, candles and covered plates.

"When I said I brought food, I meant that I brought food!" Kevin answered, enjoying her bemusement and following her into the dining room. "Is it okay if they set the meal up in here?" he asked belatedly, as they had already begun doing just that.

"Sure," Nicole answered, as she struggled to contain her pleasure over his surprise. Looking around flustered, she tried to unobtrusively pick up a scrap piece of paper from the floor and tidy up the pillows on the couch, where she had been reclining before he arrived. As she searched for any other misplaced item she reprimanded him. "You could have called first and given me a chance to straighten up."

"If I had called and you had said that you needed to straighten up, I would have just sent the housekeeping staff as well." When her eyes turned to him in shock to see if he was teasing, he continued, "Will you relax?" He captured her hand as she bent to retrieve a book from her coffee table. "Everything looks fine."

Finally the meal was set up and the wait staff left, their brisk and efficient tasks complete. The huge dining room contained a huge fireplace on one side wall. It was on the table in front of the fireplace that their meal waited.

Feeling unreasonably nervous Nicole sat down. "What time will they come back?"

"I told them to just pick it up tomorrow."

"Oh," was all Nicole could think of as a response. Silently, she wondered what else he had on the agenda for tonight."

"I just thought it would be easier since I didn't know what time we would finish," he further explained.

"Oh," Nicole repeated dumbly, feeling guilty that she had let her vivid imagination picture a far less innocent reason.

After he sat in his own chair, he halted her before she

could lift the lid off her plate. Grabbing her hand, he held her attention before he spoke. "I just want you to know that I put a lot of thought into this meal. The chef on staff came up with a lot of suggestions for what he thought would make a perfect menu. But in the end I went with what I felt was most appropriate. I wanted something that would really speak to our special past. And I wanted something that would let you know that I've never forgotten one day that we spent together. Each day has stayed with me always, like a treasured memory"

Nicole could hardly wait to see what delicacy awaited her delight. When she lifted the lid and looked down at her plate, her eyes flew up to his in stunned disbelief. "What the..."

"Like I said, I remembered..."

"But Kevin," she said, giggling uncontrollably. "Pizza?" Still looking at her plate in disbelief, she lost the battle to hold in her laughter. Privately, she couldn't help giving him credit. They had practically lived off pizza during those last two years of school, especially after Nicole had first moved into her off campus apartment and was still mastering the fine art of cooking. Many days they had both looked at the final results of her best efforts and agreed...pizza! Curious to see what was under the lid of the large plate in the center of the table, Nicole was not terribly surprised to see the rest of the pizza pie, artfully arranged with a garnish in the center.

"And," Kevin stated, as he reached in the champagne bucket, "voila!" He triumphantly pulled out a two liter bottle of orange soda which had been hidden under a layer of ice.

While she laughed hysterically, Kevin seriously poured the soda into the crystal wine glasses. Playing the moment for all it was worth, he even swirled it around as if tasting a bottle of wine before declaring, "Perfect, no doubt an excellent month for soda making."

Nicole was tickled by his foolishness. One thing about Kevin Powell was that he had always been able to make her laugh, and he was showing her that, at least, hadn't changed. She was also touched that he had remembered about the soda. Nicole recalled how they had argued many times over what to drink. He preferred dark colas and she the lighter taste of lemon-lime, until they had both discovered a mutual love of orange soda. After that compromise, whenever they splurged and could afford more than their usual tropical punch flavored packaged drink, they purchased orange soda. At one point, Nicole figured, they had both drunk so much of it that she imagined if they ever gave blood, orange syrup would come out instead.

"Pleased?" he asked as they both dug into the pizza.

"Very much so," she answered, unable to lie. "So much, that I will forgive you for lying about the cheese-cake." She didn't see any place it could be hidden on the empty dining cart left near their table.

"Always so quick to think I've lied. I'm gonna teach you to believe me, if it's the last thing I do."

"Well, where is it then?"

"O ye of little faith," he responded, moving to reveal a hidden compartment under the dining cart.

"Is my cheesecake in there?"

"What will you give me if it is?" he asked.

"The better question is, what will I do to you if it isn't?" she threatened.

"Okay, don't start threatening me, girl. Your cheesecake is in there."

"Thank you very much. I would have hated to get physical."

"Now I wish I wouldn't have told you. 'Cause I wouldn't have minded one bit."

Unable to think of a witty comeback to that last remark, Nicole primly finished her pizza. Two and a half hours later they were still seated at the dining table. The pizza had long since been finished and the candles had burned down practically to the silver candlesticks as their pleasant dinner conversation dwindled down to a companionable silence. They had discussed everything from what city had the best professional basketball team this year to what future of education was going to be like with the advent of the computer as teacher. Nicole, who had always admired Kevin as much for his quick intellect as his gorgeous body, enjoyed the challenge of his conversational repartee. When the lively conversation lulled,

Nicole admitted to herself how reluctant she was to see the date end. Sighing with regret at the same time, they both looked at each other in a silent acknowledgment of a wonderful evening.

"Do you wish as much as I do that this evening could just go on and on?" Kevin asked.

"I did enjoy myself," Nicole replied without really answering his question.

"Enough to invite me to stay for something beyond dinner?"

"I think dinner was a good start, don't you?"

"True, it was a start. But that doesn't mean it has to end just yet, does it?" he persisted.

"I'm afraid it does," Nicole answered. "Unless you have something else in mind."

"Actually, I do," he surprised her by saying. "Leave those dishes alone. They'll get them tomorrow, I promise." He forestalled her protest by grabbing her hands from their busy work and leading her into the living room and seating her on the couch. "Wait right here," he instructed as he ran out to his car.

Wondering what other he had in store for her, Nicole waited with anxious anticipation.

# Chapter 11

Getting up, Nicole peeked through the window on her heavy oak door as Kevin disappeared into a dark vehicle and emerged with a small black overnight bag. Could he be arrogant enough to think that she would invite him to spend the night because of one meal? Nicole watched his return with some trepidation. All night, as they had slipped into the easy comfort of their early relationship, Nicole had searched her heart for the answer to the unspoken question between them. Was she ready for more?

The candlelight, his ready smile and sensuous good looks made it all too easy for her to recall how they had once been in perfect accord in all areas. Even as they drifted from subject to subject in familiar perfect harmony, Nicole had wondered if that same harmonious rhythm would later be transferred to the bedroom, which was merely one floor away. It was impossible for her to forget how much she missed the intimacy of their previous relationship. Every time their hands touched or legs brushed under the table, Nicole had been blushingly aware of the magical promise of pleasure not far away. Taking a deep breath as she opened the door to him again, Nicole wondered how she would deal with the issue. Days before or even hours earlier, it wouldn't have been a question, but Kevin was so impossible to resist when he was purposefully charming and sweet, that Nicole wasn't sure she could find the fortitude she would need against him even in angry memories. Especially when her betraying heart whispered, 'That was then, this is now.'

"Kevin...," she said, not sure how to begin. Fiddling nervously with the buttons on her sweater, she barely noticed that he went to her television and promptly started fiddling behind it. "I'm don't know if I'm ready..." She broke off as it finally sank home that he was not acting as if he were preparing for a bout of lovemaking.

"Not ready for what?" he asked in distraction as he continued concentrating on his task.

"Never mind, what are you doing?"

"Just give me a minute. You always were an impatient little thing. Don't worry. I'm not going to hurt your television."

"You'd be nervous too if you knew how much that

television cost."

Stopping from his mysterious task, he looked at her in amusement. "You're kidding, right? I'll get you a televison for every room in this house, every corner of this house. All you have to do is say the word."

"Just tell me what you are doing," she repeated, neatly evading his statement.

"That's what I thought, you little coward," he said affectionately. "You just wait or go
make yourself useful somewhere. I'm almost done."

Ten minutes later, Kevin came and retrieved Nicole. Because she couldn't fathom the idea of leaving dirty dishes sitting out, she had busied herself by tidying up. When Kevin suddenly put his hands over her eyes, she halted in surprise. "What are you up to?" she asked as she automatically raised her hands to his defensively. His hands, which were covering both of her eyes, remained a secure blindfold. Momentarily struggling against the restraint, she stopped abruptly when she realized how intimately he was pressed up against her backside. Her unconscious childlike wiggling to get out of his grasp and escape his hands had caused a natural and very adult reaction.

His breath exploded like hot steam on the side of her neck at the brief brush of her derriere against his pelvis, and it was a long moment before Kevin responded in a voice that was unusually gruff, "Just come on and no peeking."

Guiding her from behind and seating her on the couch, his hands never left her eyes until he quickly sat beside her. "Keep your eyes closed," he cautioned.

"This better be good," she threatened in a teasing tone.

"Remember to keep your eyes closed. I want to see if you can figure it out. I'm going to put something in your hands and you tell me what it is. Now, Nicole, don't peek."

Feeling first the square flat portion of the object, Nicole was clueless. Kevin slowly guided her hand up a thin, short column, about the circumference of a short pencil. Nicole was at a loss. Drawing her hands quickly back she said, "Kevin, if you wanted a quick feel, all you had to do was say so!"

"Very funny, Nicole," Kevin reacted without humor. "But I know you know better. And if you need reminding, I'll be happy to oblige."

"Never mind. I give up. Can I open my eyes now?"

"Go ahead," Kevin said neutrally, some of his good humor having evaporated with Nicole's joke.

It took Nicole a minute to realize what the black joystick actually was. "You brought a video game?" Looking at him in puzzlement, she wondered why he had made such a big deal out of something so simple.

"Don't you get it?" Kevin looked into her questioning eyes, compelling her to recall long suppressed memories. "Remember how your cable was always going out and we couldn't really afford any of those expensive games?"

"And one day we were at a rummage sale and found an old Atari game system," Nicole responded, picking up the story. Memories of happier times came flooding back as he opened the gate on her memory.

"It only came with one game..."

"Pac Man."

"I beat you regularly," he added proudly.

"You cheated regularly," she corrected.

"You can't cheat at Pac Man," he protested.

"You can if you constantly try to distract your opponent."

"Kissing was not distracting. I was just being my usual affectionate self."

"Cheater!" she loudly argued. "I can't believe you found this old system. I didn't think it was on the market anywhere. This looks brand new."

"It is."

"But how," she asked in disbelief, "how were you able to get it?"

"Don't you worry about that. I got connections." He smiled smugly. "Wanna play a game for old time's sake?"

"Do you promise not to cheat?"

"Are you asking me if I'm going to keep my hands off you?" he asked in disdain. "Because I cannot, will not, promise any such thing."

"Cheater," she repeated. However the allure of their old friendly competition was too tempting to decline.

"All right then, to even the odds a little, you are welcome to put your hands anywhere you want, if you think it is going to distract me," he challenged, seductively grinning down at her.

Just like that, it was on. The game, which started out friendly enough on the couch, was soon a knockdown, drag-out fight on the floor in front of the television. True to his word, Kevin took every opportunity to distract her, playfully brushing her hair when she was concentrating, claiming as she looked up at him in disgust when she was promptly 'eaten up' that he was only trying to help her. He ran his fingers along the outside of her thighs, pretending that he was brushing dirt off her pants, and staged a thousand seemingly innocent caresses designed to distract her.

"Will you just stop?" Nicole finally asked as she shooed his octopus-like hands off her for the hundredth time. She threw her joystick down in frustration as she was again gobbled up by the hungry, blinking monsters.

"I can't help it," he sighed as if under extreme pressure. "I can't be around you and not want to touch you." Tossing his joystick to the side, he rolled Nicole, who had been lying on her stomach as she played, over so that their faces were mere whispers apart. "Touch you and kiss you." So saying, his actions quickly followed his words.

Lowering his mouth to hers, he devoured hers with a passion that belied the light teasing of his words. The dark, forceful kiss left Nicole literally breathless as she could do no more than meekly offer up the surrender his kiss demanded from her lips. Coming up for a breath of his own, Kevin looked at Nicole with dark-brown eyes that were defenseless and allowed her none of her own. Muttering softly, "Butter," he returned to the kiss far more gently yet just as firmly in its uncompromising conquest.

The tidal wave of longing that swept over Nicole came in a strong and sudden surf that was relentless in its demand for more. Struggling against the waves of passion, which were overwhelming her, Nicole tried vainly to retain her composure. "We can't...," she mumbled in protest.

"Yes, we can," Kevin softly argued while licking the protest off her still parted lips. "We've wasted so much time, let's not waste another minute." Pulling back briefly to look into her eyes as he spoke, Kevin waited anxiously for some sign from Nicole. As if sensing her hesitance, he leaned down and gently kissed her forehead, his tongue wreaking havoc on the little creases as Nicole struggled to remember her objections.

It was the gentleness that, in the end, was Nicole's final undoing. Painfully tender, the soft kisses on her forehead were like the soft rushing of spring raindrops against her skin. Lifting her head, she murmured, "Oh

Kevin," as she reassuringly brought his lips back to her own with sure fingers.

Following her lead with gracious triumph, Kevin returned to his hungry assault on her lips, again confining his attentions to the outside of their outside corners. Nicole could only moan in despair as she gave herself up to his gentle gnawing. Kevin took his time as he familiarized himself again with the succulent sweetness her lips offered. When the gentle exploration was over, Nicole sighed in relief as he coaxed her tongue out to play softly with his. Curling her toes at the electric sparks from their dueling tongues, Nicole welcomed the deepening kiss, acknowledging to herself that no other kiss had ever moved her as much as Kevin's. Nicole ran her fingers up his back to his broad shoulders as she purred in contentment.

Kevin's hands, which had found their home in her softly curled hair, started their own quest as well. Turning her slightly, so that one of her thighs found itself nestled between his, Kevin groaned at the sudden intimate touch. Moving with a steadfast purpose, his hands found their target with determined accuracy. Cupping the arch of her buttocks and softly squeezing, Kevin kneaded firmly, pulling her hips more firmly into his groin. His intimately erotic massage was as much torture as prelude.

As Nicole's hips unconsciously bucked his in a subliminal message of consent, Kevin tore his lips away from hers to travel down the side of her neck. Frustrated by the lack of access their positions afforded, he abruptly sat up. Pushing his back up against the edge of the couch and straightening his legs out, he reached for Nicole and pulled her astride his lap in one deft movement, then continued to rock her hips gently against his own as his hands started unbuttoning her sweater. In one swift movement her sweater was tossed behind the couch and promptly forgotten. Surprising Nicole, Kevin did not immediately remove her bra, even though its front snap enclosure gave him an easy access. He chose instead to turn his attention to her collarbone and the feminine cavity at the base of her throat. Breaking off, he kissed her hungry mouth briefly before returning to the base of her throat once again. With bone-melting accuracy, Kevin planted kisses across the top of her breasts.

Sketching the sculpted lace border of her bra, Kevin avoided her breasts themselves with a perverse indifference. Moaning in frustration, Nicole took her own initiative. Arching her back slightly, Nicole molded her palms to Kevin's cheeks, pulling his face softly against the lace and satin of her bra. Refusing to rush things, Kevin obstinately kissed her breasts through the satin that cupped them. Stiffening in appreciation of the delicate offense, her nipples strained themselves in eagerness, until Nicole, unable to bear the exquisite torment anymore, finally flicked the snap open and tossed the oppressive bra to the side herself. Kevin looked at Nicole with such triumph as she arched her back and presented her breasts, that she knew that he had been waiting for her to offer herself completely.

Kevin could only marvel at her glorious display, and he returned to his task with a fervor that belied his earlier indifference. Sucking exquisitely on her breasts, Kevin's mouth traced the darkened center outline before engulfing the entire nipple. Traveling from one nipple to the other, back and forth, Kevin feasted. "Hmm," he groaned. "Tastes like honey." Going back for a second helping, he corrected himself. "No, it tastes like butter." He licked the tautly erect nipple, battling the stiff tip with the point of his tongue before sucking on it again. "No," he corrected himself again. "It tastes like butter melting into honey." Palming both breasts in the cup of his hands, he brought them together in one sumptuous meal. Then tiring of the game which whetted the appetite without satisfying it, Kevin released his captives.

Trailing his mouth down the edge of her rib cage, Kevin continued his assault lower. Nicole, who had already been leaning back on his lap, was pressed into an even deeper arch as his mouth found a new target in her belly button. With Kevin's strong hand supporting her back, Nicole could only sigh as his tongue wreaked havoc on her stomach, which was already fluttering wildly.

Laying Nicole out on the floor, Kevin resumed his

kissing below her belly button as he unzipped her jeans and tickled with his tongue the indentation under the curve of her pubic bone. Nicole wiggled in a move that was both protesting and inviting. Drawing back to look at her face, Kevin tried to read her love-glazed eyes. He found the answer to his unspoken question. Kissing her lips, he quieted her tumultuous emotions before tracing his way to her waistline again.

Nicole pulled his face back up to hers and reached for his shirt which he had yet to doff, and started lifting it off. "I don't want tonight to be just about me."

"But it is," he protested as she unzipped his jeans. "This night is for you."

"No," she stated firmly as she crawled back onto his lap. Holding his head between her hands, she softly punctuated each word with a kiss. "Tonight is for us. And I don't think we should have to wait any longer." With a confidence that was fed by her newfound feeling of 'rightness,' Nicole wrapped her legs around his back as she moved fully into the embrace, pressing breast to breast, as she kissed him fully on his still parted lips.

Never one to discard a gift that was literally thrown in his lap, Kevin resumed his lovemaking with gusto. Laying Nicole onto her back once again, he slowly began peeling off her jeans. He looked at the tempting picture she made lying lasciviously displayed, wearing nothing other than her lace panties and a sinful expression, then swiftly shucked his own pants. Kevin nearly tossed them in the corner before he remembered the small foil packet still in the pocket.

Looking at him in suspicion when she saw the packet, she asked in a voice gone suddenly tremulous as doubt sneaked back into her mind and she wondered just how promiscuous he had become, "Do you always carry those around with you?"

"Only since I've been back here with you." Smiling mischievously he added, "I never knew when or if you might cave in, but I wanted to be prepared."

At that moment, with her heart in complete control over her mind and body, Nicole could not recall why she had ever protested this glorious coming together. Not wanting to remember any bad times, Nicole instead pulled him down to her waiting lips. Instantly she was made aware of another thing she had not fully recalled. His jeans had helped to conceal the fact that the disproportion in their sizes was not only in height. Now with his jeans lying somewhere in the corner, Nicole was reminded that it was not just his body that was broad and big.

Suddenly nervous as he lay wholly upon her, pressing his groin down onto hers as he deepened the kiss, Nicole could only think with trepidation of how her celibacy had not prepared her for their natural disproportion. As if sensing her fears, Kevin drew his hand down her stomach and over the satin and lace edge of her panties and cupped her intimately. Tracing concentric patterns over the satin as he kissed her, he did not stop until the satin was wet. Only then did he gently pull the panties down and cup her to his naked lower half.

Taking a moment to deftly sheath himself in the contents of the foil packet before returning to her kiss, Kevin nestled himself at the doorway of pleasure. Before leaping through, he stopped and waited until she looked up at him in questioning wonder. "I just want you to know one thing."

"What?" Nicole asked breathlessly, wondering what couldn't wait until a more appropriate moment.

"I love you," he stated simply. Those were the words that unleashed the storm. Leaning down to kiss her, he again consummated the union they had begun nearly ten years earlier.

Set adrift initially when the first wave of pleasure hit her, Nicole was just as instantly anchored by Kevin who pulled her closer to him. Wave after wave buoyed them closer together through the storm. When Nicole's pleasure intensified to the point that she could not breathe, Kevin leaned down and kissed her. They both moaned together in climatic finish.

Taking deep breaths, Nicole fought to regain her composure. Her intimate contractions forced his withdrawal and he rolled onto his back. Bereft at his absence, she felt a tiny pleasure tear roll down her cheek as he pulled her into his arms. As their sweat ran down their bodies, Nicole and Kevin held each other in a perfect, satiated silence.

What have I done? The thought echoed through Nicole's mind as she began to come back to reality. All my talk of waiting and taking our time just went down the drain. What must he think of me right now? she wondered, as the silent moment lingered on. Where will we go from here? Doubt after doubt chased themselves around in her brain, until finally her deepest fear of all voiced itself above all the others. What if his only reason for returning had been the challenge of getting the unobtainable Nicole back into his bed? And worse yet, now that he had achieved that goal, would he move on? Nicole shivered at that final thought, hurt indefinably by just the possibility.

Kevin stirred. "Cold?" he asked obliviously as Nicole began to pull away from him in a profound embarrassment that mixed and congealed into regret.

"Just a little," Nicole lied as she looked around for her underwear, which was contrarily hard to find.

Sitting up, totally heedless of her discomfort, Kevin joined her in the search for her wayward undergarments. "You're right. We probably need to make a move off this hard floor. But I just feel so comfortable I can barely move. Come here," he entreated, tugging Nicole to him for a kiss made short when Nicole hesitantly pulled away.

Avoiding his penetrating gaze and abandoning her search, Nicole quickly pulled on her sweater without the bra. Before she was forced to do the same with the jeans, she finally located her panties in the spot made vacant when Kevin rose to look for his own jeans. Desperately pulling her panties on, Nicole said, "You're right, that floor was definitely getting hard."

"And it's not the only thing," Kevin said as he looked at Nicole standing sexily defensive in her half-buttoned sweater and panties.

Nicole gulped and turned guiltily away when her eyes found the meaning of his statement. She quickly stepped into her jeans. "Yeah, well..., too bad you have to be getting back."

"I don't have to get back," Kevin contradicted as if she were completely obtuse.

"Yeah, well...," Nicole stammered. "I have a lot of things to do at work tomorrow. And I'm sure you do too..."

"Nicole, tomorrow is Sunday." Taking her hands which had been nervously fluttering about as if looking for something else to do, he locked her eyes with his own. "Are you putting me out?" Before she could answer, he added, "I hope not, because although I didn't plan for this to happen, it did. And I certainly don't intend to run away from it now. You are my wife." He stated the last sentence with a simple emphasis which cut Nicole to the core. "What we did was not wrong. We're not college coeds hiding from our parents. We're adults who just shared what I think was one of the most wonderful experiences of my life. I hope you aren't going to ruin it now by going back into hiding."

"I'm not hiding. I thought that we were supposed to be taking our time. Instead, we fast forwarded a lot, and we should probably take some time and think about it." Holding her hands out entreatingly, she argued, "I'm just suggesting that we need to think about what tonight really means."

"It means, Butter, that we still care about each other." Grabbing her hands and squeezing them as if he could transmit some of his confidence into her he continued, "It means that we still belong together in a way that time has not diminished. Can't you see that?"

"All I see is that you said you would give me time and you didn't."

"So, now once again Kevin is the evil villain. This is all my fault," he argued sarcastically. "I just overwhelmed the innocent Nicole who couldn't make a decision for herself."

"That's not what I meant. I take full responsibility for my actions."

"Good, I'm glad you at least have the courage to admit that."

"I just think that we should back up..."

"Nicole, life only moves in one direction and backward is not it!" Looking at the honest confusion and distress on her face, Kevin took a deep breath. He calmed himself down before he spoke again. "I said I would give you time, and I still will. Just don't ask me to act like tonight was some horrible mistake and pretend that it never happened. Because for me, it was special."

"It was special for me too, Kevin but..."

"No buts," he interrupted emphatically. "We both agree it was special. Can't we just leave it at that?"

"It was special," she continued as if she hadn't heard his objection. "Because it was like being magically transported back in time. But no matter how special or magical tonight was, it can't erase the last ten years." As she saw him shaking his head in protest she added, "Like you said yourself, we can't go back."

"All I'm asking is for the chance to move forward, with a new beginning. Are you going to give us that chance?"

His chocolate brown eyes nearly melted hers with their intensity. His hands squeezed hers with a reassurance that bordered on desperation. In the silent shouts of his sincerity, Nicole found her doubts quieting "Yes, I will. But..."

Whatever objections she had went unheard. As Kevin pulled her into his embrace, he whispered, "No buts." Then nothing else was heard as he devoured her lips in a kiss that banished all fears.

The kiss continued even as he swept her up into his arms and started for her stairs. He paused only when he reached the second floor to look questioningly in her eyes for direction. Nodding her head to indicate wh room was hers. Kevin proceeded in that direction while renewing the kiss.

Opening the door to her room, he laid her on the massive four-posted, king-sized bed. Nicole watched his face shyly as he took in the room she had personally redecorated to suit her taste. She waited for his response, knowing that many men would have felt overwhelmed in such a feminine setting, but she hoped Kevin was not one of them.

"I love it," he declared. "I don't know when I've seen a room that so completely
reflected its owner. It's old fashioned and it's romantic. It's chaste, yet that little hint of green lets you know there is some spice under all that ice." Leaning down to kiss her again, he whispered, "Just like you, fire and ice blended perfectly."

"You didn't think that ice was so spicy a few days ago."

"That's because I almost believed you had let all your fire go out," he replied smoothly, unbuttoning her sweater once again.

"And now?" She obediently lifted her arms for the sweater's removal.

"Now I know better." He bent his head to suckle at her breast.

"Kevin, wait," she pleaded. "I want to take a shower first."

"Don't want to wait." He shook his head in refusal

but she squirmed off the bed.

"Well, come and join me then, and maybe you won't have to," she invited as she took his hand.

Suddenly compliant, Kevin followed her eagerly into the adjoining bathroom, playfully caressing her breasts from behind.

"You are making it kind of difficult for me to walk." She stated the obvious when she couldn't extricate herself from his grasp.

"Believe me, Butter," he kissed the back of her neck, "you are making it just as difficult for me to walk."

And that comment set the tone for the sexy play which began even before they hit the shower and continued throughout the night. Rising early the next morning, feeling satiated yet exhausted by the vigorous lovemaking, Nicole watched the sun come up. She tried to awaken Kevin by running her fingers over his chest. Then she nibbled at his lips and whispered in his ear. But he turned sleepily away. Returning her attention to his broad chest Nicole let her fingers caress its musculature before wandering below. As her fingers continued their quest lower and lower, she got his full attention.

"Oh, so you are awake," she teased as he lay flat on his back and enjoyed her working hands.

"You always did know how to get my attention." He smiled without opening his eyes.

"So, I see," Nicole said, looking at the rising tent of cover. "But it's time for you to get up."

"I am up," he announced with huskiness as he reached to bring her into his arms.

Evading him, she smiled, "Good, because it's time for you to leave."

"Leave?" he asked in shock, his eyes coming fully open for the first time. "Why? Where am I going?"

"Home."

"Home?" he repeated in bewilderment. "I thought we went through all that last night."

"We did," Nicole answered, as she rummaged through her closet for her robe. "And I'm not backing out of what I said. You were right. If last night proved nothing else, it proved that there are still strong feelings between us. And I am determined to give those feelings a chance and see what can develop."

"But..." He sat up in bed and with a lazy pleasure watched her moving around naked.

"I just think it's time for you to go home now." She found the elusive bathrobe and quickly donned it.

Instantly displeased, as much by what she was saying as her sudden covering up, Kevin could only respond in disgust. "So, I guess I'm to sneak out the back door before anybody discovers I spent the night here. Don't you see how insulting that is to both of us?"

"No, I only see the need for privacy. Let's face it. You are a public figure. And I think that if we are going to work anything out, we need to do it privately." She looked at him firmly, having given the matter some intense thought while he had slept blissfully.

"We can't hide forever, Nicole. I think this may be partly where we went wrong before. If we are married, a marriage should be a public declaration before the world."

"So what do you propose we do? Hold a news conference and just announce that we are married and after ten years have finally reconciled?" she asked sarcastically.

"Would that be so terribly bad?"

"No, and when we've actually reconciled, maybe we will do that. But in the meantime, we're just working it out and now would be a little premature to come out so publicly, don't you think?"

"You still just don't trust me, do you?"

"You agreed with me last night that trust takes time. Are you going to go back on your word and not give it to me?"

Defeated, he answered, "No." Getting out of bed and looking for his clothes, he continued, "I just don't like the idea of sneaking out of here as if we did something wrong. And I don't see the big deal if it did become public. I'm proud to have you as my wife. It is absolutely one of the best decisions I ever made in my life."

Touched, yet resolute, Nicole had to ask, "But you will respect my wishes for privacy?"

"For now," he compromised.

"Thank you," Nicole replied, equally pleased and regretful that the pleasant, light and sexy mood of the previous night had faded somewhat under the dawn of reality.

# Chapter 12

Sunday fled by in a pleasurable haze. Kevin and Nicole met at his hotel for a late brunch and later after lazing around in his bed, Nicole convinced him to go to the movie. They sneaked in ten minutes after the movie started because, Kevin explained, it was the only way he could enjoy a movie without being mobbed. They snuggled and joked through the movie like any other anonymous couple. But as the lights were raised, he was immediately swarmed by the crowd, despite their best efforts to slip inconspicuously away.

Nicole appreciated her decision to hammer out their tentative reconciliation in privacy even more as she stood to the side while Kevin assumed his professional demeanor. Signing the last of the autographs, he firmly pulled her back to his side as they walked to the car. As if reading her silent concern that it would be impossible for them to establish any type of a normal relationship with his fame, he stated, "Don't let it bother you. In a couple of years they'll forget all about Kevin Powell for the next sports hero."

Seriously doubting that, Nicole decided to let his statement go unchallenged. Unwilling to mar the beauty of the day, she responded, "I always wished you would be successful and famous but then when you were, I wished you belonged only to me again."

"And I do. See how wishes come true." He reached over to buckle her into her seat and steal a kiss.

When the magical day ended, Nicole returned home, pleasantly tired and looking forward to spending time in his company again. She resolutely refused to think beyond the immediate future, for once trying to adopt Kevin's attitude that the future would take care of itself.

❧❧❧

Nicole smiled at Rose when she arrived at work Monday morning. She tried to take her mail and slip unobtrusively into her office, but Rose's sharp eyes zeroed in like a hawk on the twinkle in Nicole's eyes. She immediately went digging for answers. "Well, well, Miss Thing, what did you do this weekend that's got you glowing?"

"Nothing special," Nicole lied badly while shuffling through her mail as if she barely heard the question.

"Don't 'nothing' me," Rose persisted, not at all put off by Nicole's innocent demeanor. "You definitely didn't look like this when you left on Friday night, and today you practically skipped in here."

"Rose! You should be a writer with your vivid imagination and your gift of exaggeration. I definitely did not skip in here. And I resent the implication that I am acting like some love-struck schoolgirl."

Kevin chose that very moment to come walking out of his office. Whistling, of all things, Nicole thought in disgust. Did the man know the meaning of discretion? His eyes, which went immediately to Nicole as he approached Rose's desk for his own mail, raked her from head to toe, unknowingly hammering the nail in their guilty coffin with his sensual smile.

"Good morning, Nicole. You look ravishing today." His subtle emphasis on the word ravish, left no doubt in Nicole's mind as to his thoughts.

"Yes, she does," Rose quickly responded before Nicole could answer. "She positively glows, don't you think?" As Kevin nodded his answer without taking his eyes off Nicole, she continued her unashamed probing. "How was your weekend? Do anything special?"

"Actually, I did. I have to say I had the most pleasurable weekend I've had in a long time." As Nicole turned pure red he continued, "The best time I've had in about ten years in fact."

As he finished so outrageously, Nicole planned his

slow murder.

"Um-hmm," Rose grunted in satisfaction. "I see," she finished, as no doubt she did. Raising her eyebrows, she nodded at Nicole in victory at having put the answers together for herself.

"Kevin, I'm glad you're here. There are a few things I need to discuss with you in my office before you get started, if you don't mind."

"Of course not," he replied cheerfully. "For you, it would be a pleasure."

"I just bet it would," Rose murmured for Nicole's ears only.

Angry now at his antics, Nicole turned and walked into her office in a huff, already planning just what she would say to him about his blatant disregard of their agreement. Waiting to close the door, Nicole set her briefcase down angrily. Placing her hands on her hips in a gesture centuries old, she scolded, "How could you? Didn't we discuss the whole privacy matter? You should be ashamed of yourself. You practically flaunted the whole weekend like some kid who got lucky with the prom queen..."

He cut off her words by pulling Nicole into his arms and kissing her. "Butter, you are completely irresistible when you're angry." When she was defeated and breathless, he continued, "I wanted to do that the first moment I saw you." He kissed her softly once again on her parted lips. "Don't hold it against me if I had a little fun with you and Rose. It was either that or this." *This* turned out to be another soul-stirring kiss.

"Yes, well," Nicole stammered as she tried to regain her composure after the breathtaking kiss. "Next time, find some other distraction." Straightening her suit, she lifted her hands to her french roll to make sure he hadn't mussed her hair.

"Please don't do that," he implored as he watched her in complete absorption. "Watching you fix your jacket and hair only makes me want to rip the pins out, tear your jacket off and continue my weekend right there on your desk."

Momentarily afraid he would follow through on his words as his eyes told her he was seriously considering it, Nicole finally regained control of her heartbeat and the situation. "In that case, don't watch me," she instructed stiffly, valiantly holding back a laugh. "Oh, for heavens sake, just go to your office."

"Am I dismissed then?" he asked, mocking her discomfiture.

"Yes, you are." She shooed him out the door, wondering how she would ever get to work now with the picture his words had evoked dancing in her mind.

An hour later when Nicole heard a persistent knock at her office door, she had no doubt who was on the other side. Only one person had the uncanny knack of disturbing her at the exact moment she had finally settled into some semblance of work. Putting her pen down, she focused on the door with a stern impression.

"Come in," she said loudly enough for him to hear on the other side of the thick door. "Kevin Powell, I don't have time to put up with your antics today. Unlike some people, I do actually have things to do today." She broke off in consternation when she realized that Mike Dix was the person who had actually entered her office.

"Sorry to disturb you then if you are busy," Mike said, "but since you directed that at Kevin, I won't take it personally." He smiled, putting her at ease despite her mortification.

"I apologize," Nicole answered in dismay. "I thought you were someone else."

"Obviously, but that's okay. If it's more of you putting Kevin in his place, I don't mind." He grinned conspiratorially, referring to her embarrassing interruption of the previous week.

"Again, my apologies for today and the other day. I don't want you to think that this how we usually do business at Tolleston. Kevin just..."

"...has that effect on women," Mike interrupted her flustered apology. "I was his roommate on road trips for four years, so believe me, I know."

"Oh...." All of the possibilities of what that cryptic statement might mean floated through her brain and tortured her heart.

As if sensing her distress, Mike tactfully changed the subject. "I really don't mean to take up too much of your time today. I just thought maybe you could fill me in on a few details regarding the theft of the book. And I could give you a few details as to what we've found so far."

"Basically, I think you are pretty much up to date. I gave you my statement the other day and I don't know what new details I could give unless you have a specific question."

"I have found in cases like this it's best to go over the details as much as possible. When we spoke last time you were understandably upset about the incident in the gym. I was hoping that, now that you've had some time to cool down, you might help me put a few pieces together."

"I'll be more than happy to do the best I can."

"Great," Mike smiled reassuringly. "I do have a few questions that I hope you can help me with."

"Okay, shoot," Nicole encouraged.

"First, I was curious as to how exactly you picked the security agency you used. I mean, from all accounts, you have plenty of security right here on campus. Why was there a need to look elsewhere?"

With his eyes penetrating hers, like the detective he was, Nicole felt unreasonably nervous. "I just felt that because of the book's high value, it would be best to hire professionals. After all, the campus security is adequate enough for breaking up the occasional fraternity brawl but I didn't want to trust them with a priceless antique."

"You say this is what you personally felt?"

"In conjunction with the board of course," Nicole responded to his question defensively. "It pretty much was a decision we all made together after agreeing to sell the book."

"That's another question." Mike abruptly jumped one train of thought for another. "Why sell the book in the first place?"

"We desperately needed the money."

"What made this particular book so valuable?" Mike asked curiously.

"It was the school's first edition copy of *The Confessions of Nat Turner*, which was written by Thomas Gray from his original interviews with Nat Turner before he was executed. Because it's one of the authentic copies from 1831, it is very rare."

"And was the sale of the book was also at your encouragement?"

"Yes, it was. But again, only after the board agreed."

"But in decisions like the one to sell the book, the board pretty much agreed with whatever you told them. Isn't that correct?"

"You know," Nicole shook her head in disbelief, "you really missed your calling. I think you should have studied law. Because I definitely feel like I'm on trial."

A long moment passed as the two occupants of the room looked at each other with a new intensity. Both candidly searched for the truth behind the other's facade. He looked for honesty and tested her commitment to the school. She looked for and found depth and intelligence behind his easygoing guise. This was no dumb jock who had just happened to luck up on a 'cool job.'

"I certainly don't mean to put you on the defensive," Mike eventually answered. "But I get paid to ask the tough questions."

"And you love it," Nicole responded with new insight.

"I can't tell a lie." He held his sturdy, muscular hands out as he unabashedly grinned. "It's a great job. Besides being a football player, it's the one thing I always wanted to do. As a little kid I wanted to..."

"...play cops and robbers," she finished. "Only you're not a cop."

"No," he continued smiling, "because this pays just a little bit better."

At his last statement, they both laughed tentatively. "Okay, I don't mind tough as long as you're fair. So what else can I help you with?"

"Thanks," Mike commented with a new respect for Nicole. "I really need you on my side 'cause it may get tough. That's why I'm asking you the hard questions first."

"Well, let's go. I have nothing to hide," Nicole answered confidently, liking Mike more and more.

With a mind like a steel trap, Mike returned accurately to where his questioning had been halted. "You never did answer my question. Did the board give you any sort of fight over whether or not to sell the book?"

"You're kidding, right? It was an uphill battle all the way. If I hadn't had David in there backing me..."

"David...?" Mike interrupted.

"David Spears, the athletic coach. Before Kevin came, he was acting athletic director and so he came to all of the board meetings. I think you met him when you went down to the gym."

"Yes, I did. I just hadn't realized he sat on the board. And he was the only person to really back you?"

"Don't get me wrong. Harold also supported me. The board didn't put up much of an argument for long. It quickly became apparent that we were in a desperate situation and didn't have much choice."

"Okay, that puts us back where we started. At your instigation the board agrees to the book's sale. They also agree to use the outside security agency. Who picked the agency?"

"I'm afraid that was my decision also," Nicole answered, realizing how guilty she probably appeared.

"And why this particular agency?" Mike asked.

"Well, let me clarify. Usually the board, you were right, does pretty much give me a free rein. But in this instance they wanted to be updated at every stage. So what I did was narrow down a list of agencies I found in the phone book and they voted from the final five."

"May I ask what you did to narrow down the list?"

"Well, I had a ten-point system that my assistant and

I used together. In all honesty, he did most of the checking for me, because I was so busy working out other details."

"Who was your assistant?"

"Same person as now. Tyrone Reese."

"Is that the same young man who, according to your statement," he paused as he looked back through a small notebook he pulled from a pocket, "was the last person to be alone with the book in your hotel room?"

"Yes, but Tyrone..."

"This is the same student who discovered the gym packages, right?" Mike questioned in a mildly deceptive tone.

Nicole was not fooled. "Wait a minute. Let me tell you something about Tyrone Reese before you got leaping to any erroneous conclusions. He has been nothing but a help to me since he arrived at this school, and he has proven himself to be extremely trustworthy."

"Calm down," Mike soothed at her passionate defense. "I have to ask the tough questions, remember. No one is about to get arrested."

Not entirely soothed, Nicole decided it was time to turn the questioning around. "When we began this meeting, you said you had an update for me. I'd be interested in hearing what you've found out."

"Truthfully, not much. And the investigation is still in the preliminary stages, so right now all I can do is..."

"I know, ask the tough questions."

"You got it." He grinned, pointing his finger at her in playful affirmation. "Seriously, though, I do have enough to know it was an inside job."

"Why do you say that?"

"Because the only people who had access to the book were either Tolleston staff or security hired for that night. I've retraced every step the book took that night and watched and re-watched all of the hotel's security footage. The only people coming off the elevators that night during the time in question were either security or board members, not including of course Tyrone Reese."

"Whom I would prefer that you didn't include."

"Your objection is noted. Unfortunately, that leaves only one other possibility. That the book was taken from the school itself and never even reached the hotel. If that was the case, only key staff here had access to it before security picked the book up. Again, except for Tyrone Reese."

"Mike, I guarantee you I would be guilty of taking that book before Tyrone."

"That brings us to the gym's vandalism," he continued, ignoring for the moment her words of protest. "Only a few people had access to the gym. Again, that only leaves key staff here."

"Your theory sounds good and makes sense. But you've got to understand that this school is like a family. I just can't believe anybody here could possibly be involved."

"Would you have believed that Dean Chandler could possibly have embezzled funds from the school?" When she shook her head in the negative, he continued, "And you worked with him, side by side, day after day, didn't you?"

Realizing the truth of his words, Nicole could only nod her head pensively, not wanting to even imagine that someone she trusted could possibly be involved. "Well, what can I help you with now?"

"Right now, since I seem to have met a dead end in terms of clues, my current strategy is to try a different tack. Since I can't find our culprit, maybe I can find his—or her—," he added quickly to be politically correct, "motive."

"How can I help?"

"I thought maybe you could make me a copy of the original packets. And also a list of all the schools you were going to visit. It may be a long shot, but I have to work every angle."

"No problem," Nicole answered, eager to help. "I've got the disks right here. I saved everything on computer disks." Retrieving her file cabinet key from her desk drawer and rising to her feet, she quickly crossed to the locked cabinet in the corner of her office. Unlocking the cabinet and stooping down to open the bottom drawer, she suddenly pulled back in amazement. Both disks lay in the spot where she kept them. They were nevertheless smashed beyond repair.

# Chapter 13

"What is it?" Mike asked, jumping up as Nicole stood silently in shock. "Nicole, what is it?" he repeated as Nicole gave no response. When he moved her aside, he immediately grasped the situation.

Staring at him in bewilderment, she said, "They're ruined. How is that possible? The file cabinet was locked. You saw me unlock it, didn't you?" Seeking reassurance, she continued. "I am not crazy. This cabinet was locked when I came over here."

"Yes, it was," Mike finally answered. "But who else has a key? Who could have had access to this cabinet?"

"Nobody. Mike, this is not like the gymnasium. This is my personal office and nobody has a key to this office except me. There is a lot of personal student information in that cabinet. So when I'm not here the key to the cabinet is in my desk and the office door is always locked."

"You're sure of that?" Mike asked in disbelief. "What about your secretary? Haven't there ever been times when you have been out of the office and needed her to get something for you? Wouldn't she have a key for emergencies like that?"

"Well, of course. But..."

"So that's at least one other person with the key. Are you sure there isn't anybody else? Think hard."

"Well, Tyrone has an office key too," Nicole replied as answers started clicking in her mind. "And of course the head of security has a master key to my door. Coach Lyons and I exchanged keys. He was the old athletic director before Kevin came. So I suppose Kevin may have it."

"That's already four people with keys to this office, and anybody who can get into the office can get into the cabinet."

"But none of those people would have a reason to do something like this."

"Remember what we just talked about? Until we find out who's responsible for what's going on here, everybody is a suspect. Because whoever is behind these acts is definitely someone who is very familiar with the school."

"I just have a hard time believing that anyone close-ly associated with this school could be the culprit. I know that sounds naive and I'm sorry. But that's how I feel."

"And that's why you hired me." Taking a deep breath and releasing it, he said, "Now, let's go back again. You first said there were no other keys, but it actually turns out there are four. The first is Rose's. I met her earlier today, but I'll..."

Nicole emphatically came to Rose's defense. "No way. Whatever you're going to say, I can't agree. I know in my heart that no matter what is going on, Rose is not responsible for it. I've known her since I was a student here myself. She is like a mother to me, and I know she would never do anything to hurt me or this school."

"Okay, we'll leave her out for now. The second key you said was Tyrone's. I assume you meant Tyrone Reese, your assistant."

"That's correct. And I'll say the same for him as I did for Rose. There is no way he is involved."

Ignoring her comment, he added, "And I believe he told me that this was his freshman year. So he's fairly new here, right?"

"Right. But in that short time he has more than proven his loyalty. In fact, Tyrone is the one who helped me gather the information on the disks. I'm talking about weeks of research. We would often be the only two people here until nearly midnight and he still gave one hundred percent, without a complaint. Why would he possibly want to destroy his own hard work?"

"Okay, then that leaves security..."

"You can rule them out too. Only Officer Ballard has access to the master key and he has been head of security here for longer than either one of us has been alive. Believe me, he's not exactly the type to go rummaging through cabinets destroying computer disks."

"You do realize that you have ruled out everybody?"

"Not exactly, that still leaves Kevin," Nicole answered, giving Mike a very direct look.

"What about motive? What possible reason do you think Kevin Powell would have for doing even a single one of any of these things?"

"Look, I don't I think it's him, any more than you do... But what reason would anybody have? If I knew the answer to that question, I would know who was responsible but the bottom line is I don't. You're the one who said everybody is a suspect."

"Do you really mean that?"

"No, I don't. You're asking me to suspect my friends and that's not easy."

"Well, since both of us seem to have trouble viewing this objectively, I say we drop the question of who for now and concentrate on why. You're saying you don't have any idea of why someone would want to do this? But are you sure? Has the school received any threats lately? Could this possibly be a case of revenge from either Dean Chandler or Coach Lyons?"

"I don't think so. Dean Chandler is in one of those luxury facilities serving his prison sentence. He has taken the opportunity to 'find God' and the last letter we got from him was one begging for our forgiveness and telling us he would pray for the school. He's not thinking about revenge, believe me. And even if he was, I doubt if he would have the resources to carry it out. He didn't have any family and what friends he did have abandoned him quickly after his sentencing."

"What about Coach Lyons? Could he possibly be harboring any resentment toward Tolleston?"

"Again, I doubt it. We weren't the ones who actually discovered his improprieties. He was caught by outside authorities. Believe me, if we had discovered it first, we would have quietly terminated his position and hushed everything up. After leaving Tolleston, he managed to snag the head coach position at his former high school. Though that's not exactly college sports, he squirreled away enough funds over the years to live pretty well. If anything, Tolleston should be planning revenge against him. So, to answer your question, I don't think either one could be involved. However, we do have both of their current addresses if you would like to meet with them."

"I'd appreciate that. Meanwhile, we still have the question of motive." Thoughtfully he drummed his fingers on her desk before he continued. "The real question is, what will be gained by all of this? Ultimately, someone is aiming for a very definite objective. If we can figure out what the objective is, we'll be more than halfway there. What do you see as the eventual outcome?"

"Well, the book is obvious. With its sale, the thief gains financially."

"Obviously. But what would be the eventual outcome of some missing recruitment packages, other than slowing down recruitment?" Looking at Nicole as he continued his train of thought, he asked, "What was on the disks that could possibly profit someone by their destruction? You said nothing but names and address of schools and research, right?"

"Exactly. In an effort to boost enrollment, we were going to try going outside of our usual recruitment base. So we did research on various schools we've never actively recruited from before. The research included things like demographics of the high school and surrounding communities, names of contact people, etc., nothing that wasn't public record. The hardest part was merely compiling it all in one place."

"And what will happen now that you don't have the disks anymore?"

"Unfortunately, it will slow me down just a little bit. But," she continued as she anticipated his interruption, "it will not stop the recruitment efforts. Our purpose in getting such specific information was so that each school presentation could be tailored for that high school in particular. So our efforts will still continue; they will just be a lot more general than we'd like."

"And therefore a little less effective?"

"Hopefully not less effective." Nicole shuddered at the thought. "But I'd definitely agree that the presentations will be less personable and appealing."

"So we both agree that these actions seem to have one purpose in common: slowing down recruitment?"

"Other than the book's theft, which for all we know may not even be related."

"I think it's definitely related."

"There is one other possible objective that could be achieved with all three events." Shaking her head, Nicole mused, "And I'm sure you've actually realized it but have been too polite to mention it. But the fact is that all three make me look pretty bad as an administrator and in a different situation or circumstance might have cost me my job. Who knows, maybe if things continue this way, they still may."

"Actually, Nicole, since you brought that possibility up, I have to tell you it does look pretty bad. And it also has the feel of a personal vendetta being acted out here. Is there anyone you can think of who might be harboring some resentment against you? Someone who might have access to these buildings? A disgruntled student perhaps."

"Like I said before, nobody that I can think of. The only person from my past who might hold a grudge who has shown up recently is Kevin."

"Do you think he is here because of some grudge against you?"

"Truthfully no." She shrugged, "I realize that if Kevin Powell had wanted me off this campus he had the pull to remove me with just one phone call. But if you ask me why I think he's really here, that's an answer I'm not sure of."

"Well, that answer you'll have to seek for yourself. I'm satisfied that Kevin is not involved at all. I've known Kevin Powell for nine years and I would trust him with my life." Anticipating the question she was about to ask, Mike said, "No, I don't think I'm being objective. And yes, I will investigate him as thoroughly as anyone else. Not just to satisfy you but because I know he wouldn't expect anything less."

"Thank you. I know he's your friend, but for all we know, someone trying to get some kind of twisted revenge on him might use the school as the method."

"Well, I'll check into that angle as well." Smiling to himself at Nicole's persistence, he said, "You know, you don't exactly back down from the tough questions yourself. I see why Kevin hasn't been able to forget you."

Looking up at him in surprise at the personal statement, Nicole could only sit in wonder as Mike continued. "You know, Kevin tracked me down at two in the morning to call in an old favor and get me on this case. Now that my company has grown fairly large I no longer handle these investigations myself." He smiled in a self-deprecating manner. "I'm really just a pencil pusher now. But Kevin insisted that I take care of this personally. He simply wouldn't trust anyone else. When he finally told me you were involved, I was on the next plane. I've been curious about you for a long time."

"You've known about me?"

"Oh, yes ma'am." He grinned as he answered her shocked question. "As I've said, I was Kevin's roommate on road trips for our away games for about three years. Of course after he reached a certain status, he didn't have to share a room with anyone. But even then we remained close and often visited each other's home. He has a big picture of you in a silver frame on a bedside table in his master bedroom. And I believe he still carries a miniature of the same picture in his wallet."

"Right! I'm supposed to believe that?" Nicole asked in disbelief.

"Believe it or not, it's the truth. Those first few years he would mention you fairly frequently. Wondered how you were doing, should he call, that kind of thing."

"He wondered about me so much and yet my phone never rang once." Nicole discounted his words with sarcasm.

"Now that was something I never understood either. Then one night we were sitting up kind of late after a very disappointing loss. And I admit we were drinking just a little bit. Just enough to give me the courage to ask him why with all the girls falling all over him he was stuck on you. If you love her so much why don't you just go and get her?" I said. After all, you are Kevin Powell. What woman is going to refuse you?"

"Disgusting, that you all think women will fall at the feet of any athletic god just because he can shoot a hoop or throw a football," Nicole couldn't help interjecting.

"It may be disgusting, but very often it is the truth. Believe me, I've played professional sports so I know." Shaking his head at his own memories and misspent youth, he continued, "But Kevin was never like that. He always had a certain grace and class. And he never really took advantage of women like he could have. We all respected him a great deal for that." Winking, he grinned and added, "Of course we all broke our necks trying to pick up his rejects. But we were grateful even for that."

"Like I said, it's disgusting," Nicole repeated, shaking her head in distaste.

"That may be, but realistically that is a part of professional sports. And I'm not saying Kevin was completely innocent, but he never really succumbed like the rest of us did. And it was only because of our closeness that he revealed why."

"And did he bother telling you also that he was married at the time."

"Yes, he did."

"And you still respected his behavior?"

"I did." When Nicole snorted in disgust again, he explained, "Because when he realized that he couldn't handle his commitment, he separated. And," he continued over her objections, "there are many professional athletes who don't respect their mates enough to do that. They go home to their wives and children and play the role of perfect husband and father, all the while playing Russian roulette with their marriage and the hearts and minds of their families. And if you've ever seen the devastation caused when the truth finally comes out, which it always does, you would have to respect him for what he did."

"What neither of you understands is that what he did was just as devastating," Nicole exclaimed, refusing to let Kevin so easily off. "And it will take time to rebuild anything close to what we did have or what we lost while he was 'respecting' me."

"Well, you guys will have to work that out for yourselves. I am just happy to meet the woman who I know Kevin has never forgotten." Before Nicole could break in with more sarcasm, he deftly changed the subject. "I was hired to protect you. Believe me, Kevin was very clear on that and I was told no price was too high. I admit part of my curiosity was mixed with concern that maybe Kevin was making a fool of himself. After all, he hadn't seen you in nearly ten years, a lot could have changed in that time. You could be manipulating his feelings and loyalty while you robbed the school blind."

"And am I?" Nicole asked, amused.

"No, but I don't think it would matter if you were.

My instructions were clear. Guilty or innocent, his concern was for you first and the school second."

"So that's why you ask the tough questions," Nicole asked, trying with humor to deflect some of the weight of his words.

"You better believe it."

They stared at each other intently before they both smiled with a mutual understanding that turned strangers into friends.

# Chapter 14

After Mike left her office, Nicole contemplated his words. Had Kevin really acted as he felt best for both of them? Could he have possibly imagined leaving her as a way of showing respect? It was a selfish act in her eyes to walk away from the marriage. But would it have been more selfish to stay and cheat? She hadn't lied when she had expressed to Mike how devastated she'd felt when their relationship had ended. But she'd never before wondered how much more devastated she would have been if he had taken the course many others had. Couldn't he have easily 'had his cake and eaten it too' if he had wanted? And if so, wouldn't that ultimately have been the most devastatingly selfish act of all?

After all this time, could she really just put these questions in the past and  start over with a clean slate for both of them?  Briefly she fantasized what their relationship  would be like if she had met him today for the first time.  Oh, she knew she would still be attracted to his smooth cocoa complexion, his deep brown eyes, and his muscular build.  If nothing else, she knew that ten-carat smile would have lured her.  But would all that have been enough for them to begin a relationship if they were meeting today?  Honestly answering her own question, Nicole knew the answer was yes.  And since she knew that, didn't she owe it to both of them to give them the clean slate they both desired?

Frustrated by her own confusion, Nicole didn't realize how long she had sat debating the issue until the phone rang.  Looking at her clock, she realized the morning had slipped away from her, and she had yet to accomplish anything.  Vowing silently to remedy that by working through lunch, she answered the phone.  Nicole was not too surprised to find the object of her distraction on the other end of the phone line.

"Hey beautiful, how are things going?" Kevin asked with a smile in his voice.

"Slowly."

"Sounds like you need a break.  What are you doing for lunch?"  Kevin blatantly ignored the dismissive tone in her one word response.

"Working."

"Aw, come on, Nicky, can't you come out and play with me?" Kevin mocked in a childlike voice.

"No, Kevin. Absolutely not. I have too much work to do." She peered absentmindedly at the clutter on her desk as she refused to be budged, the thought of the smashed disks uppermost in her mind.

"Come on, Nicole, you have to eat."

"No, I don't. I have to work."

"Well, in that case, I guess the little surprise I had for you will have to wait. And I'll have lunch brought to us here in your office."

"No, thank you. I'm all right, believe me. I'll grab something a little later. You go ahead and leave me."

"No way, Butter. Never again." His softly spoken subtle reminder of their past relationship sent a tingle of regret down her spine. "Okay, you get off the phone and get back to work and I'll call and have a little something brought in for us."

He clicked off before Nicole could protest again. Grateful yet surprised by his complicity, Nicole turned her attention to the mail on her desk. Ten minutes later his words still haunted the back of her mind. What had seemed like a friendly gesture loomed instead as a cryptic threat. Knowing his persistence when he wanted to get his own way, Nicole put down her pen in defeat. Picturing his idea of having 'a little something brought in,' she put on her jacket and went to his office.

Opening his door, she found him sitting on the front corner of his desk, swinging his leg and apparently waiting for her. "It took you long enough." Rising to meet her as she walked in and closed the door, he immediately took her into his arms and kissed her.

"You knew I would come running over here to stop you."

"I would like to think you suddenly realized that a private lunch with me is too tempting an offer to refuse. But I knew your practical considerations would rule out over your heart. Especially since you knew I would make it a lunch neither you nor anyone else in this office would ever forget."

"What I knew was how stubborn and pig-headed you can be when you don't get what you want."

"As long as I get what I want, your name calling doesn't matter." Opening his legs to pull her fully into the cradle of his embrace, he leaned down to kiss her more thoroughly and added. "And this is what I've wanted all day."

Completely devoured, Nicole could barely catch her breath to protest. "Kevin, stop, one of the students might come in here."

Pulling back to deliver a light kissing smack to her forehead, he released her. "You're right. Let's get out of here. I want you all to myself for a little while."

Exiting the office together, Kevin led Nicole outside to the parking lot where a black Range Rover was parked. Previously he had taken her to the movie in his sports car. Looking at the expensive utility vehicle while she waited for him to unlock the door and let her in,

Nicole remarked, "My, my we have come a long way. Haven't we?"

She was surprised to see the brief embarrassment her light teasing caused. "It's only a car. I really just bought it because of the great value. Speed, economy, safety were all of my main concerns, and in these mountains it's certainly more practical," he uncharacteristically defended himself.

"Sure, sure," Nicole teased, enjoying his discomfort. "That's what everybody buys a luxury vehicle for, the great economy and value."

"Just get in and buckle up." Kevin cut off her teasing as he closed her door.

Once inside, Nicole was slightly overwhelmed by the extravagances of the vehicle, from its butter soft leather seats to its passenger side television monitor for watching movies. Obviously no expense had been spared in its outfitting. Briefly Nicole allowed her insecurities to rise as she wondered what a man who could literally buy anything he wanted would really be doing with her. For a moment the huge disparity in their income and lifestyle seemed too large to bridge.

Kevin chose that exact moment to grab her hand and bring it to his lips for a soft kiss, saying only, "Hey come back to me, I miss you." Those simple words coupled with his actions traversed the distance that had suddenly seemed overwhelming. Suddenly she wondered why she had any doubts about him. Surely a man who could be this affectionate and attentive could not be planning her downfall. Could he?

Breaking into the silence of her thoughts, Kevin seriously asked, "Is anything wrong? You seem kind of distracted today."

"No, everything is fine," Nicole smoothly lied, not wanting to mar the beauty of the day with pointless arguments and accusations. After all, if Kevin was behind the goings on at Tolleston College, Mike would find out. She only hoped he found out soon, before any more damage was done.

"You know, I started to wonder," Kevin continued, blissfully unaware of the doubts being argued for and against him in Nicole's mind, "when you were in there so long with Mike, what was going on. I almost started getting nervous about my old friend Mike. Another twenty minutes and I was going to start looking for an all female detective agency."

"Don't tell me you were jealous," Nicole teased.

"Okay, I won't tell you. Seriously though, was everything okay. Have there been any new developments?"

"Not really." Nicole looked out her window to avoid his direct gaze as she evaded a more honest answer. "We still don't have any idea of who could be behind everything."

"I wish I could think of something that could help."

"So you could be 'the Great Kevin Powell' to the rescue again?"

"You know, you are only going to call me that one more time. And the next time you say it, you are going to know just what Kevin Powell is truly great at." He winked with a titillating grin that emphasized the sexy threat.

"Yeah. Me and how many other women?" Nicole's teasing tone couldn't quite mask the serious question that had been floating in her mind.

"Just you." Kevin squeezed her hand softly as he answered seriously, correctly guessing the insecurity behind the joke. "I might have been good with other women, but I only achieved any kind of greatness with you. You inspire me and fulfill me in ways no one ever has or ever will."

Touched more by the earnest sincerity in his eyes than his smooth words, Nicole could not think of any appropriate response. Silently squeezing his hand back, Nicole hoped he understood her quiet echo of his words.

"Anyway, I trust Mike. If anyone can get down to the bottom of what's going on he can. So don't worry about it."

Deciding not to inform him that Mike wasn't the one she was worried about, Nicole instead changed the subject. "Where are we going?" Nicole asked as the Range Rover expertly managed the small hills leading away from the school toward the city.

"To my favorite spot."

"You haven't been here long enough to develop a 'favorite spot.'" Nicole arched one perfectly shaped eyebrow in derision as she waited for further explanation.

"I beg to differ. My favorite spot is anywhere I can get you alone." His actions bore the truth of his words as he pulled to a stop in front of his hotel.

"Kevin Powell," Nicole shook her head in protest as she viewed the hunger in his eyes, "The only way, I am getting out of this car is if you promise me I will be back at my office in exactly one hour."

"How about an hour and a half?" he hedged.

"One hour, or I'm not budging," Nicole pressed, uncaring that the hotel's valet was waiting for her to exit the vehicle as he stood with her door open.

"All right, I promise," Kevin finally agreed as he stepped out, muttering "spoil sport," under his breath.

Upon entering his suite, Nicole was pleased when she saw the elegant assortment of light lunch hor d'oeuvres which had been arranged on silver platters in the living room area. Light finger sandwiches, freshly cut fruit, and a sampling of small deserts decorated the table. Nicole busied herself with making a first selection as Kevin doffed his jacket and checked his messages.

Just as she picked up a cracker and lightly spread the crab salad onto it, Kevin purposely put down the phone and strode toward her. "You don't have time for that. You said we have to be back in one hour and I'm a man of my word."

"Well, if we're not going to eat in an hour, what do you propose we do?" Nicole asked saucily with her hand on her hip in challenge.

Taking her challenge in stride, he swiftly decided he could show her better than he could tell her. Crossing the room quickly, he swept her up into his arms and carried her, over her laughing protest, into the bedroom.

"Kevin, we have to eat," she vainly protested as he laid her on the bed.

"Believe me, I intend to," he winked in response to her words. "But I told you on the way over here that you were only going to call me 'the Great Kevin' one more time and I meant that. You will be calling me 'the Great Kevin Powell' in about thirty-five or forty-five minutes if I time it right."

"I will not!" Nicole challenged back.

"We'll see," Kevin warned as he took off his shirt and bent down toward her on the bed.

Not even a half hour later, Nicole had to give in to defeat as Kevin continued to mercilessly torment both of them. Already sheathed in protection, he nevertheless waited for her capitulation, actively teasing but not fulfilling. Finally she shouted out in frustration, "Okay, you are 'the Great Kevin Powell,' now come here."

Later, just before they reached a simultaneous, eruptive conclusion, he made her say it once more by devilishly withdrawing and asking, "What's my name again?"

Hating him, yet laughing at the same time, Nicole said it one last time before she joined him in a defeat that was also the sweetest victory.

Exhausted yet invigorated, they both reluctantly returned to work exactly one hour later. Feeling shy, as if the whole world could read her activities of the last hour on her face, Nicole approached Rose's desk. "Any messages? she asked, trying to ignore Kevin who bounded up the stairs behind her and went whistling into his office.

"No, nothing," Rose answered in distraction as she tried to read the body language between the two late returnees from lunch.

"Good," Nicole responded, finally able to fully exhale when Kevin went into his office. "Can you give me a few minutes and then join me? We need to have a short meeting."

"No problem, boss," Rose answered cheerfully, correctly interpreting the new developments between her two supervisors.

Two hours later she and Rose wrapped up their meeting. Rose, who had been as stunned as Nicole when she heard about the disks, could only shake her head in wonder. She'd been like Nicole, unable to think of a single reason why anyone would do such a thing. Not wanting to waste too much time mulling over useless guesses and suspicions, Nicole had instead chosen to focus on what needed to be done from this point. They had both agreed that as quietly as possible they, along with Tyrone, would begin again compiling as much information as possible. This time, they decided, three copies would be made of any disk. One for Rose, one for Nicole, and a third for the office vault. Further, they would immediately begin transcribing the recruitment packets content onto a disk again in case the saboteur decided to destroy what few packets they had made.

"I wonder why," Rose asked, "they chose to destroy the disk rather than just erase the information?"

"I thought about that too. But I believe the reason why they didn't do that was because they wanted us to know. Tolleston has always been a fairly safe place and I don't know if we would have even been suspicious if the disks had just been erased. I think whoever this person is, he wanted to flaunt this in our face. This way he spites us and is laughing at us at the same time."

"I just can't believe we have someone so vindictive here at this school," Rose observed in amazement. "What did Kevin say when you told him?"

Looking down and nervously plucking at the collar of her shirt before she responded, Nicole answered, "I didn't tell him."

"Why not, for heaven's sake?" Rose asked, her southern drawl more apparent as was always the case when she was truly confounded.

"Look, I know you think he's Mr. Wonderful..."

"And you don't?" Rose asked meaningfully, guessing full well what had transpired during their lunch hour.

"I'm not saying he doesn't have his moments but..." Nicole broke off, thinking of the wonderful, intimate lunch they had just shared. "But regardless, he is still a suspect."

"I guess that goes for me too," Rose stated in an offended huff.

"That, unfortunately, goes for all of us," Nicole replied firmly.

All things considered, it was not the most pleasant way to end a meeting with a woman she both valued and trusted, but it was the most honest. Sitting at her desk as she weighed her words in her mind, Nicole wondered if maybe that wasn't another motivation they had neglected to consider. For whatever reason, maybe the saboteur wouldn't be happy until they all turned on each other and destroyed the school in the process.

# Chapter 15

Sitting at her desk on Monday morning, Nicole discreetly kicked her navy blue pumps off and curled her toes at the thought of the week and the weekend that had just passed. There was definitely something special about a man who could keep a smile on a woman's face into the next day after hours spent apart. For the first time in nearly a month, Nicole allowed herself to dream about what being the wife of Kevin Powell could truly be like.

If the weekend was any indication, Nicole wondered why she had ever balked at the idea. Knowing how she felt about their privacy and the importance of being discreet, Kevin had whisked her away for a romantic weekend up in the Tennessee mountains. The cabin he said he'd rented turned out to be a virtual mansion secluded in the middle of rolling hills. It had met all of their needs for both comfort and isolation. With a well-stocked refrigerator, a full bar, several fireplaces, a sixty-inch viewing screen for watching movies, surround sound stereo system and a hot tub big enough to hold ten people in its own glass-walled room, 'the cabin' more than met Nicole's expectations. When she inquired as to how he had found this dream house, he'd explained he'd had his travel agent locate it after giving him a few specifications as to what he wanted. Once owned by a country music star, the home, which had been placed on the real estate market, was meanwhile available for lease as the owners anticipated a long wait for their exorbitant asking price of several million.

When he noticed Nicole's unmitigated pleasure upon seeing the kitchen which was built large enough to make any restaurant staff happy, yet cozy enough to have a large brick butcher's block in the center, he said, "If you like it that much, I could have my lawyer put in an offer for it. We could always buy it as a little getaway, for whenever we need to get away from Tolleston."

"We..."

"Yes, as in you and me. Our first home together. I know you really love Tennessee, and with your parents living down in Georgia, you wouldn't be too far from either them or Tolleston. What do you say?"

"I'd say..."

"Wait! Before you say no, why don't you at least

give it some thought? I know you think I'm just acting impulsively but I'm not. Make no mistake, Nicole. I intend for us to get our marriage back on track. And one good starting place would be in a home of our own."

"But..."

"Just think about it. Another good starting place would be...," he leaned down to kiss her lips, "...would be right here." Deepening the kiss, he began the sensuous campaign on her body. Later, as the heat and intensity of his kiss swept over them passionately, Nicole waited anxiously on the bed while he fumbled around in the pockets of the jeans he had carelessly discarded on the floor. Thinking he was searching for the little package of protection that never seemed to be far away, Nicole was surprised when he returned to the bed and took her hand. When he took a deep breath before starting to speak, Nicole wondered what he had to say that was so important he seemed to be gathering up the courage to say it.

Speaking at last, he said, "You never knew that you did one thing that really hurt me. Before I had ever broken a vow, you sent your rings back. Just shipped them back in a box. You didn't even bother sending an explanation with the rings. Later, to justify my own actions, I would say to myself, 'Well, she gave up on me.' Which of course is no excuse, but for a while it helped ease the guilt and pain by turning it into anger. Today I brought them with me." Opening the fist he had been tightly squeezing, he revealed the platinum and diamond set nestled inside."

"I don't know what to say...," Nicole started in bewilderment. This step she had not contemplated at all.

"I know you think we are not ready yet. But for this weekend, I want you to wear them.
For this weekend, can this be our home? Will you be my wife?"

Looking with trepidation at the hand extended to her, Nicole found her answer in the tears stinging her eyes. Holding her own hand out in affirmation, she repeated the vow-like words. "For this weekend, this is our home." Shakily she took a deep breath before adding more firmly in a voice that was strong and certain. "For this weekend, I am your wife."

Looking down at the rings, she noticed they had been inscribed. Wondering what changes he had made, she grabbed the band before he could slide it on her ring finger. The tears which had glistened her eyes rolled softly down her cheeks as she read the inscription aloud. " 'Love never fails.' "

Kevin, whose eyes were suspiciously moist themselves, stated simply, "I kept them on a chain around my neck and under my jersey at every game. Because even when you weren't there, I knew I wanted you with me."

Tenderly placing the rings on her fingers, Kevin pulled her back into his embrace for a kiss that was mixed, like her ring, with the fiery passion of the large diamond she wore and the platinum-like strength of a love that was unyielding.

Nicole, who had thought she remembered all of the heights Kevin could take her to romantically from before, found that there were still new peaks they could conquer together. Although he was not the eager, hormone-driven machine of his younger years, Nicole found that, like wine, he had aged very well. Before, his love-making had had the intensity and fervor of first love and the stamina of the young. Now, with age, he had learned that getting there was sometimes the best part and he had learned to appreciate, savoring the journey. Together they had savored each other with mind-numbing, tasty delight.

Now returned to work, Nicole could only eagerly anticipate their next interlude. As she admitted to herself, she also began to secretly dream of the day when she could openly claim her husband and all of the rights that entailed. She especially looked forward to the more pleasurable ones as she curled her toes again and squirmed in her chair.

Hearing Kevin's voice outside as he barked out a gruff hello to Rose, Nicole sat up anticipating the knock which she knew would come. Instead, she was surprised when her door flew open unexpectedly and then was slammed shut with a loud bang.

"Just what kind of person are you?" Kevin demanded angrily.

Not expecting this attack, Nicole straightened her back in bewilderment. "What are you talking about?" Nicole skipped the pleasantries as he had also done.

"Why don't you tell me?" he answered cryptically.

Struggling to keep track of the conversation, Nicole put her shoes on in defense as she prepared herself for battle. What could have agitated him so much first thing in the morning? When he had dropped her off last night, they had parted on very agreeable terms. He had even called her after he arrived at his hotel room and settled in for the night. They had talked for hours more, as if they hadn't just parted, until Nicole finally had to beg off, explaining that she simply had to get some rest after her exhausting weekend.

"I don't know what you're talking about. Why don't you just calm down and tell me what's going on?"

"I don't know what's going on. Before I left my suite this morning I got a call from my attorney. Can you guess what for?" Kevin asked, an intimidating figure as he glowered at her.

Nicole, who had considered hiring an attorney when he first appeared, with the purpose of dissolving their marriage, had never done so and therefore she could not imagine why his attorney's call should make him so angry with her. Refusing to be put on the defensive by his unwarranted actions, Nicole took a deep breath and as calmly as she could, she repeated her request. "I can't guess what your attorney wanted, so why don't you tell me?"

"My attorney," he sneered the word, "called me to ask if I wanted to give my consent to cooperating with the investigation into the school. It seems he was contacted by a private detective over the weekend who wanted access to some of my financial information. Naturally my attorney was not at liberty to discuss such private information without my express consent, so he contacted me to see if I wanted to give it. What I can't believe is that if you wanted to know something about me, why you just didn't ask me yourself."

As she began to understand why he was so upset, Nicole tried to explain. "Mike is just conducting regular background checks into everyone involved with the school."

"Don't you dare try and palm this off on Mike," he angrily rebutted her defense.

Growing angry herself, Nicole said, raising her voice to match his, "I'm not trying to palm anything off on anyone. The truth is that everyone involved with the school is going to be investigated. And why do you think that you should be above scrutiny just because you are 'the Great Kevin Powell.' " As soon as the words were out of her mouth, Nicole wished she could call them back. "Look, Kevin, I didn't mean that. Like I said, everyone is being investigated."

"And this is what you were doing when you were screaming out that I was 'the Great Kevin Powell?' "

Conducting a little investigation of your own, doing your own brand of undercover work," Kevin countered, cruelly bringing up the fact that she had shouted the words in a moment of passion.

"That's not fair. You can ask Mike..."

"I did ask Mike, even though I didn't have to. I've known Mike for the last nine years. Mike is closer to me than my own brother. And I know that there is no way Mike would have ever thought I would be involved in something so childish and petty. But I had to ask him anyway, 'cause I just couldn't believe that the woman I love..., yes, that I love, no matter how hard it is for you to accept that or even apparently understand what that means..."

"Kevin, give me a chance to explain..."

"Explain what? How the woman I love gave the go ahead for the investigation into my possible motives for destroying not only her life but this school and the lives of innocent students."

"Kevin I...."

"Or maybe you could explain why you never once mentioned to me about the computer disks being destroyed. We have been together nearly every day since it happened, yet you never once mentioned it."

"I just..."

"Maybe you were just too busy building up any defense you could against me. As long as you had your secret, then if I messed up and disappointed you, you could always fall back on your suspicions as your excuse. I can hear you now justifying your own insecurities by saying, 'Well, I thought he might have been involved in the school sabotage anyway.'"

"That is not true," Nicole violently objected. "The two issues are completely separate."

"You cannot separate the two. You can't claim to be building trust on one hand and then withholding it on the other."

"Look, you are taking this way too personally..."

"When my lawyer calls to tell me that my wife is having me investigated for theft, I have a tendency to take that a little personally!"

"Will you give me a chance to explain? Or are you just going to do the exact thing that you are accusing me of doing, although, believe me, I understand how difficult it is to trust when your feelings are hurt. How easy it is to lash out with accusations rather than listen to the uncomfortable truth."

"All right, go ahead. Explain away."

"When the incident first came up with the computer disks..."

"Which you never felt it was necessary to mention. In fact you looked me in my face and lied when I asked you if anything else had happened."

"As I was trying to say, when the incident came up with the computer disks, I didn't feel it was necessary to mention it. You said trust Mike. So I did and he was handling it."

"I never said trust Mike over me," he loudly remonstrated, angry that his own words were being used against him.

"Oh come on, it wasn't a question of choosing him over you. It was a question of
putting my faith in the investigator you hired."

"You will never make me believe that Mike advised you to keep this from me. Mike and I trust each other, something you obviously don't know the meaning of."

"I'm not blaming this on Mike..."

"Nicole, answer this: Do you trust me or not?"

"It's not about trust. Trust takes time. We were supposed to be building trust, building our relationship."

"You don't get it, do you? Without trust, we don't have anything to build upon."

"If you'd just calm down, you'd see that even if you aren't directly involved, maybe these events are happening because someone is angry at you or even angry that you are here at all. I mean, we have to face the fact that none of these events occurred until you arrived."

"Even if...? Nicole, do you honestly think I had anything to do with what's been going on?"

Carefully trying to phrase her words so that they would be effective without offending, she paused before answering, not realizing the lethal silence offended more than the words which followed it. "Maybe...not...directly, but..." She broke off in confusion as she struggled to find the right words.

"Forget it, I have the answer I needed to hear." Turning angrily, he slammed out of her office and a few minutes later, Nicole heard the door to his own office slam with a finality which shook even her office door, a conclusiveness that made Nicole put her head down on her desk in a moment of quiet despair.

Nicole was not too surprised a few minutes later to hear Rose knock softly on her door before entering to check on her. Seeing Nicole's red-rimmed eyes, she quickly went to Nicole's side to give her a comforting squeeze. "Oh honey, are you okay?"

"Yes, of course," Nicole answered, quickly composing herself, embarrassed by her brief lapse. Nicole repeated her answer in a stronger voice. "I'm fine."

"I take it he found out about the disks?" Rose asked, not really expecting an answer.

"And blew it totally out of proportion." Exhaling as she rolled her eyes in disbelief, Nicole stood up to pace around the room in a burst of nervous energy. "I swear that I don't understand that man. If I had come to him asking him if he was involved, he would have been angry. He would have accused me of not trusting him. So instead, I don't mention it at all, and he's still angry, saying that not mentioning it was a sign of not trusting him. Rose, it's like I can't win for losing."

"Is it really so hard to understand? To a man like Kevin, trust is everything."

"And he was supposed to be giving me time to develop it. I mean, let's not forget that he is the one who caused me to lose what trust I had in him in the first place."

"That's what's probably really bothering him. Maybe he's afraid that you won't ever be able to forget it. Will you?"

"Honestly, Rose, I don't know. I want so bad to believe that he is all that he seems to be. Don't you think I realize how great it would be if he were the person that he claims to be? But I just can't forget that he seemed so wonderful before and look what happened."

"I don't claim to know all of the facts of what happened before. I just know that you are going to lose a good thing because you're letting your fears rule your heart. And you'll never be happy in any relationship until you learn to take people on faith."

"That sounds so good when you hear that said. But it's so hard to do, especially with someone who has already betrayed your trust. And honestly, I don't know if I can find the faith within myself to ever try it again."

"Well, I'm sorry to hear that because I think the two of you make a wonderful couple," Rose added softly.

"No sorrier than I am," Nicole admitted as she subconsciously reached for and held the rings that now circled her neck on a silver chain.

# Chapter 16

As the days wound down toward the monthly board meeting, Nicole filled with dread. It was hard for her to fathom that only a month had passed since Kevin's arrival, yet so much had changed in that brief span of time. The board meeting, which was scheduled for Friday, was only one day away, and still Kevin had not spoken one word to her since the unpleasant encounter in her office on Monday.

The strained climate in the office was definitely felt by anyone who set foot on the administrative floor that housed both of their offices. Poor Rose, Nicole thought with remorse, she had the unfortunate position of being thrust between the two of them. With neither one desiring to be the first to breach the ever-widening gap, Rose had become their messenger as each childishly refused to speak directly to the other. Luckily, they were both so wrapped up in their demanding job that there was rarely a need for messages to be carried across the office floor. But how much longer could this situation go on? Nicole wondered.

Tyrone, ever her staunch defender, had immediately taken her side as soon as he had noticed the tension. Although he had no knowledge of what had happened to put the two of them on the 'outs' with each other, he was certain that it was no fault of Nicole's. Once he had made the decision that Kevin had somehow upset Nicole, he went out of his way to snub Kevin, despite the friendship that had been growing between them and his own previous feelings of hero-worship for the athletic star. Kevin, who of course noticed the youthful disdain, took the frequent brush-off in amused stride. If anything, Tyrone's interference only seemed to increase his contempt for Nicole, as if he imagined she felt she needed to hide behind a mere child.

Mike, who called not long after Kevin left her office on that fateful day, had tried too late to warn her of Kevin's discovery. He explained that he had vainly tried to reassure Kevin that this was all part of a standard investigation, but that Kevin had been unwilling to listen to reason, even from an old friend. Trying to console her, he vowed he was certain that Kevin would eventually calm down and realize how foolishly he was acting. As the days approaching the meeting neared, Nicole began to have her doubts that Mike's prediction would be fulfilled.

Even David had unwittingly been drawn into the fray. When he had called that Monday to innocently invite Nicole to lunch, she had gone eagerly, happy to get away from her tormenting thoughts. It was his unfortunate bad luck that they left the floor together at the same time Kevin exited his own office. Nicole, who had seen the jealous ire light up in Kevin's eyes the moment he saw her with David, had tried to quickly direct him down the stairs. But David, who was apparently a glutton for punishment, had tarried, offering a quick friendly greeting. Cut to the quick by Kevin's unnecessarily harsh response, he'd looked to Nicole in confusion. Nicole, who had been on the receiving end of Kevin's silent, withering glare, could only shake her head. Offering no explanation for Kevin's discourtesy, she instead used body language to tell David to just 'let it go.' Returning to the office with Nicole about ten minutes late from lunch, David was subjected to Kevin's anger again as he was tersely ordered into his office. Later David told her that Kevin had given him a blistering speech, chastening him for being late, stating that 'if he didn't want to work, then maybe he should move on and let someone who did have the job.' David had with his easygoing nature taken the rebuke in stride, only asking Nicole innocently, "I wonder what's eating him?" Feeling guilty, Nicole had not answered.

An uncomfortable sense of deja vu overwhelmed Nicole as she stood in front of the huge mahogany doors of the board meeting room on Friday morning. Although she was on time for this meeting, she was filled with as much apprehension as she had been at the meeting which had sent Kevin hurtling back into her world. Looking around self-consciously, she saw Rose watching her in amusement.

"What are you waiting for, girl? Get on in there," Rose encouraged, increasing Nicole's sense of being sucked into a time warp.

Opening the doors, Nicole saw that everyone was seated and apparently enjoying casual conversation as they waited for her arrival. Feeling grateful that at least this time she was not embarrassingly late, Nicole sat down in the only open seat, which was, not entirely to Nicole's surprise, next to Kevin.

"Good morning, Nicole," Hal said cheerfully. He waited patiently as everyone else added their greeting, all except for Kevin, who merely nodded mockingly. "Now that you're here we will open the meeting." With his direction, the meeting began with the reading of the minutes, followed by various topics of 'old business.'

Kevin was asked to give a report on the athletic department. Nicole watched him enviously as he coolly explained changes in the program that he had already begun. "My biggest concern at this point is for the future welfare of our athletes,' he stated. "As many of you know, even though we have had various athletes recruited from our school in the past to play professional sports, including myself, the majority of them will not play beyond the college level. Even if they are one of the lucky few who make it beyond college, many will find themselves at the end of their professional careers living only minimally above the poverty they lived in before their careers began. Although this can often be attributed to frivolous immaturity, it is just as often because of ignorance. As the old saying goes, 'A fool and his money are soon parted.' "

"So what are you proposing?" Harold asked, enthralled by Kevin's suave professional demeanor.

"I would like to see us place a new emphasis on education. After all, we are an institution of higher learning. I'm launching a program which would create mandatory 'study tables' for our athletes with tutors available to help them with any area of study. Flex time for the weight room would also be initiated so that athletes would be encouraged to work out before breakfast, so that they have more evening hours available for study. In the coming fall semester, we will begin our practice a little earlier than the usual two weeks before school begins. Hopefully, as many of our athletes as can, will come. That way, by getting the jump on their physical conditioning, when school begins they will not have to focus as much on recovering from a long summer off and can immediately start focusing on school. To encourage this,

I will sponsor a two-week football camp, and right now I'm signing up professional athletes to come and work out with our students. Hopefully, this addition will also help encourage recruitment in the area of athletics."

"Wonderful, wonderful," Harold gushed as he moved on to the next item on the agenda.

Nicole waited with apprehension as the topic of the book's theft approached. As if she had conjured up the subject with her thoughts, Harold asked the dreaded question. "Nicole, at this time can you give us an update on the investigation of the theft?"

"Well Chairman Wright," Nicole began by using his more formal title for the board meeting, "as we discussed at the last meeting, Michael Dix was hired to investigate the theft. Unfortunately, at this time the investigation is still continuing and right now I don't have any- thing specific I can report. I do feel confident that Mr. Dix is doing a competent job as he investigates both the theft and several other new developments," Nicole concluded briefly, hoping that her vague answer would suffice.

"What new developments are there exactly?" Harold asked, not satisfied with the brevity of her answer.

"Well...," Nicole began, as she brought the board up to date on both the vandalism of the gymnasium and the destruction of the computer disks.

"You mean all of these occurrences have taken place in the last month and you did not feel the need to notify a single member of the board?" Harold asked with blustering anger. "Can you explain why you didn't share this information immediately?"

"Yes, Nicole," Kevin spoke sarcastically. "I think we'd all like to know why we were kept in the dark."

"Simply because, in speaking with Mr. Dix, we felt it best that this information be kept as quiet as possible."

"You both felt, *Miss* Blakely, or you felt?" Kevin interjected his question before she could complete her explanation.

"We both felt," Nicole stated heartily, refusing to be baited by Kevin Powell. Besides, the last incident was discovered only ten days ago. Because it happened so close to the board meeting, I felt it would be best to present the information at one time to everyone."

"You felt...," Kevin muttered for Nicole's ears only.

"Well, be that as it may, you should have at least notified me," Harold rebuked. "Now, you said you felt very confident with Mr. Dix. Is he actively investigating every lead?"

"I can answer that question personally," Kevin replied before Nicole could. "He is looking into every possibility. He has even investigated me." Looking around the room, he joined the others in self-deprecating humor. "Apparently everyone is under suspicion."

"Well, certainly not all of us...?" Harold asked, clearly shocked at the idea.

"Everyone, just ask Nicole," Kevin responded without humor.

They all looked at her as the seriousness of Kevin's words struck each member of the board at the same time. "Mr. Dix assures me that a basic background check on everyone, including myself, is just standard procedure," Nicole explained.

"But did you explain to Mr. Dix that some members of this community have proven their loyalty with service that probably extends years before his birth?" Harold asked, nonplused.

Unable to meet Kevin's eyes, she replied, "As I stated, this background information is not directed at any of you personally. It is just standard procedure."

"Very well." Harold finally left the powder keg topic, obviously displeased. "Miss Blakely, are you able to give us an update on how your recruitment efforts are going?"

Swallowing hard, Nicole squirmed in her seat, which suddenly felt uncomfortably hot, before she responded. "Well, as I explained, we lost a great deal of information in the two incidents that I just recounted for you. Therefore, unfortunately, all of our plans have been shifted back a few weeks."

"Surely you are not trying to tell us that a full month has gone by and you have done nothing?" Harold asked, growing angry at her evasiveness.

"I just..."

Kevin interrupted before she could defend herself. "Miss Blakely has had her hands full in recovering months of valuable research. The information on the discs that were destroyed was invaluable. She could have gone to her various recruitment activities without it. But Tolleston College would have appeared unprepared and unprofessional, an image we are not seeking to reinforce. She has worked tirelessly to regain in weeks what took months to compile, and many evenings I have watched her stay well into the night. I personally worked until after midnight on the original packets, along with other volunteers, and I know firsthand the hard work she is trying to recoup." At his staunch defense, Harold was slightly mollified.

"Well, of course no one means to imply that Nicole is not working hard. However, the loss of valuable time cannot be taken lightly. Students have to apply by certain dates to garner the full amounts of financial aid that many of them will need to attend. We also need to have a certain number of students to meet our own goals."

"And no one understands that and is working harder toward those goals than Miss Blakely," Kevin replied, still not looking at Nicole, as he had not done all through his fierce words.

"I'm happy to see the two of you working together on this. I'm sure with two such bright young minds, you'll soon have the problem well in hand." Harold wisely changed the subject.

Feeling incredibly guilty, Nicole could not remain silent. In spite of Kevin's zealous defense, she knew in her heart her best efforts had not been given to the school, as she had been so distracted lately. Speaking up, she said, "Chairman Wright, I want to apologize to the board. I can't let you leave here today under the mistaken impression that Kevin and I are working on this project together. The truth is that although he has consistently offered to help, I have heaped all of the responsibility on myself. And it is for this reason that I alone am responsible for the disastrous results we have today. While what Mr. Powell intimated about my working double time to catch up it true, it is even truer to say I wouldn't be in this position at all if I had shared the responsibility with him as you had requested."

"Miss Blakely," Harold spoke into the silence, "those are very serious words."

"I understand that, and I will accept whatever penalty the board imposes. Even if it means relieving me of my duties."

Kevin spoke firmly into the silence, mocking Nicole's self-martyrdom. "I don't think that will be necessary at this time. Do you?" He posed the question to Harold, his tone allowing for no dissent.

"No, of course not." Hal quickly huffed the words out and changed the volatile subject. Soon after the meeting ended. Nicole was able to slip quietly away as the fawning board members stayed behind to heap praise on Kevin.

Sitting at her desk, Nicole replayed the events of the

meeting in her mind. No one could have told her that Kevin Powell would end up giving her much needed support. If someone had told her, she would not have believed it. She could think of no possible hidden agenda for his defense. If he had wanted to tear her down, he certainly had had the opportunity to do so. Indeed, at the beginning of the meeting, she'd thought that was what he was going to do. Unconsciously she had even begun bracing herself for his attack. Instead, he had come to her defense when that attack had sprung from another source. She had no doubt that his subtle unspoken message to the board to 'leave her alone' was the reason she was let so easily off the hook. Had she misjudged him? Reflecting on events of the last month, Nicole realized that although she still felt she had no reason to trust him as her mate, she had no reason to distrust him with the school. She knew she owed him an apology.

Moving quickly before she could lose her nerve, Nicole left her office and crossed the great divide to his. Knocking softly on the door, she waited for his approval before she entered. Closing the door behind her, Nicole noted the brief surprise on his face before he closed his expression off.

"Yes, Miss Blakely. May I help you?"

Inhaling deeply, Nicole reminded herself that although Kevin was not going to make it easy, it was still necessary. "Kevin, I want to apologize."

Putting down the letter he had been perusing as he

leaned back in his chair, Kevin sat up for the first time, giving her his full attention. "Go ahead," he said gruffly.

"I'm sorry. I realize I might have misjudged you about the school." Even though his expression didn't change, Nicole knew that he heard her by the sharpening of his glance. "Your return caught me a little off guard and I have reacted in a way I'm ashamed of. Please forgive me."

"So you're apologizing about the school?" Kevin asked for clarity, his expression still shuttered.

"Yes, of course, the school. You've been here working just as hard as I have and I know you are doing so out of what I now believe is a genuine concern for our students. And I'm sorry that I might have doubted your intentions. I hope you'll forgive me."

"Forgiven," he replied, dismissing her as he picked his letter up again, clearly expecting her to leave. When she didn't, he looked up from his reading and asked, "Was there something else? I thought you'd said all you had to say about the *school*." He sneered the last word unpleasantly.

"Yes, there was," Nicole began as his once shuttered look gave way to open disgust. Bravely, Nicole continued anyway. "About us..."

Putting down the paper again, Kevin asked, "What about us?"

"Kevin, you have to understand that trust takes time..." She broke off hesitantly as Kevin picked up his reading, exhaling angrily, clearly dismissing her when she didn't say what he wanted to hear.

"Nicole, we've been through this a hundred times and I don't want to hear it. Now I have work to do, and I'm sure you do as well."

"Kevin, I'm trying to apologize," Nicole forced out through frozen lips.

"Don't bother, if it's that same old tired line!" he vehemently protested.

"Well, what do you want from me?" Nicole cried out in frustration.

"Everything!" Kevin snarled. Quieting down some, he continued just as strongly, "Everything you have to give. All your love, all your trust, all that loyalty you spread around to everyone else. I want that for me. Because that's what I'm offering to you. And if you can't give it back to me, then I don't want anything from you at all." Ending with his frostbitten words hanging in the silence between them, he returned to his letter, dismissing her again.

"And you don't see that as being at all unfair when you're the one who messed up in the first place?"

Looking up at her with eyes that were unnaturally bleak, he answered, "I can't apologize enough for what I did. But neither can I apologize again. Either our love is enough to move us past it, or it's not. You've made it abundantly clear that your love is not strong enough to carry you over my mistakes. Do you know why I had the ring engraved as I did? Because at my lowest moment, the point at which I couldn't forgive myself, that bible verse came to me. And I realized what it means. I failed you. People fail people. But 'love never fails.' And that gave me hope that maybe there could be some small chance for us. As long as our love did not fail." Shaking his head as if to ward off any softening of emotion, Kevin returned in defeat to the work on his desk.

"Can't we at least talk about it?" Nicole asked weakly.

"I don't see that there is anything left to say," Kevin answered without looking up. As the silence grew, Nicole left the room holding the rings with the powerful verse in her hand, wondering bleakly if he was right, and everything between them had been said.

# Chapter 17

Hanging up the phone on Friday evening, Nicole smiled to herself. David was such a glutton for punishment. All week he had labored under a workload that had increased dramatically as Kevin flooded him with assignments. Resolutely, David had refused to give in and had made a point of asking her out to lunch each day despite Kevin's obvious disapproval. Now with a little arm twisting, he had managed to convince Nicole to have dinner with him. Still feeling a little wobbly from the combination of board meeting and her scene with Kevin, Nicole had very reluctantly given in to his teasing persuasion. His final argument won his case when he pleaded that Nicole had refused every dinner invitation since Kevin's return. "It's like none of us mere mortals can have any fun since he's been here." His uncharac-

teristic resentment surprised her, but it helped her realized that she had neglected him considerably in her preoccupation with Kevin, and so she gave in. As she prepared to leave for the weekend, Nicole heard David's
knock on her office door fifteen minutes later.

"Come in." She raised her voice so he could hear her
through its thick mahogany wood. "What did you do, run
all the way over?" she asked David as he entered her
office, grinning mischievously.

"You bet," he answered. "Anything for you, babe."
Helping her into her jacket, he waited while she turned
off her desk lamp and led him out of her office.

"You're gonna call me that just one time too many,"
she vowed as she turned her attention to her coat jacket.

"Oh, I hope so!"

"You don't even know what I might do yet," she
laughed.

"Whatever it is, bring it on. I hope it's a spanking. I
don't know if I ever mentioned that I'm into that."

"You are a mess." She couldn't help laughing.
"Let's get out of here."

"Your wish is my command," he said as he escorted
her out of the office door.

As they both turned around, Kevin chose that
moment to exit his own office. When he looked at them
both coldly, they froze in their tracks like naughty school
children caught ditching school. "Good evening, Coach
Spears. You're here a little late for lunch, aren't you?"

"Actually, it's dinner, Kevin," David responded smoothly. "I just thought I'd take my number one girl out." Reaching out his arm, he pulled Nicole close to his side for a playful squeeze. "We haven't had much time to get out since you've been here. Isn't that right, babe?"

"Oh, I'm sorry, babe," Kevin said in disdain as he looked at Nicole as if noticing her for the first time. "I didn't realize you were his 'number one *girl*.' And he must be your number one *boy* as well." His patronizing emphasis on the word *boy* left no doubt that he considered David as beneath him.

Before Nicole could refute the insulting innuendo, Kevin's office door behind him fully opened to reveal Carlista Cunningham, who was just finishing a call on her cellular phone. Clicking the phone closed and putting it into her brown leather purse, she turned to Kevin.

"Sorry, about that phone call. I'm all set now. Are you ready to go?" She practically purred her question as she laid one elegantly manicured hand on his coat sleeve and looked around him as if she hadn't known she had an audience. "Oh I'm sorry. Were you all busy? I didn't see you standing there. If I've interrupted a little business meeting, I'll be happy to wait in the car."

"No, there's no need," Kevin demurred. "Apparently we were all just going out to dinner at the same time." Looking at the two people facing him, Kevin added as if seized by a sudden thought, "You know, since we are all going out, we could make it a foursome."

Struck with horror at the very thought, both Carlista and Nicole cried out simultaneously, "No!"

Quickly trying to assess the reason for Nicole's distress, Carlista slyly added, "Now, Kevin, don't be silly. Can't you see the two lovebirds obviously want to be alone together?"

Kevin, whose eyes had hardened with contempt at the word lovebirds, stared at David's arm still draped casually around Nicole's shoulder before answering concisely, "Let's go."

Both David and Nicole stepped aside to let the glamorous couple pass down the stairs quickly. Nicole, who had been absorbed in her own distaste at watching another woman drape herself onto Kevin, didn't at first notice the imperceptible pressure David was applying to her shoulder. When she did, she stared at his face in astonishment, never before having seen such undisguised venom in him. Trying to understand what could cause such hatred, she remembered that just weeks earlier, Carlista had been draping herself around David at the charity auction.

Reaching her hand up to lightly pat his in a show of support, Nicole softly said, "Come on, let's go. They're not worth upsetting our evening."

"He thinks he can just come here and have anything he wants, take anybody he wants too," David declared venomously, obviously referring to Kevin.

Not knowing quite what to say to him in his current mood, she squeezed his hand again. "Hey, don't let it get to you."

Shaking his head as if awaking from a stupor, he smiled sheepishly. And instantly Nicole knew the David she loved had returned. "You're right. Come on, babe, what are we standing around here for? Your chariot awaits."

"My chariot or that rusted out old tin can you call a car?" Nicole grinned.

"Hey, don't make fun of Mabel. She may be slow but she's steady. Besides, she's the love of my life."

"I thought I was the love of your life?" Nicole stopped walking to put her hands on her hips demanding an explanation.

"You are. You are," he reassured her softly as he helped her into the car. But don't let Mabel hear you say that. She's extremely jealous and I'd hate for us to have to walk back." They both laughed at his silliness as he put on his seat belt and started the car.

Two hours later, Nicole said good-bye to David who dropped her off at home. It wasn't until the door closed behind her that she allowed herself to react to her long day. Walking to the couch, she carelessly dropped first her purse onto it and then her body as an overwhelming fatigue set in. She felt as if she had been on an emotional roller coaster all week. Nicole didn't know how much more she could take. Closing her eyes, she briefly opened them to check  if the message light on her answering machine was blinking.  When she saw it was not, she closed her eyes again and chastised herself for looking when she knew Kevin was not likely to have left a message today, of all days.  How had she gotten into this position? she wondered.  And how would she ever get out?

The simple truth was she loved him.  Nothing had brought that home to her more than when she saw him descend the stairs with Carlista on his arm.  It had taken all of her poise to not go tearing down the stairs after them and rip the couple apart.  She wanted to shout to the world, "He is my husband."  But was she really ready to take such a step?  Today, Kevin had made it clear that nothing less would do.  But again she asked herself, was she ready?  Kevin seemed to think she should be, even if she wasn't.  His words about love never failing had really hit home for her.  And she wondered with uncomfortable introspection if her love had failed him.

She wasn't sure of anything other than the fact she was tired of debating these issues in her mind.  She needed to get away.  Momentarily she allowed herself to fantasize about the 'cabin' in the mountain that she and Kevin had shared.  She wished she could just snap her fingers and be magically transported back to that place in time.  Knowing that was not to be, Nicole thought of another solution.  Wondering why she hadn't thought of it earlier, she quickly crossed over to the phone and called Rose.

"Hi, Rose. I hope I haven't caught you at a bad time?" Nicole greeted Rose when she answered the phone on the third ring.

"Don't I wish," Rose answered scoffingly. "Nine o'clock and Luther is already fast asleep." Rose's jokes about her romantic life or lack thereof were little more than idle humor. Everyone knew that Rose and Luther shared the kind of loving and happy marriage of more than thirty years that others just dreamed about. "What's wrong?" Rose asked.

"Nothing," Nicole lied. "I just wanted to get away. And I thought I'd call and let you know where I'm going to be. I know last weekend when you couldn't reach me, you just about called the police."

"Just about, honey, I did. You nearly scared me to death. The only reason the police didn't come is because Luther made me hang up the phone and told me to mind my own business. Can you imagine?"

Laughing, Nicole responded, "No, I can't. What must he have been thinking? Doesn't he know that my business is your business?"

"No, he doesn't. But I just keep trying to tell him." The two women broke off into companionable laughter. "Anyway, hon, where are you headed? Or better yet, should I ask who with?"

"Actually, this trip I'm going it alone," Nicole answered with regret. "You know the bus is leaving to pick up the students from Washington High School who are staying for the weekend campus tour, and I just thought I'd ride down there with Jim to go pick them up."

"So you just wanted to get away, hmm?" Rose questioned, waiting for Nicole to fill her in on the rest of the story.

"I just need a break, that's all," Nicole evaded, not wanting to get into another discussion with Rose on the subject of Kevin. Yet, secretly she hoped Rose might have some helpful advice.

"Aw, honey, he's really getting to you, isn't he?"

"I'm just so confused right now."

"There's nothing to be confused about. You love him, don't you?"

Nicole waited a long time before she finally breathed out the words she had been holding inside. "Yes, I do."

"Then just tell him."

"It's not that simple. And even if it were, I don't think he'd be willing to listen to me right now."

"Why wouldn't he listen? It's what he's been waiting to hear."

"Because I left it too late. He doesn't think I trust him anymore."

"And do you?"

"I'm willing to try," Nicole hedged.

"There is no try with trust. Either you do or you

don't," Rose explained softly.

"I just feel like I don't have a choice. He left after work for dinner with Carlista. And Rose, I swear I never wanted to rip another woman's hair out so badly. And intellectually I know it's just a case of 'the grass always looks greener on the other side of the fence.' " But that still didn't stop me from wanting to murder her."

"Honey, love is like that. I can't tell you how many times I almost blew up the garage because it seemed like Luther loved those cars more than me." They both laughed at her foolishness. "But truthfully, love can make you feel so irrational sometimes. But you don't give in to those moments. You just hold on to the truth of the love you feel in your heart and you trust your partner. Even if he's hurt you. Even if he will hurt you. When you are in love, you open yourself up to that possibility. You take that risk, and maybe you get lucky like I did with Luther." Nicole envied the love she heard in Rose's voice as she continued speaking. "You realize that the reward far outweighs whatever small risk you took."

"All of that sounds good. But like I said, I think it's too late. You saw how he's treated me lately. He won't even speak to me, let alone listen to me..."

"Then you make him listen. And believe me, I know how hard that can be. There is nothing worse than a mule-headed man. I know because I married one. But you let your heart speak those words if they're the truth.

His heart will hear you. Believe me."

Taking a deep breath, Nicole confessed, "Truthfully, I'm scared."

"I know, honey," Rose soothed, hating to hear the despair in Nicole's voice. "I've been there. Luther and I have gone through the same thing. All couples have at some point. But you'll see. If you open up just a little bit, it will be like taking a brick out of a dam. And all the little things that seem so solidly between you now will come crashing down as if they had never been. Trust me. Better yet, trust yourself. Your heart has not misled you."

"We'll see. Maybe I'll try again when I get back," Nicole offered.

"Okay, then. Well, have a safe trip. You tell Jim I said we have precious cargo. So he needs to just take his time or he'll answer to me." They both laughed at the picture of Jim, the school's near retirement age bus driver, rushing anywhere. Ringing off, Nicole went to bed, throughly exhausted .

The cool crisp morning breeze played with Nicole's hair as she made her way across campus to the old stable where the buses were parked. Looking over her shoulder, she noticed Kevin's car parked in the lot outside of the administration building. Wondering what he could possibly be working on so early in the morning, Nicole nearly walked straight through David who was exiting the stable.

"Well, good morning. What in the world are you doing up so early?" Nicole asked by way of greeting, knowing that David particularly hated rising early and avoided it whenever possible.

For a moment he stared at her, looking positively guilty before he responded. "Well, good morning to you. I could ask you the same question. Don't tell me you've decided you couldn't live without me after all and decided to track me down."

"Huh! I don't think so," Nicole responded lightly. "I'm riding up with Jim to get the students from Washington High School. Don't tell me you had the same idea?"

David's normally light skin seemed to actually pale and then redden as he took a deep breath before answering. Alarmed, Nicole reached out her hand to steady him. "Hey, are you all right? You don't look well."

"It's nothing," David finally responded, seeming at last to catch his breath. "I'm fine, it's just all this morning air. I told you it wasn't good for me," he joked weakly as Nicole still looked concerned.

"That's why I'm surprised you're up in it. Where are you headed?"

"Well, you know Kevin has us all getting up for these Godawful early work out sessions in the weight room. We won't even have the official go ahead to play until the fall but we're already conditioning. I was just cutting through on my way to the gym."

"That must be why Kevin's up on campus too. I saw his car in the administrative building parking lot on the way over here."

"You did?" David reacted as if stunned before clearing up his words by adding, "I'm surprised. I didn't think our lord and master would actually be joining us so early in the morning."

"Well, I'm sure he's on his way to the weight room right now. You'd better catch up. I'd hate to get you into any more trouble."

"Forget him. How about you and me playing hooky and spending the day together?"

"No, don't be silly. I'm going to get the kids."

"Jim can get them. That was the original plan anyway. Come with me. We never spend any time together any more."

Nicole refused again. "We had lunch every day this week and dinner last night. Besides I just want to get a change of scenery."

"Well, wait for me then. We'll drive down to Atlanta today. You always like that."

"No, maybe another time. Now, run along like a good boy before Jim leaves me."

David stood as if undecided on what to do before finally releasing her hand. "Okay," he eventually said with obvious great reluctance. "But have a safe trip. And do me a favor. Be sure you put your seatbelt on for the trip. You know how dangerous driving through these mountains can be."

"Fine," she agreed, squeezing his hand since he seemed to need reassurance. Then she stepped away and made her way to the bus waiting in the stable.

# Chapter 18

"Good morning, Jim," Nicole greeted warmly as she stepped into the old stable which now served as housing for all of the school's vehicles.

"Good morning, Nicole," he replied just as warmly. "What can I do you for this glorious day?"

"Jim, every time I see you, you say it's either a glorious or a blessed day. Are there any days that are not glorious or blessed?" she teased.

"Not as long as I'm alive to see them. That's the blessing right there."

Nicole and Jim exchanged affectionate smiles. Their friendship had been cemented long ago, when Nicole had first entered the school as a student. "I thought you might like a little company for your trip down to Washington High School today. You don't mind, do you?"

"Certainly not," he responded. "Especially not if it's your company. You haven't come around in quite a while. I've missed you."

"Not as much as I've missed you, Jimbo." Nicole smiled sincerely. "I've just been really busy. You know how it goes."

"Nope, can't imagine," came his slow response.

Nicole laughed. Everybody knew that Jim was one of the reasons that southerners had a reputation for moving slow. He definitely believed in taking time to relax and smell the roses. Which was just one of the reasons he was so beloved at the school. He always had ample time for everyone, and even when he didn't have, he made it. His generous spirit, which accepted everyone at face value, could put anyone at ease. Steady as a rock, he was for many students the grandfather they had never had or known.

"Jim, I've needed you to help me keep everything in perspective."

"Yup, I heard you were having a little difficulty up yonder. I knew eventually you would work your way down here to tell me about it."

"And I will," Nicole promised. "But not today. Today I just want to relax and get away. And hopefully forget for a little while that I have any worries."

"Well, you know what I always say..."

" 'Don't worry, be happy,' " Nicole finished his sentence for him. "You know Jim, there's a nasty rumor going around that you didn't make that saying up. Some people are saying that was actually the title of a song a ways back."

"Now some people might say that, but only 'cause they don't know I let that fellow borrow it from me. But don't get me started, you know I could tell you stories."

"Yes, I know you could. But I suppose we better get started if we want to pick those students up before night-fall."

"Well, you know what I always say..."

Nicole asked the expected question. "What's that, Jim?"

"No worries, no hurries. It's the only way to live life."

Grateful for his comforting presence, Nicole boarded the bus. It was only after she sat down in the passenger seat directly behind Jim that David's warning echoed in her mind. Reaching down to buckle her safety belt, she recalled that on this older model bus, there were none. With typical lack of foresight, the designer of the vehicle had provided a seatbelt for the driver only. Oh well, she thought, when was the last time Jim had had an accident on this bus?

They traveled northeast through the Great Smokey Mountains to Washington High School, which was located near the Tennessee, North Carolina border. Nicole anticipated the trip would take about five hours. They

hoped to arrive at approximately noon, quickly load up
and return to the campus by six-thirty p.m., just in time
for the last serving of dinner in the dormitory cafeteria,
and hopefully in time for an intramural basketball game.
Later the students would be treated to a fraternity/sorori-
ty 'step-show.' Nicole could imagine their excitement as
many of them would be watching a 'step-show' per-
formed live for the first time. She remembered very well
her own sense of amazement and excitement the first
time she saw the syncopated rhythms stomped out by
energetic fraternity members.

Traveling through the mountains, Nicole allowed her
mind to wander as she blocked out Jim's tuneless, quiet
singing. Relaxing back in her seat, she remembered
when she first arrived at Tolleston, the excitement of set-
tling into campus, the thrill of being truly independent
for the first time in her life. Thinking of those days fond-
ly, she allowed her mind to also remember those early
days with Kevin. They had experienced so much pure
joy just in being together. Nicole wondered how had
they ever let those days slip away.

She remembered the weekend they had spent in
seclusion at the cabin. For a small moment in time, she
conceded, it was as if those magical peaceful days of
their early relationship had been revisited. Could that
magic stand up under the harsh glare of daily reality?
Reaching up to hold the rings still hanging from the silver chain she now wore, Nicole realized that if there

were any chance they could have those good days again, it would be worth whatever occasional bad days might come with them.

The only chance they would ever have would be the one she gave them. Nicole made her decision. Reaching up, she opened the clasp on the necklace and slid the platinum rings off the chain. While she admired the rings in her hands, she remembered the cheap pair they had purchased in the Las Vegas chapel where they were married. She still recalled the joy on Kevin's face when he had finally been able to afford this far more expensive set. Taking the old pair off her hand, he had attempted to throw them away when Nicole had stopped him, saying she didn't care if the first rings came from a Cracker Jack box, she would treasure them always as a symbol of his love. Lovingly she had placed them in her antique jewelry box where they remained to this day.

As he slid the more expensive pair onto her hand, he had repeated his vows. " '...In sickness and in health. For richer for poorer...' " At which point they had both laughed, counting their blessings as they acknowledged even then that 'poorer' would never be a problem for them. They considered themselves one of the luckiest couples they knew. " '...Until death do us part.' " Nicole had quietly repeated the vows with him as she admired the token of his love on her hand. "You'll always have my heart," he'd promised solemnly. "So you better always have these rings!" he'd threatened jokingly, completely ruining the tender moment. Then they'd kissed and celebrated their union, intimately.

Sliding the rings onto her ring finger, she contemplated the meaning of the words engraved on them. 'Love never fails.' Silently and solemnly, she vowed she would not fail him again. If marriage was a commitment, then at that moment she committed herself to whatever their future would hold, and promised to reassure him of that the next time she saw him.

Looking out the window, she breathed a sigh of relief. Now that she had made her peace with her decision, Nicole could truly enjoy the view. As the bus began its descent down the narrow mountain highway, Nicole noticed that it seemed to be picking up speed. Joking with Jim she asked, "Changed your mind about hurrying?"

"I'm trying to slow her down, but I think something's wrong with the brakes. You just hold on back there, little lady."

Growing alarmed as the momentum of the bus increased, Nicole could only shout, "Jim?"

He was not able to respond. Jim's entire focus was on stopping the out-of-control vehicle. The evergreen trees that had looked so tranquil just minutes earlier now flew by in a mass of menacing green, too fast for Nicole to even recognize them as individual objects. Heart racing, Nicole looked anxiously from window to window, as if she could somehow find a miracle that would stop the careening bus. "Jim?" she whimpered as the full desperation of their situation hit her.

The bus was sailing along the slick surface of the recently wet asphalt as if it were a plane on a runway preparing to take flight. Nicole could see out of the small square pane of her window just where such a reckless flight could land them, because she literally could look out over the edge of the mountain as the bus hugged the guardrails so tightly that sparks flew from it in protest. Terrified thoughts chased themselves through her mind, each coming and going in an instant, as each second was stretched to an eternity. She lamented, "I never got a chance to tell him I love him." On each of the occasions since his return that he had said I love you, she had remained stubbornly silent, not wanting to repeat the words for fear it might indicate capitulation on her part. Yet, he had not relented, repeating them often while making love, while joining her for dinner, in the middle of the day on a coffee break. When she had asked why he said it so often, he had answered, "I want you to hear it now for all the times I couldn't say it before. And I want you to know it for all of the times you felt it was no longer true. I do love you and I always will."

The bus which began fish-tailing its way out of the last curve in the road went into a full headlong skid sideways as it tried valiantly to correct itself. As she held onto the seat in front of hers with a terrified death grip, Nicole prayed, "Please God, don't let me have decided too late. Please give us our second chance." In that moment she vowed if given a second chance, she would treat love like the precious commodity it was.

Jim, who was doing some praying of his own, could do nothing as the momentum of the bus completely snatched all control of the vehicle away from him. Helplessly, his elderly yellowed eyes met hers in the rearview mirror of the bus.

As the bus rolled down the bumpy, unpaved slope with tires squealing as Jim still futilely applied the hand brake, Nicole heard the loud protesting shriek of the axle as it gave way. Almost as if it had been tripped by the broken axle, the bus tumbled onto its side and continued down the embankment toward the wall of the mountain. Thrown from her seat, Nicole tried to brace herself as she was hurled against the roof. Her purse and various other unsecured small objects from the bus's floor, came rolling toward her face.

A loud crash, followed immediately by what seemed like a burst of light, finally stopped the bus. A stillness encased the mangled vehicle briefly, before, mercifully, all went black.

Just as suddenly as the light went out, it seemed to miraculously turn back on. Praising God, Nicole opened her eyes into a blinding flashlight. "Can you hear me?" the emergency technician repeated his question.

Never so glad to hear such a ridiculous question in her life, Nicole could only nod dumbly.

"Okay, don't move," he cautioned when she nodded her head. Curtly and efficiently, he began explaining exactly what was going to happen next as the emergency medical team worked to extract her from the crippled bus.

She struggled to remain awake, as shock and exhaustion swiftly set in. With sheer determination, Nicole gripped consciousness. She couldn't pass out again until she knew. "How's Jim?"

"You mean the old guy?" the paramedic responded, too busy to use tact.

"Yes, how is he?"

"We've already taken him in," came the response as he evaded her question.

Too tired to realize that the vague answer gave no tangible information, Nicole quieted.

As she lost her battle to exhaustion, she mumbled, "Kevin..." Then all went black again.

# Chapter 19

Nicole felt herself go hurtling towards the roof of the bus. "Kevin!"she screamed in panic. Desperately flinging her arms, she jolted awake.

The hand holding hers instantly tightened as she came back to reality. "It's all right, it's all right," Kevin's unusually gruff voice soothed in cracking tones. Sitting on the edge of her bed, he continued holding her hand. "You're all right. You're in the hospital. I'm here."

"You're here." Nicole sighed in relief as if those words made perfect sense. Her dazed mind accepted his presence as if he'd been conjured up by her nightmare alone. She hovered for a moment in the peaceful state between dream and awareness, and it was another long minute before she again emerged.

"What happened ?" she asked hoarsely with a voice

that seemed raw.

"You were in an accident on the bus." Kevin's voice caught uncharacteristically on the word *accident*, as if pained by the mere mention of the word.

"The bus...," Nicole repeated dumbly, her eyes closing briefly as she tried to remember. In a flash that made her head hurt, the memory exploded back into her consciousness. Wincing, she closed her eyes again as those last horrifying minutes before she blacked out replayed in her mind's eye. Squeezing his hand as she sought to bolster herself, she opened them again when he squeezed back.

"How did you get here?"

"I came as soon as I heard. Look, let me go into all of the details later. Right now, I have to get the doctor. He made me swear on my life that when you woke up, I would send for him right away. Since it was the only way he would let me wait inside the room, I better make good on my promise." Smiling gently, he started to rise from the bed where he had been sitting. Before completely standing up, he leaned down to bestow a bruising yet gentle kiss on her lips. Withdrawing until he was only a hairbreadth away, he added as he exhaled, "God, just don't ever do that to me again. I was scared to death. Do you know I almost lost you?"

Still in a highly-charged, emotional state, Nicole could only tearfully nod her head. "I know, 'cause I almost lost you too."

Leaning down once again Kevin returned to her lips with a fierceness that belied any previous tenderness. Wrapping his arms around her through the confining hospital sheets, he broke off the kiss only when she winced.

"God, what am I thinking? Let me get the doctor. I'll be right back." His distinctive lightning moves served him well as he bounded off the bed and hurried out of Nicole's hospital room door.

Twenty minutes later, Dr. Agnew stood looking at Nicole, well pleased with himself, nodding his salt and pepper head approvingly, as if he alone had been responsible for Nicole's miraculous condition. He folded his stethoscope into the pocket of his white laboratory coat as he announced his findings. "Well, I personally think that a few bruised ribs and a small knot on the back of the head are a small price to pay, considering the accident you were just in."

Looking at Kevin as if completely dismissing Nicole, he added, "She just needs a little rest. I think she is doing very well. No doubt in the coming week, she'll notice several other bruised areas." He smiled graciously, his olive-colored skin wrinkling with satisfaction. "I'm going to prescribe some pain pills, because as the adrenalin in her system wears off, she will certainly feel each bruise and laceration. You can get the prescription in the morning when you pick her up."

"So she will need to stay the night then?" Kevin ignored Nicole's dissenting shake of her head as he questioned the doctor directly.

"Yes. Nothing to worry about, just standard procedure when dealing with any type of trauma to the head."

"All right then, I'll see you tomorrow. And I can't thank you or this hospital enough. I won't forget it, I promise." He grasped the doctor's hand in a firm handshake that cemented an unspoken vow of gratitude more binding than his words.

Suddenly self-conscious, the doctor actually blushed as he accepted the words of praise, his swarthy, leathered skin turning rose-colored. Because even with his meager time for viewing any type of entertainment, he was aware of who Kevin Powell was and what his gratitude could mean for the hospital. Thanking his lucky stars that he had agreed to switch shifts to do a colleague a favor that Saturday, he shook the legendary athlete's hand.

"Excuse me," Nicole interrupted. "I don't want to stay here overnight."

"If Dr. Agnew says you need to stay..."

"The doctor also said that I'm fine. And actually, now that I'm up, I feel fine."

"Now that you're up," Kevin thundered incredulously. "Nicole, you were out for two hours."

"That was just my body's way of shutting down, so it could rest. If I need any more resting, I'll do it at home."

The doctor raised his hands disapprovingly when Kevin turned to look to him for assistance. "I strongly recommend that you remain here. You never know exactly what side effects could occur during the night. However, if you really want to go, I can only advise against it. I can't keep you here by force."

"Good, because I want to go home." Looking up at Kevin who stood close to her bedside, she once again squeezed his hand. She hoped he understood the message she was trying to convey as she added, "I want to be with my husband. That's really all the medicine I need."

Those words he had waited so long to hear decided the matter as far as Kevin was concerned. "What if a nurse stayed nearby during the night?"

"Well, that would certainly be the next best thing, if she decided to leave the hospital," the doctor hedged.

"Good, then let's see if we can arrange that." Kevin was clearly placing full responsibility on the doctor, despite his use of the word *we*. "In my hotel there are two penthouse suites. Your nurse and whatever equipment she needs can occupy the one next to mine. I'll have a car sent around to retrieve her and I'll have the bill taken care of before she arrives. Is that okay?" Before the doctor could protest again, he added, "Right now, the news of the accident hasn't hit the media. But when it does, if they believe my wife is in this hospital, they will blitz this facility. I think if we left now, as quietly as possible, that would probably be best for all of your patients. Don't you agree?"

Dr. Agnew gave in as he accepted that he was being

given a command and not a request. "Certainly, uh, Mr. Powell, as long as a nurse is nearby, I think your, uh, wife will be fine." Discomfitted by the sudden loss of power, he could barely continue. "I'll just leave and make those arrangements right now."

"Again, thank you for all you've done."

"One more thing, doctor," Nicole spoke before the doctor could vacate the room. "There was an elderly driver of the bus. What is his condition?"

"I'm afraid he's still critical, at this time."

"Oh no," Nicole gasped in dismay. She turned to Kevin accusingly. "Why didn't you tell me?"

"Because I didn't want to upset you. Right now he's in surgery for some internal bleeding. But the doctors anticipate he'll have a full recovery. He was wearing his seatbelt and that apparently did help. The officer at the scene said that if he hadn't been wearing it, he would have catapulted through the windshield from the force of the impact."

"Poor Jim," Nicole lamented, feeling terrible. "Does Ladybird know?" Nicole referred to Jim's wife of the last forty years as concern for him and his family swamped her.

"Yes, she does. I made sure I called her before I came, and she and Rose drove down together."

"I want to go and wait with the two of them."

"You need to go home. The doctor has already said that you need rest." Not allowing her to interrupt, he continued, "No, Nicole," in a tone that allowed no further argument. "I know you care about him, but you are going home."

"Well, can I at least stop by to give Ladybird my well wishes?" Nicole asked petulantly, too tired to put up much argument.

"Good afternoon, little lady," Mike said as he walked into the room. "You're looking very well for someone who was nearly at death's door a few hours ago. Kevin here almost lost his lunch when I told him about the accident. Luckily, you had my business card in your purse, so the hospital contacted me right away. I had to force him to ride with me or he would surely have been in one of those operating rooms upstairs. He could barely stop his hands from trembling and he wanted to drive."

"Please don't remind me! I have never been so scared in my life and I hope I never have to go through something like that again. You just don't know, until it's your loved one and not some anonymous story on the news, how devastating some coolly reported accident is for the loved ones who can't do anything but wait. I thought I would go out of my mind just trying to get here."

"Lucky for you I got you here safe and sound," Mike baited Kevin.

"I certainly can't argue with my luck today," Kevin answered as he took Nicole's hand again and returned to his seat on the bed.

"Are you going to stay the night? Because now that I know Nicole is all right, I think I'll head to the accident scene and the police lab and get a look at the bus before they foul up any evidence."

"Do you think this could have been planned?" Nicole asked in disbelief as all of her senses came completely alert. "Jim said the brakes just seemed to fail."

"I don't know," Mike answered honestly. "But I get paid to be nosy. So I'm going to get down there and find out what I can."

"Well, you be careful," Nicole warned. "If this was planned, then you could be in a lot of danger."

"Sweetheart, if I find out that someone did this on purpose to you and Jim, then believe me, I am not the one who'd better be careful."

"Don't worry about him," Kevin interjected, not one to be ignored for very long. "The bus would have to fall on his head to crack that thick skull. Just ask any of the linebackers who played against him." They all shared a laugh as they briefly neglected the more serious questions that needed to be answered.

It was in this state of easy camaraderie that David found them. Knocking lightly before entering with flowers, he stopped short when he saw the two men near her bed. "Oh, I'm sorry, I didn't realize you had company."

"Don't be ridiculous, come on in," Nicole welcomed him as he handed her flowers.

Kevin was the first one to break the awkward silence

among the four occupants of the room. "I'll go see about the hospital bill and getting it forwarded."

"Thanks, Kevin," Nicole said as he left the room.

"And I will go pay my respects to Jim's wife and Rose upstairs. Before I leave, I do need to talk to you about a few leads I have," Mike said before he too departed the suddenly uncomfortable room.

"Okay, sure," Nicole answered as he left the room, leaving her alone with David in a silence that remained awkward despite the fact that they were now alone.

"So, I see Mr. Football got here in time to play the big superhero again. Isn't it funny how he always seems to be coming to your aid?"

"David," Nicole gently reproached him, "that's not fair. He only heard about the accident because I had Mike's card in my purse."

"I'm sorry," David grinned sheepishly, once again slipping into his usual easygoing manner like a man donning a mask. "I don't want to upset you. When I heard about the accident on the news, I practically flew down here. Are you all right?"

"Yes, the doctor just left. He gave me a clean bill of health. I can go home now."

"Good, do you need a ride back to campus?"

"No, actually Kevin's taking me." Knowing that David deserved the truth, but unsure of how to begin, she patted the side of her bed that Kevin had just recently occupied with her hand. "Come sit down," she commanded in a soft voice.

Instead of moving he stood transfixed as he stared at her hands. Looking down to see what he was looking at so intensely, she realized it was her wedding ring. His eyes which traveled slowly back up to her face in puzzled shock probed hers for the unspoken answer.

"David, sit down," she again commanded softly.

"What's going on, Nicole?"

"David, you and I have been friends for a long time. And I know that there have been times when you hoped our friendship could one day travel along more romantic avenues. And truthfully, there have been times when I wished I had those feelings for you." Taking a deep breath, she sighed before she continued with the words she knew would cause him pain. "But I could never develop those feelings because I have never been able to forget Kevin Powell." Exhaling again, she proceeded as he didn't seem ready to interrupt. "I have loved him for a long time and I hope to love him for a long time yet to come."

Sighing deeply David finally said, "Well." Shaking his head as if in a daze, he repeated the one word. "Well. I can't say I haven't known for a while that you didn't return my feelings. But this still comes as a little bit of a shock. And should I take it from that blinding light on your hand that he has asked you to marry him?"

Swallowing hard, Nicole answered truthfully. "Actually we are already married." As David eyes widened in surprise, Nicole explained, "We were actually married years ago, but different circumstances kept us apart until..."

"...until he showed up here a month ago."

"Yes. And I'm sorry I never told you before, but I was confused myself about how I felt."

"But now you're sure?"

"Yes, I've never been so sure of anything in my life."

"I can't exactly say I'm ecstatic. But if he makes you happy, that's all I want. And of course if you ever change your mind, you let me know."

"Thank you, David. And I will, I promise," Nicole answered, drawing him down into a light hug.

"I guess if you're okay, I better go upstairs and check with Ladybird about Jim."

"Okay, and tell her I'll be up as soon as I finish here." He nodded his agreement as he left the room, sending her a last shaky smile that belied the lightness of his tone. Lying alone after he left, Nicole pondered their friendship. She prayed fervently that they would survive this development with their friendship intact. As she lay pensively looking out of her hospital room view, Mike entered.

"Hey, are you all right?"

"Yeah, I'm just sitting here thinking about how you never know when life is going to throw you a curve ball. Just when you think you understand it or yourself, you realize that there's still something more to learn."

"Speaking of which, I have a little information I just learned myself."

"News already about the crash?"

"Not quite, but..." He moved closer to the bed and lowered his tone. "Guess which former professional football player is a minority owner in Tennessee Peaks?"

"Kevin? He's never mentioned it to me."

"Or to me either. So I did a little digging into what Tennessee Peaks' activities are, and I found that currently their primary concern is buying up as much of the land as possible in the area of Tolleston College. They plan to build a multimillion dollar resort there. The only blight on the resort will be this tiny, historically black college that sits in shouting distance from where their wealthy guests will be vacationing."

"I knew that they had made an offer for the school about two years ago, but I hadn't heard anything else."

"And maybe that's because they decided if they couldn't buy the land, they could find another means to close the school down."

"But you can't believe that Kevin would have anything to do with something like that?"

"I don't want to think it, but Nicole, you are the one who pointed out that none of these events occurred until he arrived."

"I was just angry. I don't really think that Kevin had anything to do with all of this."

"And I don't want to believe it either. But I have to

investigate the facts, not my feelings."

"Listen Mike, I've spent the last few years hiding behind a wall of facts. Now I'm going with my heart, which is what I should have been doing all along."

"Well, just ask him for an explanation. Maybe he can provide one. Like I said, I only recently received this information so I still have a little more checking to do. So of course I'm giving him the benefit of the doubt. But meanwhile I'm going to ask him and you should do the same."

"I don't have to ask. I trust him completely."

"Ask him," Mike repeated firmly.

Walking in the door and catching the tail end of their conversation, Kevin asked, "Ask me what?"

"Nothing," Nicole answered, ignoring the raising of Mike's eyebrows. "Nothing at all. I'm ready to go, are you?"

"We can go upstairs and visit with Ladybird for a little while. The hotel said a car will be here for us in about an hour."

Waiting patiently as Kevin bundled her into the wheelchair that the hospital insisted upon until she left the premises, Nicole left with Kevin. Observing him as he patiently tended to her and still managed to be solicitous of Ladybird, Nicole knew she had made the right decision. Now that she finally intended to get their marriage on the right track, she was going to stick with her unspoken decision to trust him completely.

# Chapter 20

"It feels so good to just get out of that car. I don't know if I'll ever enjoy a ride through the mountains again." Nicole breathed a sigh of relief when she and Kevin arrived at his suite. The ride over in the hotel's limousine had seemed to fly by as Kevin had tried to keep her distracted with lighthearted chatter about inconsequential matters. Now as she watched him doff his jacket and throw his key card carelessly onto the foyer table, she felt decidedly nervous.

"The nurse is installed next door and you're with me now, so you can relax." When Nicole raised her eyebrow in mocking humor, he corrected himself. "I hope being here with me is a little less terrifying than a ride through the mountains would be."

"Only a little," Nicole answered, awkwardly

attempting humor.

"You said you wanted to come home, and I figured you didn't mean your house on campus."

"You're right. I didn't. I guess I just feel a little nervous now that we're actually here. I know that there's a lot we need to discuss and there's so much I want to tell you..."

"That's where you're wrong." Kevin reached for Nicole who stood indecisively in the center of the suite's living room area and removed her jacket. Tossing it onto a chair, he took her hand and guided her to the couch where he soon joined her in sitting down. "You don't have to tell me anything. When I saw those rings back on your fingers where they belonged, that told me everything I needed to know." Pulling her into his embrace, he reclined her across his lap and cradled her in his arms. "When Mike told me about the accident..." He shook his head as he relived the moment of despair. "You can't know what that felt like inside. All I could think of were my last words to you. I know it seemed like I didn't care about the relationship anymore, but that wasn't the truth. The truth was that I wanted you, needed you, and I just didn't know what I could do to make it possible to keep you, and the frustration was killing me. I felt like I was losing you. Then when I heard you were in such a bad accident, I cursed myself for my own lack of faith. Here I was doing the very thing I accused you of doing, giving up on us. I just hope you can forgive me for that."

Nicole found and held the hand that was caressing the side of her cheek. "Only if you can forgive me first. It's funny how just when you realize you're about to lose everything, how clearly things sort themselves out. Suddenly everything in my life got prioritized real quick into two lists, the things that mattered and the things that didn't. And I realized loving you was the only thing that mattered."

He placed a reverent kiss on the hand that still caressed his cheek before turning softly to her mouth. Their lips met in a kiss that searched for the truth of their words in each other and found it. In that one kiss, hearts healed and bloomed like flowers coming alive with spring.

Breathing deeply, they took a break. But although the contact of tongue against tongue had ended, their eyes held just as intimate an embrace. Breaking the silence first, Kevin asked, "Does that mean you will marry me and be my wife?"

"I am your wife!" Nicole proudly protested. "But yes, I'll marry you...again." She smiled the answer, knowing there was no other she could give.

"And this time, you'll actually live with me?" he persisted.

"Of course. Do you think that you'll ever get away from me again? But I do think we will have to find something a little more permanent than this suite, lovely as it is."

"I'm way ahead of you," Kevin said cryptically. "Wait here a minute," he instructed as he slid her off his lap back onto the couch. "I'll be right back."

Nicole waited impatiently as he went into his bedroom. She heard him shuffling things around before he returned triumphantly with keys dangling tantalizingly from his fingers. "You're giving me the keys to one of your houses?" she asked, not really surprised. It was a well-known fact that Kevin Powell owned several homes around the country.

"Nope,' he answered swiftly. "At least not yet," he clarified as she now looked puzzled. "I own three houses in this country and I have time shares in a couple of others that I use for vacationing. But this is not the key to any of those houses. This opens the door to our home. The first home we ever lived in together as man and wife."

"But we never lived anywhere together as man and wife," Nicole reminded him in confusion. "Nowhere except...oh my God, is that the key to the mountain cabin?"

"You mean our first home."

"Kevin. My God. I can't believe you did that," Nicole exclaimed in excitement. "I don't know what to say. You know I fell in love with that cabin the first moment I saw it. I just never expected you to buy it!"

"I had no choice. I can't imagine any other person ever living in the house that was made for you. It's yours, Nicole. I only hope you'll be willing to share it with me."

"Oh my God! What a question! It's not mine. It's not yours It's *ours*. I'm so excited! I wish we could drive there right now. Heck, we have the key. I guess we could."

Laughing at her excitement, Kevin tried to calm her down. "We'll get there soon enough. But right now, young lady, the doctor said you are to rest. So you are not going anywhere tonight more exciting than bed."

"And will anything exciting happen to me there?" Nicole asked with seductive teasing.

"I don't know. You know what the doctor said. We have to take it easy on those ribs. Thinking about it now, I think it would probably be best if I slept out here on the couch. I'd hate to crush you."

"Whatever you say, Kevin," Nicole pouted, then added seductively, "of course you can't crush me if I'm on top." She winked as she sashayed into the bedroom. Closing the door as if to wish him goodnight, she was not at all surprised to find him entering behind her.

"You know, in retrospect, I think I may need to keep a closer eye on you."

"Uh-huh." She smiled knowingly. "Probably need to do a hands on inspection as well."

"I think you're right. You know you can't always trust these doctors."

"Uh-huh. Well in that case." Nicole unzipped her

fleece sweater and pulled it over her head and also unclasped the front of her bra. "I better get undressed so you can do a thorough examination."

"Everything looks pretty lovely from here," he answered, raising one eyebrow as he stepped closer to remove her bra. "But I may need to get a little closer. I hope the patient has patience. Sometimes these examinations can take hours." Slowly raising his hands to cup her breasts, he added, "Yeah, I definitely see a couple of hours of work here."

"Oh, I hope so," Nicole replied huskily. "Take your time. I wouldn't want you to miss a spot."

"Believe me, I won't. In fact...," he bent his head lower and kissed the crevice between her breasts, "this spot looks a little tender. Tell me, how does this feel?"

Taking a deep breath, Nicole replied, "You're right, that does feel a little tender. But if you move just a little to the left. I think that spot..."

"Right here?" Kevin asked with his mouth plastered to her skin.

"Ah, yeah, that's it." Nicole sighed out her answer. "But maybe, just maybe, a little bit lower."

"Right here?" he asked again as he complied.

"Yeah, that's it," she answered again. "But maybe a little bit more in the center," she suggested.

Again he followed her directions. Each time the command was different, to the left, to the right, lower. Nicole was enjoying being in charge but Kevin had a suggestion of his own. "You know, it might be a little easier to give a complete examination if you were lying down. After all, I wouldn't want to miss a spot, especially if you still want me to go a little lower."

Nicole was undressed and flat on the bed with a speed that even Kevin couldn't compete with. When she noticed his amused astonishment, she defended, "Hey, I'm only doing this for my health. That doctor didn't look at me nearly as closely as you are."

"That's because he had his own health to consider," Kevin observed before joining her and resuming their play.

Hours later, as he had promised, they lay satiated in each other's arm. Basking in the afterglow, Nicole said wistfully, "I wish it could be like this all the time."

" Hey, I resent that. I don't know about you, but I think I'm good for a couple of more years at least."

Slapping his chest in playful protest as she snuggled closer to his side, Nicole explained, "I meant this sense of peace. Lying here in your arms I can't imagine any problems. I just feel so safe and secure. Like all my wants and needs have been taken care of and there is absolutely nothing to worry about ever again. That's why I wish I never had to leave this bed and face the outside world again."

"I know. I feel the same way." Squeezing her shoulders, which were pressed halfway between his chest and muscular forearm, he lifted up just a little as he looked for and found two of the hotel pillows which had earlier been tossed aside during their love play. Propping himself up slightly, he adjusted Nicole's position so that her head nestled on top of his collarbone and her body cleaved to his side once again. Using his hand he smoothed her curls which lay softly against the nape of her neck. "Comfortable?" he asked as she practically purred in her new position.

"Very much so."

"Enough to ask me the question Mike told you to earlier?"

Stalling for time, Nicole feigned ignorance. "Question?"

"Nicole, are you ready to trust me yet? Or do you still feel you need more time?" The stillness of his hands, which had been caressing her back, was the only indication Nicole had of the tenseness behind his softly spoken question.

"No, I trust you completely."

"Then why don't you ask me?"

"Because it's not a matter of trust. It's about knowing your mate. And I know in my heart that you could never be behind something like this accident today."

The hand which had resumed tracing the curls on her shoulders stopped in sudden attention. "Is that what Mike thinks? That I had something to do with the accident?"

"He thinks Tennessee Peaks is involved. They've

been buying up a lot of property for their resort, continuing with their plans as if they suddenly don't mind that Tolleston College has rejected all of their offers to buy the property."

"Why would Mike think that it had anything to do with me?" Kevin asked, puzzled.

"Because apparently you own the largest minority share of stock in the company."

"I do?" Kevin asked, surprised. "He's sure of that?"

"Very sure. That's what he wanted me to ask you about. That's what he is trying to figure out. Exactly what is or was your relationship with Tennessee Peaks?"

"Whatever relationship it was, believe me, it must be a very silent partnership. So silent I don't know anything about it."

"Are you saying you don't own any stock in the company?" Nicole asked, feeling confused.

"No, I'm not saying that. If Mike investigated and found that information, it must be true. And he knows from our friendship over the years that I like to keep a very tight watch over all of my investments. In the past, nothing was bought or sold without my express permission. And, believe me, I missed out on a couple of great deals and lost money sometimes because of that policy."

"But that was in the past..."

"Exactly. When I retired everything changed. I realized that I had made enough money to keep myself and my family financially secure for the rest of our lives. To hold onto that security I put a lot of money in trust, I invested more in property and in long term bonds and annuities. With a portion of what was left, I instructed my stockbroker to invest wisely. Over the years we have worked so closely together that he knows my preferences and dislikes. So I trust his judgement, but even with that trust we still meet quarterly to discuss my portfolio. I wanted more free time to spend working for the school and on my marriage. I finally got wise and decided to let my money work for me and not the other way around."

"So it's possible he bought it without your knowledge."

"Yes, but only in the last three months. I definitely did not own any stock with Tennessee Peaks in the previous quarter."

"Now you see why I didn't want to ask you at all. I knew you couldn't possibly be involved."

Stretching his neck down, he kissed her lightly on the lips. "And I thank you for that. However, trust is not the only thing we've got to work on."

"Dang and here I was getting so good with the trust thing," she playfully interrupted.

"You are. But communication is just as important. When we have issues like that which come up, you've got to feel comfortable enough to discuss them with me. I won't be able to read your mind, so we've got to be able to talk and share our feelings."

"You're right, I know. It's ironic because people

would look at us and think that you're the strong silent type but really, it's me. I guess I've held back a lot of things I should have said to you over the years." Brooding, she rubbed her hand in circles across his chest, unconsciously imitating his motion on her back.

"Imagine how much sooner we could have gotten to this point if we had just talked things out. And I'm not saying that it is all your fault. I know I haven't always made it easy for you to open up and express yourself. But I am saying that we have got to do better."

"You're right, Kevin. I will start by telling you things right now."

"Okay, shoot."

"I think you and I both...," she paused for dramatic effect before she held her nose and continued, "...could use a shower."

She laughed and then gave a quick yelp as he lightly smacked her bottom in response. "That's not exactly what I meant."

"I know, but total communication has to start some-where, and we have been back about six hours now."

Looking over her shoulder at the clock, he reluctant-ly started pulling back the covers. "All right then, let's get up and at 'em. But after this, I am getting some rest. Otherwise, in another six hours, I'll be the one needing a doctor." Their soft laughter and play continued into the shower, and despite his protests to the contrary the play continued for the rest of the night.

Nicole awoke with the rising of the sun, unable to rest later in her unfamiliar environment. Soon, she vowed to herself, she would be very familiar with any place where Kevin slept. Nicole released her self from the steel prison of his arms. Pulling on his discarded tee shirt, Nicole paced the room nervously. From the suite's window she quietly watched the spectacular show the sun made with its ascent over the mountain tops from the suite's window. A discomfiting anxiety gnawed in the back of her mind. She knew she was overlooking something very important right under her nose, but she couldn't figure out what it was.

Disgusted, she padded barefoot into the living room and closed the door to the bedroom. When she plopped down on the couch and turned on the television, she was surprised to see a picture of herself on the screen. Reaching for the remote again to remove the mute function, she remembered David had told her the story had made the news.

"Channel 6 News has just learned that Nicole Powell and Jim Elliot, both of Tolleston College, were the two unidentified victims in yesterday's bus crash. The accident which Channel 6 News first reported to you last night..." The bright-eyed and bouncy news reporter went on to give more details, including a 'live at the scene' update.

But Nicole only heard one phrase repeated over and over again in her mind. "...First reported last night."

Hadn't David told her that he'd heard about the accident from the news? But if they'd first reported the crash last night and the victims had been "unidentified," how had he gotten to the hospital so soon?

"...Make sure you put your seatbelt on," David had insisted before she'd boarded the bus. Suddenly everything made so much sense. Like why he had been at the bus stable so early in the morning, and why he had been so shocked to hear of her leaving with Jim. His reddened and guilty look, his insistent offers to get her to make other plans for the day. Everything was crystal clear. David had to have been involved in the bus crash!

Sick to her stomach, Nicole could hardly fathom the idea. She remembered the day she had loyally defended him to Mike in her office. She had been more willing to believe Kevin responsible than David, her best friend. Every conversation replayed itself in her mind in a series of blinding flashbacks. He'd checked every day. "Any new developments?" And like a fool, she'd answered every time. She'd unknowingly helped him every step of the way. The vileness of the betrayal threatened to rise up into Nicole's throat as she thought of how completely she had trusted him. Yesterday that trust had almost cost her and Jim their lives.

Knowing she had to confront him, Nicole jumped up off the couch to look for the jeans she'd worn the day before. Dressing quickly, she debated whether to wake up Kevin.

Through all of her moving around he had not budged one bit. She smiled as she momentarily reminisced, and decided he'd more than earned his rest. She snatched her keys, purse and jacket and was halfway through the door when she remembered their words of the night before. "Total communication."

Walking back to the coffee table, she futilely tried to think of a note she could leave that would explain the situation. Unable to concisely detail her suspicions, she finally just wrote, "Needed to get back to campus. I will return as soon as I can and explain everything. I promise. Love, Nicole." Not exactly a full explanation but she hoped it would do. She comforted herself with the thought that hopefully she would be back before she was missed.

# Chapter 21

Nicole waited until David finished putting his suitcase into the trunk of his car before speaking. "Looks like it's going to be a long trip," she said to his back.

Waiting a long moment before he responded, David finally answered, "Not really," without turning around.

"Do you mind if I ask where're you're going?" Nicole persisted.

"Nowhere special," he answered, cool as a cucumber, and turned around to face her. " I just thought I'd take that trip to Atlanta that I mentioned yesterday. Do you remember?"

"Yes, as a matter of fact I do. It was right before I got on the bus that almost took my life and Jim's."

"Well, uh..." He stuttered to an end, not sure of her

mood as she stood with every inch of her body language issuing an unspoken challenge. "I've got to get on my way if I'm going to be back in time for school tomorrow." He brushed past her and began to open his car door before her words stopped him.

"Is there anything you want to tell me first?"

"Like what?" His voice was much softer and more somber than his usual teasing tones.

"David, please," Nicole pleaded, her voice growing tremulous from the pain of this confrontation. "Please don't make me do this. Don't make me drag it out of you." When he turned around as if in confusion, she continued in an angry whisper which shouted his betrayal, "I know it was you. You were involved in that bus crash, if not everything else that has been happening at the school."

"Is that what you really think, Nicky?" he asked as if greatly pained. "Or is that what your husband has brainwashed you into believing?" He sneered the last question in disgust.

"Don't...don't you dare try to blame him or anyone else when all along it was you. You were the one holding my hand and stabbing me in the back. What were you trying to prove? You almost killed two innocent people, and for what? Was it money? What? Answer me, dammit!" Nicole shouted in frustration as David remained silent and still throughout her angry tirade.

"I can't answer you because I can't believe what

you're saying. Have you forgotten that it's me, David." Shaking his head in disbelief, he asked, "What could make you think that I could ever be responsible for any of this?"

Nicole stared at him for a long hard minute, steeling herself against her heart. Finally she asked in slow, measured tones, "How did you know about the accident?"

"What?"

"The accident, how did you know about it?" she repeated.

"I told you, I heard it on the news."

"David, it wasn't reported until this morning. An *exclusive report, this morning*," she said, stressing the words which condemned him. "The details of the accident, including our names, were just released this morning." Grinding each word out through a voice that was raw with angry hurt, she repeated the painful question, "So tell me again how you knew."

"Does it matter? Anything I say now, will it even make a difference? Haven't you already tried and convicted me? Where's your loyalty? I thought you knew me?"

"Loyalty! Don't you dare stand here and try and defend yourself with that word, when you don't even know the meaning of it! Now answer the question and quit stalling. If you weren't involved in tampering with the bus then... how...did...you...know?"

"Before I answer, tell me. Do you really think I was involved, knowing me as you do? Do you really believe that, after all we've meant to each other?"

Nicole could only answer with the heartbreaking truth. "Yes, I do."

"Ah, Nicole." He took a deep breath and slowly exhaled it before shoving his hands into the pockets of his jogging suit. "I am so sorry to hear you say that. Because I never wanted to hurt you of all people."

Nicole saw too late what he had been reaching for as he waved the gun toward her. David closed in on her left side quickly before she could think, and pressed the nozzle of the gun into her back as he pushed her toward the car. Whispering into her hair which was pressed against the side of his face in a dangerous embrace he repeated, "But don't think for one moment that I won't if I have to." He pushed her over onto the driver's side, then on over to the passenger seat, and climbed in himself.

As the danger she was in sank home, Nicole reproached herself. Had she really thought he would confess all and go meekly off to jail as soon as she confronted him? Had she been naive enough to believe that their friendship would keep her out of danger a second time? Obviously it hadn't been a very real friendship to begin with. *Now what?* she wondered. "Where are we going?"

"I was going to pick up the book, make a nice, quiet sale and vanish from your and Kevin's happy little life."

"The book is here?" She had assumed, like everyone else, that it had long since been stolen away.

"It was my little insurance plan, just in case my other arrangement didn't work out."

"You mean your plan with Tennessee Peaks to drive Tolleston out of business," she guessed.

"Good for you, babe, you did your homework. That's right. Who would have thought that one little school could have so much resilience? But with the book it really doesn't matter. As the kids would say, I'm getting 'paid,' regardless."

"Well, where is it? Back there?" she asked, nodding her head toward the trunk of his car.

"Nope," he negated flatly. He drove from his faculty apartment toward the administration building. "In there," he answered as he pulled to a stop outside of the building which was abandoned for the weekend. "Out," he ordered. She exited from her side with him close behind her. He was careful never to let her get more than arm's length away from him as he guided her up the stairs of the empty building and forced her to unlock the door. "Don't you realize yet that people always overlook the obvious."

Struck by the irony, Nicole commented, "I know I certainly did."

"Well, don't beat yourself up too bad, Nicole. I was actually your faithful servant and lapdog for many years. But come on, I mean after a while a man just has to cut his losses and go on."

"Is that what this is?"

"No, actually I guess this just falls more into the line of an early retirement." Smiling, he halted on the executive floor. He watched Nicole's face as she looked on in puzzlement when he unlocked the door to Kevin's office. "Surprised?"

"Yes, very. Especially since I know Kevin doesn't have a book shelf in his office to hide the book in plain view like you suggested."

"Ah, Nicky, you're too literal. I said, hide it in an obvious place. The most obvious person in the world to have stolen the book was Kevin. But you just refused to believe that, didn't you. A couple of times I could almost see you accusing him but you always held back. What was wrong with my plan? What kept you from believing it was him?"

"Love," Nicole answered simply.

"Whatever." David discounted her one word reply with a roll of his eyes. Crossing the room quickly, he pulled back a heavy antique painting of one of the college's founders to reveal the safe. "You wonder how I could risk leaving the book in here with him? It was never in any real danger, because I knew he didn't know about the safe. Very few people did. It was one of Dean Chandler's additions before he was unfortunately found out. He used to hide his dirty little secrets in here. Now who do you suppose let that little kitty out of the bag?"

"You..." Nicole's open-mouthed response made David laugh.

"The one and only. I'm afraid I just couldn't let him go on reaping all of the benefits and then sticking me with the measly cut he was willing to share only after I discovered his little sideline. It was awfully nice of him to go down without taking me with him, wasn't it? Of course he knew that I was aware of other accounts that have never been discovered, so I suppose he had his reasons for keeping quiet."

"All this time..."

"It boggles the mind, doesn't it." Making the final spin on the safe's dial, he slowly opened the metal door.

Watching him, Nicole realized that in his greed he had turned his back on her completely. This was her chance to escape as she stood closer to the door than he. But if she left now, even if she got away, he would still surely escape with the book. She doubted she would have enough time to get away, call the police, explain what had happened and have them track him down before the book disappeared forever. Feeling responsible for the entire mess, Nicole stood indecisively by Kevin's desk and twisted her rings nervously. *I can't leave but I've got to leave them a clue,* she thought.

Looking around frantically, she saw nothing she could unobtrusively use that would leave some type of message. She decided to make use of the only thing she had. She slipped her wedding band off her finger and laid it softly down on the corner of his desk. Since that was the best she could do, Nicole prayed it would be enough.

After retrieving the book, David closed the safe and headed for the phone on Kevin's desk. Dialing quickly, his eyes on Nicole, he spoke into the receiver. "I've got the merchandise. Unfortunately, I've picked up another package along the way. Yeah, Nicole. If only she was that easy to get rid of," he laughed in response to whatever the person on the other end of the line said. "Don't worry. I've got everything under control. It just means a slight adjustment on the location of the sale, that's all." Shaking his head negatively, he responded again. "No way. I'm not going anywhere without my money. I don't know who else may be on to us and I've got to hold her for insurance. You just tell our buyer to hold his horses. And I'll call you both back with the new location." Clicking off while the person on the other end was still obviously protesting, David again turned to Nicole. "Let's go."

Scared to even breathe for fear it might draw attention to the band, which he had miraculously not yet noticed, Nicole mutely nodded her head. David grabbed one arm and shoved the book into her other as he held the gun to her back, and they retraced their steps back to the car.

❧❧❧

Kevin had awakened as soon as the outer door closed. His first thought in the morning, after Nicole, was always for food. Putting his two favorite passions together he assumed that she must have ordered room service. He sat up in bed listening, and waited for his surprise breakfast. When he heard nothing and neither the breakfast nor Nicole appeared, he got up to investigate.

Instinctively he sensed something was wrong the minute he opened the bedroom door. His brown eyes zeroed in on the hastily written note on the coffee table. Nonplused with the brief message, he ordered his own room service and took a shower while he waited. Three hours later he was still waiting.

Frustrated at not being able to reach her by phone at either her home or her office, Kevin went looking for Nicole. With every mile that drew closer to the campus, his feeling of anxiety increased. Steeling himself against his unjustified fears, he kept repeating to himself, "She's okay. She's okay." But instincts of a lifetime warned him otherwise.

Pulling onto the campus, he breathed a sigh of relief. From his vantage point 'up top' as it was commonly called, he could see Nicole's car parked in the student parking lot not far from the center of campus. Why, he wondered as he shut the powerful Range Rover off, had she chosen this lot instead of the one closer to her home or office? He went first to the gymnasium, the nearest building. When she wasn't there, he checked all of the other buildings within walking distance of her car. Walking back to the center of campus, he looked 'up top' in frustration to the only building left, the administrative building.

A check of her office and then each of the three floors in the building yielded no results. Returning to his office, Kevin looked out of his window toward the faculty housing where he could make out the roof of Nicole's home. Deciding to call her once more, he went to the phone on his desk. He was in the process of dialing when he noticed the ring. The light playing off the platinum made it seem to radiate. He stared at it, afraid to pick it up for fear of what it might mean. Holding the ring tightly in his hands, he closed his eyes in quiet despair as all of his fears congealed into the icy knot that was now his stomach. He mentally replayed her words of the previous night. "You'll have to kill me to get it back, because I'll never take it off again." Nicole was somewhere in trouble, but where?

"Look, Mike, I know how Nicole seemed to you the last time you spoke. But I'm telling you, there is no way she voluntarily left this ring here," Kevin insisted for the second time to his friend. Balling his fist in frustration as he looked at Mike sitting across from him, he wondered not for the first time why he had bothered to call his friend. Mike was wasting time with all his inane questions. It was almost as if he thought Kevin was involved.

"Kevin, I know you think you are God's gift to women, but she seemed pretty upset when I told her about Tennessee Peaks..."

"But I explained all of that to her last night..."

"And all I'm saying is that maybe when she woke up this morning she decided she needed some time to think over your explanation. Now before we go looking for kidnappers or worse, maybe we should just give her some time to cool off."

"And what I'm saying is that she wasn't upset. Believe me, if she was, Nicole is not the type of woman to silently suffer. She would have definitely let me know she was upset about something. And she would never have willingly taken off her ring. Think about it, man! You're the detective. Why is her car sitting in the parking lot abandoned?"

"She went for a walk..."

"Thanks, Mike, for your expert detective work. You can go now because right now, if you're not helping, you're hurting. Every second that we waste on your stupid theories my wife is in more danger."

"Look..."

"I mean it. Good-bye..." The two old friends exchanged tense glances.

"All right, all right. Let's just say that I go along with *your* stupid theories. You're gonna need my help."

"Then be some help, dammit!"

"The first thing we should do is call the guard shack and see if they saw her leave the campus with anyone. There's only one way on or off the campus if you're not on foot, and either way you have to pass by security."

"Thank you. You see, now you're being helpful," Kevin added sarcastically.

Ten minutes later he was grim-faced as he hung up the phone. "She left here about two hours ago..." Exhaling deeply, as if he couldn't believe his own words, he added. "She left with David Spears. Neither one of them mentioned where they were going."

# Chapter 22

"Kevin, keep calm. We still don't know if Nicole is in any danger. For all we know, they might have had to check on a student in trouble."

"Then what were they doing here in my office? And why did she leave her ring? I told her not to take it off again and she said she never would. Why would it be off if she wasn't trying to tell me something?"

"Even if that's true, you're still going to have to calm down," Mike repeated as Kevin angrily paced the room like a leashed tiger waiting to strike.

"You tell me how calm you'd be if it was your wife!"

"If it was my wife, I'd realize that I would not get her back by reacting to my emotions. Now is the time to think."

"While you're thinking, they're getting further

away."

"And because they already have a head start, it is even more important that we think clearly, because we can't afford to waste any time."

That got through the angry haze clouding Kevin's mind. He'd been punching his hand into his fist for the last ten minutes. All the while they had argued, Mike had been careful to stay out of striking distance, just in case Kevin actually lost control and exploded on the nearest target. Mike watched Kevin pulling himself back together by sheer strength of will. As his fiery blaze of anger cooled into ice crystals, Mike didn't know what was worse: to have Kevin working beside him with hot-headed, directionless temper or with the icy calm that promised certain retribution. Never before having seen his friend so provoked, he was glad that he was not on his 'bad side.'

"So what do we do first?" Kevin asked in an ice crystal voice.

"We find out why were they in this office. If David is involved..."

"He is."

"If David is involved and Nicole either confronted him or surprised him earlier down by the gym, why did they need to come back here to your office? Do you see anything out of place?" he asked. When Kevin shook his head in frustration he said, "Let's split the room and search every square inch. There must be something we're overlooking."

Before Mike completed his sentence, Kevin had already begun, grateful to have anything to do. It took less than ten minutes to discover the safe. Kevin could not believe that he had been in the office a month and never before realized it had a safe. The safe was still unlocked. Although empty, it nevertheless established a reason for why David and Nicole might have returned to the office.

"So he brought her back here to get money or something he left in the safe," Kevin speculated. "Maybe he needed money for his escape."

"Possibly..." An amazing thought struck Mike. "Maybe the book was right here all along."

"No way."

"Think about it. I've had every contact I could think of watching for the book to turn up on the underground market, with no results. Maybe the reason is simply that it hasn't been sold yet. And if he hadn't had time to sell it, then he would definitely need to hide it. And what better place? You said yourself, you never suspected once about the safe."

"But it's so obvious."

"So was the safe. But just stay with me. If he came back here to retrieve the book, then he's got to be anxious to sell it. He might already have a buyer. I mean, the book is hot so he's got to dump it soon. Nicole has already 'busted him,' so he's got to get rid of that book quickly and quietly because he doesn't know who else may be on his tail."

Kevin's heart nearly stopped as he expanded on David's theory. "He's going to have to get rid of Nicole too."

"But not right away. She's his insurance policy in case something goes wrong with the sale. What we've got to do is get to her before the sale."

"But we don't have any way of knowing if he even has a buyer," Kevin protested in frustration.

"It's a longshot, but we could run a quick check on this phone and see if any calls were made today and if so, to whom. I'm sure I can get someone at the police department to do it for me. It may take a few hours though."

"Actually there just may be a quicker way. Last week Rose brought me a call log to sign, verifying my long distance calls. Apparently after the embezzlement, they had a program similar to a hotel's installed on the phone system, so that all calls from each phone are logged for number, date and time. I guess to stop future embezzlers from padding bills."

"So where does this log print up?" Mike asked, impressed.

"On her computer," Kevin replied. "I guess between the two of us, we could figure out how to pull up the information."

The clock slowly ticked off another half hour before

they found the data for calls made that day. There were only two. The one Kevin made to Mike and a very short phone call to a number Kevin recognized from the card still in his wallet: Carlista Cunningham.

"Why would he call her?" Kevin asked aloud. "She's nobody. I can't believe she would be involved."

"Sometimes nobodies have the most to gain."

"We'll see about that," Kevin warned as he grabbed his jacket and raced to the door.

Mike grabbed him before he could get away. "What do you think you are doing? Are you going to run over there and blow the only lead we have?"

"I'm going to get over there before we *lose* the only lead we have. She could be on her way to Mexico for all we know. Hell, they could even be holding Nicole at her apartment."

"Listen to me, because doing exactly as I say may be the only chance we have," David commanded. "You are going to call Carlista and invite her out for a friendly dinner."

"I'm not going to play footsie while they're holding my wife somewhere!"

"That's just it, somewhere could be anywhere. And right now the only advantage we have is that they don't know that we've put the two of them together. So if you want your wife you are going to stick to Carlista until she leads us to Nicole."

"What if you're wrong and she doesn't know anything?"

"Do you have any other ideas or leads? If so spit them out. Otherwise, call her and make the date." Mike held the phone imperviously while Kevin battled his fears.

When the call ended he looked at Mike with an icy stare and threatened, "This better work."

"It will, trust me," Mike returned, knowing that more than their friendship was on the line. "Anyway, while you're doing that, I'm going to search her house. When she gets back, I'll tail her. Eventually the two of them are going to have to meet up again."

"Sounds like a plan, except I'm making one change. We're both going to tail her."

"No, way..."

"Do you really think that there is any way in the world that you are going to confront the man who took my wife and I won't be there?"

Viewing the deadly certainty in Kevin's eyes, Mike knew that there wasn't.

🌺🌺🌺

"Where are you taking me?" Nicole asked the trite question after they had driven for a half hour through the mountains. Although her recent experience had left her leery of looking out the window as David maneuvered the narrow highway, her survival instinct forced her to keep watch. Although she had somewhat lost her bearings, she could tell they were definitely not heading toward Atlanta.

"Can't you tell? Don't you recognize this road, or were your eyes so full of stars when you traveled this way with Kevin that you didn't see anything but him?"

Looking out the window again as the weight of his words sank in, Nicole realized where they were headed. "You're taking me to the cabin," she said needlessly. "But how did you know...?"

"You really thought you had me wrapped around your finger, didn't you. I suppose you thought I would just meekly accept any bit of fiction you tossed my way," he scorned. "I realized right away that you were lying as soon as you told me you had no plans for the weekend. But what I couldn't figure out was why Nicole, my very best friend, would lie so boldly to my face. So I decided to follow you. When you met Kevin at his hotel, I was hooked. I couldn't let it go until I knew what exactly was happening. Little Miss Innocent, Miss No David, Miss Stop David, was sneaking away for a weekend rendezvous. I guess you were just holding out for the big bucks all along."

"David, it wasn't like that..."

"How was it then? When I looked you in the eye and asked you if you had known he was coming, you made it seem as though it was as much a surprise to you as it was to the rest of us."

"It was," Nicole hotly defended herself.

"Just stop it. You're just as much a liar as every other woman I've ever met or known!" He was so angry that spittle flew from his mouth. "I came so close to strangling you with my bare hands every time you looked at me as if you truly cared about me, when all the while you were sleeping with that..."

"David, it wasn't like that."

"Do you think I'm so stupid that I can't see what happened? Oh, I was your fool for a long time. I actually thought you were different. I thought I was being noble and proving myself to you by waiting patiently. I could have waited forever, couldn't I?"

"David, what we had was real, and I always treasured our friendship. But I always made it clear that we were only friends."

"Yeah, but you never once mentioned why, did you? I guess your marriage just slipped your mind." He rolled his eyes in disgust and focused again on the highway. After a long, uneasy silence, he continued, saying in a more somber tone, "Originally all of this was for you."

"It couldn't have been. You had to know that I would never accept anything that would hurt the school in any way."

Continuing as if he hadn't heard her speak, he said, "I could have left Tolleston. I've had plenty of money for some time." He glanced over at Nicole. "I thought seriously about leaving when Tennessee Peaks first made its bid for Tolleston." Shifting in his seat he continued, "I didn't leave because I still held out hope for you."

Choosing to ignore his reference to her, Nicole said, "We weren't interested in their offer then or now. You can't possibly believe that will change."

"Several million dollars, Nicole," he said resentfully. "More money than either of us will ever see in our lifetimes and the board turns it down." He shook his head in disbelief. "For what? For principles, for students who don't even respect their teachers enough to even show up for class half the time. For alumni who don't even bother to show up once a year for homecoming, let alone donate a dime. Why should we be the last vanguard to hold on out of loyalty to a school which no one else is giving their loyalty to? Why not sell?"

"Because we have to preserve it for those who will appreciate it. We owe that commitment to our ancestors who passed on this beautiful heritage to us. True, all of the students may not appreciate it right now. Some don't even appreciate it in later years. But think of the ones who do, the people like Bill Cosby, Oprah Winfrey, Spike Lee, and yes, the Kevin Powells who along with so many others were educated in the 'black college system' and who have given back. For many years these colleges were the only ones available for blacks to attend. And they are as important today as they were then. As a race, we have to be willing to educate our own children or at least make that opportunity available to them."

"Ah, Nicole, that was the lovely idealism I fell in love with," he sighed wistfully. "Until of course I found out that it covered a lying cheat," he finished in a scorning tone. "Face it. The future of the 'historically black college' looks pretty bleak. Nobody even cares anymore. Why not just sell the property? You'd be better off just giving the money to the community than hanging on for the few who come."

"I suppose that's what you were going to do. "Your intentions are so *honorable*."

"My intention was to help myself. Surely you support that, don't you? A brother helping himself?" he asked sarcastically as she didn't bother attempting an answer. "And, of course, to help you. I saw it was over for Tolleston, and I thought I might try and build a little nest egg for us. But I didn't know you already had quite a comfortable little nest." He laughed as he pulled into the long circular driveway of the 'cabin.'

"What are you going to do? Neither one of us has a key," Nicole lied.

"What I've wanted to do ever since I first realized this was your little love nest with Kevin. It took all I had not to bust out every window. Now I guess I can."

"No wait," Nicole capitulated, unable to bear the thought of the house being vandalized "I have the key."

"A liar to the end, huh, Nicole?" he asked as he took the key from her reluctant hands.

As they opened the door and David ushered her in

first, Nicole shivered. She wondered whether the goose bumps she felt were because of the coolness of the cabin or some instinctive premonition. Where, she wondered, was Kevin? Had he gotten her message and if so, had he understood? Now she needed him to have faith in her. To believe that she would never have taken that ring off if she hadn't been in danger. Had he believed in her or had he simply thought she had fallen back into her old mistrusting ways and abandoned their marriage once again?

# Chapter 23

"Are you sure you can't come in for a drink?" Carlista practically purred with passionate promise as she ran her hands up and down the front of Kevin's jacket.

"I'd love to, but not tonight," Kevin lied smoothly. It took every ounce of fortitude he had not to take her long hair and wrap it several times around her manipulative neck until she revealed where Nicole was hidden.

"But it's so early. Why it's barely even eight o'clock."

"Sorry, Carlista, but it will have to be another time."

"I hope that's a promise." Carlista lifted her face up expectantly for a kiss.

"I promise," Kevin said, adding silently to himself, *to make you and David pay*. Leaning down to her uplifted face he placed a soft kiss on her forehead to seal his oath. "Goodnight."

"Goodnight Kevin," Carlista responded wistfully. "And please give Nicole my well wishes. I heard about her terrible accident, and I was just horrified. Thank God she wasn't more seriously hurt."

Angered at her gall, Kevin nearly ruined the whole pretense with an expletive filled response. Instead, he swallowed his outraged words and merely responded, "Sure."

Afterwards, he parked his vehicle two blocks down and jogged back to the spot where he had noticed Mike parked earlier when he returned Carlista to her home after their dinner.

"What did you find out?" he asked immediately by way of greeting.

"Not much more than we already knew or suspected. I found receipts from dinners she apparently shared with David. Lucky for us she's been logging all of their meetings on her expense accounts as business expenditures. She made payments to David on numerous occasions, including unusually large ones the day after the auction, the day before the accident, and today. She also had copies of reports she submitted to her superiors, notifying them of her progress in closing the school down. She was far too crafty to actually admit in writing that she had sabotaged the school. However, the payments are pretty conclusive evidence that they are both involved in some pretty shady dealings."

"I can't believe that she would be so foolish as to write everything down."

"Well, like I said, she was very crafty. All of her expenses are listed under research and David is listed as an information liaison with Tolleston College. In court, with a good lawyer, she could possibly have slipped through the huge cracks of justice."

"Why do you say could have?" Kevin asked curiously.

"Before, from all appearances, David seems to have made all the moves. At least I'm assuming he did the legwork, because he had the access. Even so, in court it might have been difficult to prove that he was anything more than an overzealous employee."

"And now?"

"Now they've both crossed the line into kidnaping. The book they could have possibly plea-bargained down, and the sabotage would have been difficult to prove as a separate charge. Even if it had been proved, it also could have been reduced to misdemeanor vandalism. But what district attorney is going to plea-bargain down the kidnaping of the wife of one of America's most beloved sports heroes?"

"That just means they will be even more desperate and places Nicole in that much more danger."

"That's why we'll wait out here all night if we have to. Eventually Miss Cunningham is going to lead us right to Nicole."

"I just pray we don't get there too late." Kevin spoke gruffly, expressing his worst fears.

"Trust me," Mike responded fiercely to his friend's concerns. "He is not going to do anything to hurt her. She's his insurance policy."

"Because of me?"

"Yes, because of you. You are the biggest bargaining tool in her favor because of your fame. However, the same is true in reverse."

"My fame is working against her?"

"Yes." Mike uttered the one word response regretfully.

"Then that's the biggest irony of all. At this moment I would give it all away just to have her back." His words sank like heavy stones in the ocean of silence that engulfed the vehicle as they continued their wait.

ﷺ

Nicole paced the bedroom that David had assigned her in helpless frustration. Once again she cursed her own stupidity. What had she been thinking? She'd the chance to escape right in the palm of her hand but she had not taken it. Now the seriousness of her actions weighed on her mind. What had seemed so noble, stay with the book, now seemed foolish. Priceless though the book was, it wasn't worth her life. As she paced, she began to realize that she might pay for her impulsiveness with her life. After all, David had to know that not only was she now a witness to his crime, she could also charge him with kidnaping, and the longer he held her against her will, the deeper the hole he was digging for himself. Truthfully, she was more shocked by how much repressed anger and resentment he had been able to conceal for all these years than she was by the crimes themselves. He had a dark side she'd never suspected.

The previous day she had prayed to God that He save her from injury during the bus's crash. Today she prayed that God would be with her, but she acknowledged she was probably going to have to save herself. Grateful that David had not tied her down, she began to plan. Somehow she was going to have to trick him into letting his guard down.

After thinking through various scenarios, she finally settled for the best chance she thought she might have. "David," she called from the top of the stairs.

A short while later they were seated together on the couch drinking brandy.

"David, do you really know what you are doing?" she asked in a sleepy voice. "It's not too late to turn back the clock. Nobody ever has to know about this."

"Including your husband?"

"Even him. It can just be between us for the sake of the friendship we once had."

"Once had... " He sighed regretfully. "You could almost make me forget."

"We could both forget," she encouraged gently.

"No, we can't."

"What will you do with me when this is over? How far will you take this?"

"I won't kill you, Nicole. I promise."

"You can't promise me that." Tears glistened in her eyes as she looked at him steadily. "As I sit here facing my death, at least have the respect to look me in the eyes and tell me the truth."

"Nicky, I swear to you I just need enough time to get away. And then I'll leave you somewhere where you'll be found."

"In the middle of the woods?"

"No. I don't know. Damn, can't you just leave it alone? I said I won't kill you. Now leave it alone, will you. I haven't even had a chance to think."

Not wanting to press him too hard, Nicole let it go. Feigning tiredness, she yawned sleepily and reclined on the couch. "All of this activity two days in a row...I can barely keep my eyes open."

"Go on back upstairs and go to bed. This will all be over soon."

"I tried to sleep up there, but I couldn't get comfortable. My back was hurting too much from the accident. I took three pain pills but I still feel it."

"You took three pain pills and then drank brandy?"

"I'm not worried," Nicole answered, pulling the bottle out of the pocket of her jogging pants. "See? As long as I'm not driving or operating heavy machinery I should be okay."

"Let me see that," David commanded. Snatching it from her hand, he read aloud, "Do not mix with alcohol."

"While driving...," she murmured sleepily.

"Period," he corrected.

"Maybe that's why I feel so fuzzy-headed and sleepy. You haven't drugged me, have you?"

"No, you drugged yourself. Come on, upsy-daisy."

Reaching down with his hand, he tugged her to her feet. Pretending dizziness, Nicole collapsed backwards, pulling David with her. At the same time she reached out, as if attempting to break her fall. Her hand closed around the bronze figurine on the lamp table. Catching David off guard, she jumped back to her feet and in one smooth movement swung the heavy figurine with all the force in her. Powerful in her anger and fear, her one swift blow was enough to knock him unconscious.

She checked his throat for a pulse. Getting one, she realized that there was no telling how soon he might regain consciousness. She found his keys and gun, then sprang for the door, only to remember she didn't have the book. Stealing another quick look at him, she ran into the study where she had seen David place the book.

When she grabbed the book, she dropped the gun, acknowledging to herself that she wouldn't have the heart to use it on him anyway. Slipping back through the living room, Nicole never took her eyes off his unconscious body, afraid every step of the way that any minute he would awaken and she would be under attack. With her back to the door, she turned the knob that would open the way to freedom. As soon as she felt the cool night air kiss the back of her neck, she turned and fled. She almost had David's car door open when she heard the mocking voice at her back.

"Going somewhere?"

Nicole spun around in disbelief. She had been so focused on David that she'd never once checked outside the cabin.

Carlista was pointing a gun directly at her. "Please don't rush off. We'd love to have you stay a while." She ripped the book from Nicole's hand. "I believe that belongs to me." Then she took in Nicole's expression. "Surprised?"

"Not really. Wherever there's a stinking mess lying around, there's always a filthy rat. I pretty much figured out that David couldn't have acted alone. I admit that I wasn't sure who was involved. But I knew that someone at Tennessee Peaks had to be.

"Good for you. Though I don't know how much good that information will do you if you're not alive to tell it. Now get back inside."

A flash of movement out of the corner of Nicole's eye was her only warning. "Nicole!" Kevin shouted as he grabbed her out of the way as Mike tackled Carlista and wrestled the gun away. Luckily, she'd been so confident she'd never released the safety, and not a shot was fired.

As Nicole took refuge in Kevin's arms, she thought her heart would pound a hole out of her chest. "Thank God, thank God," was all she could declare over and over as he squeezed her tightly.

"Are you all right?" he finally choked out.

"Yes, I'm fine. How did you find me?"

"Mike put it together. Once we figured that Carlista was involved, we watched, waited and hoped. And I can tell you, no night has ever been longer."

"I know..." She looked into his eyes while he scrutinized her face, still trying to reassure himself that she was all right.

"It's good to see you, Nicole." Mike smiled his understatement as he pulled Carlista to her feet, securing her hands in cuffs.

"It's good to see you too," she smiled as she turned back to Kevin. "It's good to see you both."

"Why are you doing this to me?" Carlista demanded. "I'll have my lawyer..."

"Save it, sister," Mike answered, ignoring the threats she continued to sputter.

"Where's David?" Mike asked.

"He's inside. I managed to knock him out."

"Good for you," Mike said, impressed. "Now that I know you can take care of yourself, I'll tell your husband not to worry so much the next time something happens."

"There won't be a next time," Kevin declared as they all entered the cabin, "because I'm never letting her out of my sight again. This kind of stress can kill me," he said grimly.

They found David still unconscious, a miracle Nicole was grateful for, having glimpsed the murderous intent in Kevin's eyes. While they waited on the police Mike called, Nicole filled them in. Kevin held Nicole's hand the entire time in an angry silence that jangled her nerves. Gone was the effusive lover who had greeted her outside. It was almost as if something had congealed within him as soon as he entered their house. Nicole could only wonder why.

# Chapter 24

After the police finished their questioning and made their arrests, Nicole walked Mike to the door. She saw his concerned look as he glanced at the still silent Kevin. "Give him a break Nicole, he was really worried," he whispered.

Closing the door behind Mike, Nicole faced her husband. "Do you mind telling me just what the hell is wrong with you?" she demanded.

Kevin exploded off the couch as if her words had set off dynamite. Towering over her he snapped, "You tell me! What the hell were you thinking, going off to confront kidnappers and thieves by yourself!"

"First, I didn't know he was a kidnapper and second, Kevin Powell, I didn't need you. the great superhero, to go fighting my battles for me. I know you get a kick out of thinking only you can take care of problems, but I thought I could handle it myself."

"And look how well you handled it..."

"I was practically home free before you got here!"

"*Practically home free!* Carlista was holding a gun on you. What were you going to do, Miss I-Can-Handle-Everything- By-Myself?"

"Look, this is ridiculous." Nicole paced away from him in exasperation. "You're making me sound ungrateful that you and Mike got here in time. And I'm not ungrateful. I don't want to think about what would have happened if...well luckily, we don't have to think about it."

"And that's all I can think about." Kevin grabbed her hand before she got too far. "What if I hadn't gotten here? Do you see that your lack of trust in me almost got you killed?"

"This doesn't have anything to do with trust."

"Of course it does. If you had trusted me, we would have confronted him together."

"I wanted to let you sleep, and I left you a note."

"A note with not a damn bit of important information. Something like, 'I think David tried to kill me last night and I'm going by myself to ask him,' would have been a tiny bit more helpful. You do remember last night and our little talk about communication."

"I'm sorry. Maybe I didn't use the best judgment..."

"*Maybe*?"

"But I still don't understand why you are so angry at me."

"Because I almost lost you forever!" he shouted, squeezing her hand in frustration. "And I realized just what that would mean," he continued in a more subdued tone.

"What would it mean? You'd already lost me for ten years."

"It would mean," he pulled her into an angry reckless kiss, "...it would mean I couldn't breathe because you are my air." He kissed her again. "It would mean I couldn't think because you are my thoughts." Kissing her once more, "It would mean I couldn't love because you are my heart."

"Oh...." Nicole couldn't think how to respond with his desperate kisses raining all over her face.

"It means," he shook her lightly, "...it means you've got to trust me, communicate with me and share your life with me. Because I'm giving you all of mine."

Nicole took his face firmly in her hands and locked her eyes with his. "I do trust you. I will communicate with you. And I give you my life to share." She forcefully kissed him. "I promise."

"And I promise to treasure those gifts always and never again take them for granted." Kevin sealed his words with a kiss that healed more wounds than time.

# INDIGO

## Winter, Spring & Summer 2001

### January

| | | |
|---|---|---|
| Ambrosia | T. T. Henderson | $8.95 |

### February

| | | |
|---|---|---|
| The Reluctant Captive | Joyce Jackson | $8.95 |
| Rendezvous with Fate | Jeanne Sumerix | $8.95 |
| Indigo After Dark Vol. I | Angelique/Nia Dixon | $10.95 |
| In Between the Night | Angelique | |
| Midnight Erotic Fantasies | Nia Dixon | |

### March

| | | |
|---|---|---|
| Eve's Prescription | Edwina Martin-Arnold | $8.95 |
| Intimate Intentions | Angie Daniels | $8.95 |

### April

| | | |
|---|---|---|
| Sweet Tomorrows | Kimberly White | $8.95 |
| Past Promises | Jahmel West | $8.95 |
| Indigo After Dark Vol. II | Dolores Bundy/Cole Riley | $10.95 |
| The Forbidden Art of Desire | Cole Riley | |
| Erotic Short Stories | Dolores Bundy | |

*May*

| | | |
|---|---|---|
| Your Precious Love | Sinclair LeBeau | $8.95 |
| After the Vows | Leslie Esdaile | $10.95 |
| (Summer Anthology) | T. T. Henderson | |
| | Jacquelin Thomas | |

 *June*

| | | |
|---|---|---|
| Subtle Secrets | Wanda Y. Thomas | $8.95 |
| Indigo After Dark Vol. III | Montana Blue/Coco Morena | $10.95 |
| Impulse | Montana Blue | |
| Erotic Short Stories | Coco Morena | |

# ORDER FORM

**Mail to: Genesis Press, Inc.**
**315 3rd Avenue North**
**Columbus, MS 39701**

Name _____

Address _____

City/State _____ Zip _____

Telephone _____


*Ship to (if different from above)*

Name _____

Address _____

City/State _____ Zip _____

Telephone _____

| Qty. | Author | Title | Price | Total |
|------|--------|-------|-------|-------|
|      |        |       |       |       |
|      |        |       |       |       |
|      |        |       |       |       |
|      |        |       |       |       |
|      |        |       |       |       |
|      |        |       |       |       |
|      |        |       |       |       |
|      |        |       |       |       |
|      |        |       |       |       |
|      |        |       |       |       |
|      |        |       |       |       |

|  | |
|---|---|
| Use this order form, or call 1-888-INDIGO-1 | **Total for books** _____ <br> **Shipping and handling:** <br> $4 first book, $1 each additional book _____ <br> **Total S & H** _____ <br> **Total amount enclosed** _____ <br> *MS residents add 7% sales tax* |